The Diehard

The Diehard

Jon A. Jackson

GROVE PRESS   New York

Originally published by Random House, Inc., New York

Published simultaneously in Canada
Printed in the United States of America

FIRST GROVE PRESS PAPERBACK EDITION

Library of Congress Cataloging-in-Publication Data

Jackson, Jon A.
    The diehard / Jon A. Jackson.
      p. cm.
    ISBN 0-8021-3707-5
    1. Mulheisen, Detective Sergeant (Fictitious character)—Fiction. 2. Police—Michigan—Detroit—Fiction. 3. Detroit (Mich.)—Fiction. I. Title.

PS3560.A216 D54 2000
813'.54—dc21
                                          00-028792

Grove Press
841 Broadway
New York, NY 10003

00 01 02 03   10 9 8 7 6 5 4 3 2 1

The Diehard

One

All happy families are like one another, says Tolstoy, and each unhappy family is unhappy in its own way.

If the rule applies to childless couples, it applied to the Arthur Clipperts.

It is not rare to be healthy and unhappy. One may even be young and beautiful and unhappy. And young and beautiful and rich and unhappy. Ask Jane Clippert.

Before dawn Jane got out of her sleepless bed and went downstairs to the kitchen. She smoked cigarettes and drank stale coffee. In the first light she counted seven snowflakes falling straight down from the seamless gray sky. There was a foot of old snow in the backyard already. From down the street came the faint scraping noise of a shovel.

Jane Clippert clenched her jaws and dragged on the raw cigarette. Her eyelids felt tight and dry.

At seven-thirty, her husband Arthur came downstairs and into the kitchen. He was dressed for work in a suit of rich brown wool. He looked prosperous, confident, well-shaven, sane, handsome and forty. He was in excellent physical shape, only slightly heavier than he had been when sportswriters had called him "The

3

Flying Clipper." In those days he had won more athletic honors than any man in the history of the University of Michigan.

"Good morning, dear," he said. He picked up a white pot that sat warming on the electrified sideboard and poured himself a cup of coffee. He sat down at the table and picked up the morning *Free Press.*

Jane Clippert did not look at him. "Page two," she said.

Arthur Clippert's face darkened when he saw the headline on the article: THREE MORE INDICTED IN MASSIVE COMPUTER FRAUD.

"That's all of them now," his wife said, "except for one."

The toast popped up. She got up and buttered it and brought a pot of strawberry preserves to the table. She picked up her cigarette again and looked out the window. Her husband munched on jam-smeared toast and read the article.

DETROIT (AP)—Three more top executives of Fidelity Funding Corporation were indicted late yesterday by a Federal grand jury on charges of carrying out a computerized insurance fraud.

The fraud has been described by investigators as the largest in the insurance industry's history. The indictments were only the latest in an exhaustive seven-month investigation that has seen the indictment of nineteen other executives and key employees of the once powerful corporation. Only one other major officer of the company has thus far remained free of any taint of scandal.

Indicted yesterday were Marshall Goodrick, a vice-president; Calvin Decker, a trust officer; and sales manager Theodore H. Brown. United States Attorney James Clarke Dunn refused to comment on whether or not an indictment was also being prepared for Arthur M. Clippert, former chief counsel of Fidelity Funding.

The giant financial conglomerate, once described as a Cinderella of the industry, tumbled into bankruptcy last June. It has been charged that executives and other employees mass-produced phony insurance policies and sold them to other insurance companies.

This was done to make earnings appear higher and to inflate the price of stock of a subsidiary, Fidelity Funding Life Insurance Company, officials claim.

On at least one occasion, investigators say, the false policies were created during a late-night party at the company offices, with as many as twenty male and female employees participating and while a substantial quantity of beer and whiskey was consumed by those present.

Clippert muttered something under his breath.

"What?" his wife asked.

"Nothing," he said.

"You said something."

"Oh, it's just that they always have to get that bit in about whiskey."

"Well?" she said.

"Well what?" He put the newspaper down.

She did not reply. The smoke from her cigarette brushed her eye and she squinted.

"I'm going to New York this morning," Clippert said.

"You never say anything, do you?"

Clippert sighed. "Don't always accuse me of never saying anything. Of course I do. Just because I don't go around pouring my heart out to everyone . . ."

"I'm not everyone. I'm your wife."

"Yes, you are." He smiled. "And you are beautiful, even if you didn't get enough sleep last night."

Jane Clippert's jaw tightened. Arthur's smile faded.

"What do you want me to say?" he asked.

"Oh, God," she said. She stubbed out the cigarette in a large brass ashtray. "Arthur, Arthur! How long can this go on? You sit there so calm and innocent, smiling and patting me on the head. You're standing on the edge of a cliff, Arthur! Aren't you worried? Don't you need me? I'm your wife. Your wife! Not some pretty little mindless secretary who doesn't mind being tumbled after lunch."

Clippert looked grim. "I know who you are," he said. "And I know what I need. You're the one who is being unrealistic. You're the one who is playing games."

"Art, they are going to indict you. The money won't help. In fact, it'll be the worst kind of evidence against you. You have to go to them first. Give them the evidence they need."

"I don't have any evidence, remember? You have it." He

seemed calm. "But I won't be indicted. No, no, you can count on that."

He watched her quietly for a moment, then he took a pipe and a leather tobacco pouch out of his coat pocket. He filled the briar slowly and carefully and lit it with a wooden match, sending up a cloud of blue smoke. He leaned forward and looked at her very seriously.

"Jane, I'm not kidding. This is no game. I'm willing to give you one more chance. Just tell me. Tell me and I'll wind up a little business I'm involved in just now, and then you and I can take a nice long vacation. Just you and me. We could go to Rio again." He smiled and sat back. "How would that be? You always loved Rio. Or, hell, we could go anywhere." He waved his hand. "We could go around the world. Take a year doing it!"

Jane looked at him out of a dead face. At last she said, "No, Arthur. I'm going to give *you* another chance. Until New Year's. That's all."

Clippert closed his lips tightly. He stood up, relit his pipe and patted his pockets, assuring himself that everything he needed was with him.

"I have to catch a plane," he said.

He went to the front entrance closet and returned with overcoat, hat and a thick briefcase. He put on the coat and hat, picked up the briefcase and nodded at his wife.

Jane stood. Although the house was quite warm it made him shiver to see her near nakedness outlined by the wintry light from the window. She wore only a gauzy peignoir and her opulent body was quite visible beneath it.

It was precisely the type of feminine beauty that most attracted him, but he made no move toward her. Nor she toward him.

"So long," he said. He went out the kitchen door into a narrow passageway that connected the house to the garage.

"Good-by," she said, but he was gone. He entered the garage and got into a new Lincoln Continental. He pressed a small electronic device and the garage door automatically started up. He started the engine and then backed the car down the clean, dry pavement. The garage door came quietly and automatically down.

There was no traffic on the residential boulevard. Arthur drove away.

Jane watched from the front window. She reached up casually and tugged at the ends of the ribbon that held her peignoir, then let the garment slip off her shoulders and settle lazily onto the carpet. She stretched out her arms, pushing the curtains wide apart and leaned forward until the nipples of her breasts touched the cold glass and contracted. She wondered if anyone could see her. The only person visible was an old man down the block, scraping at the snow on the sidewalk.

The only other signs of life were plumes of smoke rising straight up from the chimneys of the huge mansions that stood well back from the boulevard. And there were the lights of Christmas decorations on houses and lawns. Across the way was a painted plywood Santa Claus, sitting in a sleigh piled high with toys, with eight reindeer stepping across the broad snow-covered yard, led by a red-nosed Rudolph.

On her own lawn there were Christmas carolers. They were very English with Victorian beaver hats and bonnets, bright scarves. Their mouths were open and a banner over their heads said, "O Come, All Ye Faithful."

She turned back to the living room. In the corner stood a six-foot Scotch pine. There were no electric lights on it, and no tinsel. Just all her old and treasured childish decorations. Wooden bells, angels, candy canes, a wooden Gingerbread Man and several very elaborate and fragile balls. On the top of the tree was a yellow star.

"New Year's," she said aloud. "I'll give him till New Year's, and then I'll go to the U.S. Attorney myself." She felt a twinge of guilt. How could a wife betray her husband so? Perhaps she couldn't. No, she didn't think she could, if it came to it. But, she could make him think she would.

He's slipping away from me, she thought. I've got to get him back. But what if he went to prison? Would he come back to her from prison?

For a moment she regretted not taking up his round-the-world offer. But then she thought, He's lying.

The trouble was, she didn't know Arthur. After six years of

marriage she didn't know who he was. He was already thirty-four when they married. He was already famous. He had a life, a set personality that she could not penetrate, though it had seemed to her at one time that she could.

She wished her father were alive to advise her. He'd know what to do, for sure. Old Axel Bodnar was no stranger to these situations. He had started out as a plumber and ended up with a fortune from the manufacture of plumbing fixtures. The Bodnar Bath, the Bodnar Kitchen—in six of ten homes built since 1947.

Along the way, Axel had picked up more than a couple indictments. He had endured a long and violent labor dispute in which three men had been killed. He had been big and brutish and had never pretended to be polite or respectable. He laughed at indictments. He knew who he was. But he had wanted something different, something better, for his Janey.

Axel Bodnar thought the Flying Clipper was just what Janey needed. So did she. So Axel got him for her, but not until he saw that Arthur was not just a swivel-hipped halfback, but a shrewd lawyer on the way up. Jane wondered what Axel would think now.

She left the nightgown lying and walked with swaying breasts up the broad staircase to the bathroom. She ran hot water into an enormous tub and sprinkled in blue and green crystals. This was her morning luxury. Sheer voluptuousness, to be perfectly private in her warm bath, adrift in exotic oils and scents, staring up into the steam fantasies.

A man stood shivering in the dark garage. He stood next to Jane's shiny blue Audi. He walked softly to the door that led to the kitchen.

He was a small man, skinny, wearing tight black leather gloves. They did not warm his hands, and his light jacket did not warm him either. He stood just beyond the kitchen door, shivering, listening. At last the faint rush of running water came down to him and he opened the door. The warmth of the kitchen was delicious. On the table were cups and saucers, half-eaten toast.

The man picked up a piece of toast from Arthur Clippert's plate, spread strawberry preserves on it heavily, and took a small bite. He chewed quickly, like a small animal.

Two

There was a note on the refrigerator door: "Honey. Gone to Stony Point. Sorry. You have to get your own breakfast. Ma."

Mulheisen stood in his undershorts staring at the note stupidly. He scratched his thinning sandy hair and then seemed to understand. He was annoyed. What the hell was Stony Point? he wondered. Birds. Bird watching.

"You're cracking up, Ma," he said aloud.

He put on a kettle of water to boil, then ground a handful of coffee beans in the electric grinder. He put the ground coffee in a paper filter and set that in its holder on the coffee jug.

If his mother had been there she would have made him coddled eggs, perhaps. Instead, Mulheisen rummaged in the refrigerator for something immediate. The refrigerator was crammed full of food. He opened a beer and sipped, to take off the taste of last night's whiskey and cigars. He found a casserole dish with leftover macaroni and cheese. He dipped his fingers in and broke off a hunk and chewed it. He took two more hunks while standing before the open door. Finally, he took the dish out of the refrigerator and set it on the table.

The water boiled. He poured it over the coffee. While it

dripped through he ate more macaroni with his fingers. He drank the beer.

The *Free Press* headline said, "Collusion In Russ Grain Deal." Mulheisen turned to the sports section and read about the hockey game. The Red Wings had lost on a last-minute goal by the Islanders. Mulheisen was depressed. He couldn't bear what had happened to the Red Wings in the last few years. The whole league had gone to hell. It really depressed him.

He drank coffee and ate the rest of the macaroni. He read the comic section, glanced at the editorials, scanned the news generally. "Shooting on East Side" caught his eye. A bar shootout, but not in his precinct. He didn't finish the article.

"Three More Indicted In Massive Computer Fraud" did not interest him. He stumped up the stairs to dress. Through the bay window of his room he could see the Detroit River. Two ships were downbound, running for the St. Lawrence Seaway, trying to beat the ice that was closing the shipping season. Mulheisen thought they might make it to Cleveland, maybe even Buffalo. Ice was already clogging the channel here. One of the freighters had a red hand painted on the funnel.

Mulheisen put on brown slacks, a light-brown shirt and a dark tie. He didn't like to be stodgy, but he hated to be stylish. Before he put on his beige cashmere coat he slipped a Smith and Wesson .38 Airweight Chief's Special into the back of his belt.

He was a well-built man, nearly forty. He was just under six feet and had a small but noticeable bulge at his waist. He had a high forehead and his eyes were set so deeply that it was not easy to see that they were pale blue. His most notable feature, however, was his teeth. They were long teeth, slightly bucked, and they were distinctly separate. For this reason the street people called him "Fang." It was "Sergeant Fang."

He was late, as usual. He should have been at the precinct already and the precinct was twenty miles away. He wasn't supposed to live outside the city limits of Detroit, but like many other cops he circumvented the rule by maintaining a phony address in town. It cost him fifteen dollars a month.

The telephone rang just as he was going out the back door. It was Inspector McClain, from Homicide.

"Glad I caught you, Mul. I got one in your precinct."

"Where?"

"I forget the address. It's just off Agnes on Seneca. You'll see the house."

"Indian Village?" Mulheisen asked.

"Right. And your asshole inspector is down here, Buchanan, getting in everybody's way. Get on down here. I think this could be a big one."

Three

The skinny man walked quickly through the house. He picked up a portable color television, an expensive vase, an original painting off the wall. He took everything back to the kitchen and stacked it by the door to the garage. The bath water was still running.

He went to a small desk in the study and tried the drawers. Locked. With a light metal bar he carefully pried the drawers open. There was some cash. He put it in his pockets without counting it. He riffled through the other papers and then tossed them back into the drawer. He looked around for a safe. Then he remembered—upstairs.

He was halfway up the stairs when the water stopped. It was very silent in the house. He crouched on the staircase and listened. She must be just lying there in the bath, he thought. After a long time there were some splashing sounds. He went up the stairs, past the bathroom door which was open just a crack. He went on into an all-white bedroom.

He opened a jewelry chest and picked out its contents, stuffing his pants pockets. He quietly slid her dresser drawers open and looked through each drawer, running his gloved hands through the silky underthings.

The splashing continued.

Near the window, next to the unmade bed with its white blankets rumpled, there was a desk. He sat down and carefully looked through the papers. Most of them were letters from friends. There were a few from the Detroit Bank and Trust. He tossed it all aside.

The safe was set in the wall, behind a clock. He set the clock down and tried the safe. The splashing stopped. He listened, hand poised at the safe's dial. Then the water started running again. The bath must have cooled, he thought. He turned the dial again. In a few minutes the safe was open. He took out all the cash and put it in his pockets. There wasn't that much.

He took a pistol out of his pocket and walked out of the big bedroom into the hall. By the bathroom door he stopped and leaned closer, peering through the tiny crack. He stared at the naked shoulders of the woman in the bath. He began to breathe harder and felt a stiffening in his crotch. Without thinking he put a gloved hand on the door and it opened an inch wider.

Jane Clippert's eyes were half-closed in sybaritic pleasure. She stretched out her arms and splashed more foamy water onto her breasts. Then she looked up and saw the man. Her mouth fell open and they stared into each other's eyes. Then he dropped his gaze back to her naked breasts and she yelled.

At first the man stepped backward, then he pushed the door open and came into the steamy bathroom. He raised a hand to his lips, as if to caution silence. It was the hand that held the pistol.

This time, seeing the gun, Jane screamed. At that the man rushed to the tub and grappled with the woman who had half risen. "Be quiet!" he yelled. He struggled with her.

But she was bigger than he was, and stronger. She slipped on the bottom of the tub and fell back into the water, pulling the man with her. He floundered in the hot, soapy water. They were both yelling. And then he momentarily regained his balance, long enough to strike her on the head with the pistol barrel.

She slid down into a cloud of suds. The man struck at her head again. When the hot water reached her mouth she spluttered and fought back from confusion and shock, struggling to rise. The man was on his knees in the water, between her legs. A wet, gloved hand pushed her face down into the water.

Jane looked up between the gloved fingers and saw a narrow face that needed a shave. He knelt between her thighs, pushing, and she thought, Rape. He wants to rape me. The man's face was contorted and his mouth opened and closed. He was talking, yelling, but she could hear nothing. Her head roared and pain ballooned. He raised the pistol again and struck at her.

He's afraid, she thought. But he's hurting me. A terrible fear grew in her that the blows were doing something bad to her head, spreading numbness and weakness. She blocked a blow with her forearm. The pistol fell on her stomach and then disappeared into the soapy water. Her forearm was numb.

With both hands he forced her down into the water, pushing on her head. Once again water rushed into her mouth and nose. She coughed and threw his hands off. She sat up. She grabbed instinctively at him for balance and he fell forward on top of her.

"Goddamn!" he yelled. He thrashed wildly at the woman. She clawed at him and wrapped her long legs powerfully about his hips. With a great effort she managed to roll over so that now she was on top, straddling him. He lay on his back, fully clothed in the hot water. Her right forearm was across his neck and he was strangling. When he tried to breathe he only took in water.

He felt the pistol under his hip. He seized it by the barrel and lashed out. The butt struck the side of the tub with a *bong*. The woman grabbed his gun hand and held it. With his free hand he punched at her and hit her full on the nose.

Then her weight was gone from him. He sat up in the tub, choking and coughing, rubbing at his stinging eyes. When he could see he looked wildly about him.

Jane Clippert crawled away toward the bedroom on all fours. Through blinking, burning eyes the man stared after her. She lumbered out of the bathroom like a wounded bear. Blood and soap bubbles ran down her wet back. Her breasts hung down between her arms and swayed as she crawled. Blond hair hung bedraggled and bloody. Her naked buttocks disappeared through the door.

The man slipped on the tub bottom in his shoes and scrambled out. His feet squished in the shoes. He grabbed a towel and mopped his face. He flung the towel away and went after the woman.

She was crouched against the foot of the big white bed, a white telephone in her hand. It was the kind of telephone that has punch buttons in the receiver. Slowly she punched out a number.

"Stop!" yelled the man. She looked up, open-mouthed.

He fired the gun. Something hit her in the shoulder and she dropped the telephone. He fired again. And again. He stood in the doorway, not ten feet from the woman, and blasted away at her. Six shots. But only two of them hit her. The air was acrid and the room seemed to ring with sound of the pistol shots.

Jane Clippert lay sideways against the foot of the bed, trying to think what was happening. She looked down at her body. There was so much blood that she couldn't see any specific wounds, but there was pain in her right side and in her shoulder and she could hardly lift her right forearm. She looked up at the man in the doorway who was gawking at her. He was soaked, dripping, his pockets bulging, a smoking pistol in his hand. Then he ran away, down the stairs, his shoes squishing as he went.

She picked up the telephone and began to punch out the number again.

In the kitchen the man stumbled over the piled-up appliances and fell. He got up slowly, exhausted. He realized that he couldn't leave yet. Above him, on the wall, was a wooden rack containing a set of French cutlery. He fumbled in the rack with his wet gloves, then knocked it off the wall and shook out a long carving knife.

Something wrong with this phone, Jane thought. It was making a kind of siren noise. She pressed the disconnecting button and got a new dial tone. She punched out the number again.

The man was back. She could see that there was quite a lot of blood on him. He held the gun in his left hand and something else in his right. Then she saw what it was. She dropped the telephone to the floor and tried to rise. She fell back, onto the bed.

"Arthur Clippert and Associates, Attorneys," said a woman's voice. "Hello. Hello? May I help you?"

The line went dead.

When she came to she was still on the bed, on her back. The man was gone. And then she saw the knife. Or rather, she saw the handle of the knife. It was sticking out of her chest. It was very hard to breathe. She heard a slight whistling sound and felt a small, dead weight in the center of her chest.

She tried to lift her hand to the knife but she couldn't seem to reach it. She quit trying. Somehow she was able to roll sideways off the bed, onto her knees. It took all her strength to rise to her feet. She took a few steps toward the telephone but when she tried to bend down she knew that it would be impossible. It was easier to stay erect, to walk. So she walked. She wavered and tottered, supporting herself with a hand against the white wall, trailing bloody handprints.

Down the stairs, one at a time. It seemed to take hours. At the bottom she turned toward the front door and with great effort turned the knob until the door swung open. She stepped outside, onto the porch.

She knew it must be cold, but she couldn't feel it. She couldn't feel much, except the dead weight in her chest and a pounding in her head. She couldn't see clearly.

Very strange, she said to herself, look at me. Walking down Seneca in broad daylight and stark naked. Bad girl. She wondered if the old man who had been shoveling snow could see her, but apparently he had gone.

She felt drunk and delirious. She staggered, putting a foot carefully before her, then lurching her weight after it. She stopped and squinted at the bright Christmas display on her snow-filled lawn. The carolers were knee-deep in snow. They looked over her head, ignoring her nakedness, singing away in total silence with their mouths in O's.

The snow was deep enough that she was able to scoop up a handful by barely stooping. She brought it to her mouth but could not taste its cold wetness.

She stumbled along the sidewalk to the house next door. The Mercer's house. The walk had not been shoveled yet but the little porch had been swept off and someone had sprinkled salt on it. She could feel nothing underfoot, but knew in a distant way the coldness of the concrete and the graininess of the unmelted pieces of salt.

Edna Mercer was out in the small greenhouse attached to the rear of the house. It was her favorite place, especially in winter. She moved about in the heavy warm air, picking dead leaves off plants and squirting the plants with distilled water from a spray bottle. She barely heard the distant chime of the doorbell.

Now why doesn't Martha get that? she wondered. The bell chimed again and again, as if someone were leaning against it. Then Mrs. Mercer remembered. Today was Martha's day off. It was too early for Henry to come down and answer the door. He would still be in the upstairs bathroom. It took the poor man hours each morning, sitting on the stool, to accomplish his business.

So she went off to answer the doorbell herself, grumbling amiably.

Four

Mulheisen spotted the scene from a block away. The sidewalks were lined with neighbors. Uniformed officers stood around talking to one another and keeping the neighbors from getting too close. A police ambulance was parked in the driveway of a large Georgian brick mansion. There were several patrol cars parked along the curb, and the van from the forensics lab was parked right in front of the house.

Mulheisen had to park a half-block away and walk back. "Hi, fellows," he greeted the patrolmen. "Buchanan still here?"

"Yeah, Sarge. Him and Lieutenant Johnson, right inside."

A reporter from the *News* walked over. "Big murder, eh, Mul?" he said.

Mulheisen looked mystified. "Don't know anything about it," he said. He turned to the patrolman. "Is there a body here?"

"Sure is," the patrolman said. "A broad. Inspector McClain's here, too. He's over there." He pointed a gloved hand at a large Tudor-style house with mullioned windows, exposed beams. There was an elaborate caroling scene on the lawn.

"What's over there?" Mulheisen asked.

"I don't know," the patrolman said. "Somebody said that was where the broad lived, but this is where she died."

18

Mulheisen looked up and down the street where groups of people stood looking at the Georgian house. It was a neighborhood of mansions, built in a confusion of styles and effects. They were mostly built in the early boom of Detroit's industrial success. All of the streets in this neighborhood had Indian names, so the area was called Indian Village. Over the decades the neighborhood had been engulfed by residential growth. First working-class people from central Europe, then came the hillbillies, and now, finally, the blacks. It was nearly all black around Indian Village now, but the Village itself remained an enclave of the grandiose manner. It was mostly inhabited by the now elderly offspring of the original giants of the automobile industry. There were very few new houses in the Village and the old mansions were too expensive and inconvenient to maintain, even for wealthy people. Some of them were only partially occupied, whole wings and floors were closed off.

"Don't they have some kind of private police patrol here?" Mulheisen asked the patrolman.

"Yep. Triple Security. They got a couple men over there with Inspector McClain."

Mulheisen turned back to the man from the *News*. He had been joined by two more reporters. "I guess the guy to see is Inspector McClain, fellows." They nodded and trooped back to the Tudor house. Mulheisen went on into the Georgian.

The corpse lay on its back just inside the door. Mulheisen squeezed around lab technicians and photographers and into the living room. The body on the floor was that of a bloodied and severely brutalized young woman. She might have been beautiful once, but now her face was battered and swollen, lips cut and nose broken. The handle of a long knife stuck out of her chest.

It was a terrible sight, even for Mulheisen, who had seen men with their noses torn off, with brains spilling from their shattered skulls. It was made more horrible by the realization that this mutilated mess on the Oriental carpet was once an exceptionally handsome creature.

"What the hell? Are those bullet holes, too?" Mulheisen pointed to the bluish marks on the shoulder and abdomen.

The City Physician stood by. "I would say so," he said. He was a careful man. He was willing to attest that the body in evidence here was indeed that of a deceased young woman. The police could remove it to the morgue as soon as they liked. He would not, of course, offer an opinion on the cause of death, despite the massive evidence. That was the job of the pathologists who would perform the autopsy.

A Homicide detective named Joe Greene stood off to one side with his hands in his pockets. He ignored the chatter of an inspector who stood beside him. This was Precinct Inspector Buchanan of the Ninth, a small and handsome man who did not look like a policeman. He looked like an undersecretary of a foreign legation. Next to him was his Lieutenant of Detectives, Stewart Johnson. Stew Johnson had a perpetual beard shadow and his uniform never fit properly. He was only slightly overweight, but looked obese. He was the perfect lieutenant for Buchanan, being intelligent without being imaginative or independent, and he was solidly loyal to his precinct inspector.

Buchanan and Johnson saw Mulheisen at the same instant. "Where the hell have you been?" they said in unison.

"Outside," Mulheisen said. He looked at Joe Greene. "You handling this?"

Greene looked pained. "Guess so," he said. "Not that I don't already have a dozen cases going. This one could be a bitch if we don't get the bastard quick. The newspapers'll be all over it like flies on shit."

The ambulance men were placing the body on a stretcher. The knife handle still protruded.

"Looks like she might have been a showgirl," Mulheisen said. "Who was she?"

"Mulheisen," Buchanan said, "this is Homicide's case."

"I'm just asking," Mulheisen said.

"Mrs. Arthur Clippert," Joe Greene said. "She lived next door. Her husband's some kind of lawyer. We haven't been able to get hold of him, yet."

"What happened?" Mulheisen said.

"Mulheisen," Buchanan interjected, "let's just leave this to Homicide, eh?"

"Sure, sure," Mulheisen said.

"Seems like she came strolling in here about an hour ago,

naked as a jaybird, and dropped dead on this lady's carpet. The lady of the house, a Mrs. Mercer, answered the doorbell and here's her neighbor with a knife in her chest. Mrs. Mercer is upstairs now with her husband and a doctor. One of your precinct boys is taking her statement."

Mulheisen turned to Buchanan and Johnson and smiled, showing his teeth. "Who's upstairs?" he said.

"Ahab," Johnson said. "Ahab" was the nickname of Hassim Ayeh, the youngest and newest member of the Ninth Precinct's detective squad.

"Well, what's the deal?" Mulheisen asked.

"This case is going to be controversial," Buchanan said. "I think the precinct would do well to leave it to the big boys downtown. Of course, we'll be glad to assist them, but it's really Homicide's jurisdiction."

Mulheisen looked at Joe Greene out of the corner of his eye. Greene was studying a cigarette. "That sounds all right," Mulheisen said.

Buchanan was clearly relieved. "There will be a lot of press attention," he said. "The department could come under a lot of fire if it isn't wrapped up quickly."

"I think I'll just go up and see how Ayeh is doing," Mulheisen said. Greene went with him. Buchanan and Johnson looked after them with suspicion.

It was a winding staircase with a spindle railing, old-fashioned and elaborate, like the wainscotted hallway. In the first bedroom an elderly woman sat in a rocking chair with a sweater about her shoulders. Nearby, on the bed, sat an old man. A man in a dark-blue suit holding a stethoscope stood watching while Ayeh talked to the lady. Ayeh was tall and thin with a large hooked nose. He was trying to be polite and gentle with his witness, but she looked wary of him. Mulheisen thought she might still be in shock. Ayeh looked up with relief when he saw Mulheisen and Greene in the doorway. "Excuse me, ma'am," he said, and came out of the room.

"Can't get much out of her, Mul," he said. "Still in shock, I guess. And the doc isn't too happy with me, either."

"What have you got?" Mulheisen asked.

"Her name is Edna Mercer, his is Henry. They live alone

except for a maid named Martha James who comes five days a week, not including today. Mrs. Mercer was in the greenhouse this morning—they got a greenhouse out back, attached to the house. About eight forty-five she heard the doorbell ring. She let Mrs. Clippert, her neighbor, in. Mrs. Clippert collapsed just inside the door. Mrs. Mercer fainted. Her husband came downstairs a few minutes later and he nearly fainted. But he called the doctor and the police. He called the police at eight fifty-seven, according to our records."

"Mercer is the name?" Mulheisen said.

"Yeah. They've lived here for a long time. Mr. Mercer was the president of a big tool company. He's retired. I think Mrs. Mercer's father invented the hydraulic clutch or something. You want to talk to them?"

"Okay," Mulheisen said. He nodded to Greene and then went back into the room alone. He said hello to the doctor and introduced himself. "How are these folks doing, Doctor?" he asked.

"They've had quite a shock this morning," the doctor said. "I'd like to see them rest."

"Yes," Mulheisen said. "I'd like to ask just a few questions and then we can clear out of here and leave them in peace." He turned to Mrs. Mercer. "You're Mrs. Mercer? I'm Sergeant Mulheisen." He cocked his head. "Mercer? Mercer. Now where have I heard that name?"

On the dresser was a photograph of Mrs. Mercer in a long evening gown. There was a sash across the bodice.

"You're in the Eastern Star, aren't you?"

"Why, yes," Mrs. Mercer said.

"Maybe you know my mother," Mulheisen said. "Mrs. Cora Mulheisen, from St. Clair Flats."

"Oh my, yes," Mrs. Mercer said. "I've known Cora Mulheisen for years. And your father, as well. He was the Water Commissioner. He was in Scottish Rite."

Mulheisen nodded enthusiastically.

"What lodge are you in, Sergeant?" asked Henry Mercer.

Mulheisen shook his head ruefully. "I'm afraid I don't belong to any lodge right now," he said. "This business of mine gets kind of hectic, you see. Crazy hours and always on call. I used to play

22

ball for Demolay when I was a kid." He turned to Mrs. Mercer. "I'll bet you can't guess where Mother is this morning. Bird watching."

Mrs. Mercer shook her head. "In this weather? Where does she get the energy? We all ought to be down in Florida. If it wasn't for my plants I think Henry and I would be down there all winter. But you can't get anybody who will take proper care of plants."

"That's what I try to tell Mother," Mulheisen said. "But she won't listen. I tell her that there are birds in Florida, too." He looked up at the doctor. The doctor smiled and nodded, then quietly left the room.

"I guess you folks have had a terrible experience this morning," Mulheisen said. "How well did you know Mrs. Clippert?"

"Oh we've known Jane since she was just a child," Mrs. Mercer said. "Her father bought the house next door more than twenty-five years ago."

"Her father was Axel Bodnar," Mr. Mercer said, "of Bodnar Bathrooms, you know? Jane was his only child and her mother died just after Jane was born. We never knew her mother. And then when Jane married Arthur, Mr. Bodnar gave them the house."

"So the Clipperts have been neighbors of yours for quite a while," Mulheisen said. "Pretty good neighbors, I guess?"

"We don't see an awful lot of them," Mrs. Mercer said. "I guess Mr. Clippert is a very busy man. They travel a lot. Jane used to come over and have a cup of tea, now and then."

"How did the Clipperts get along with one another?"

"Why, I think they were happily married, if that's what you mean," she said. "They have always been very pleasant when we've seen them. I'm sure they were very much in love."

"I see," Mulheisen said. "I'm just trying to get a picture of things in my mind. Now, you were in the greenhouse when the doorbell rang. What time was that?"

Mrs. Mercer straightened her glasses. "I'm not sure, but I suppose it was between eight-thirty and a quarter to nine."

"And you were upstairs, Mr. Mercer?"

"That's right," Mr. Mercer said. He looked kind of embarrassed.

"So you went to the door," Mulheisen said to the woman, "and what happened?"

Mrs. Mercer looked down at her hands folded in her lap and was silent.

"You opened the door . . ." Mulheisen prompted.

Mrs. Mercer took a deep breath. "I opened the door . . ."

"And Mrs. Clippert was there," Mulheisen said. "Did you see anyone else?"

"No. No, I was so shocked. I don't believe I would have noticed anything else. At first I didn't recognize her, you see. I mean, I didn't—I couldn't imagine what was happening. She had no clothes on, you see, and . . . there was a lot of blood."

Mrs. Mercer looked down again. She was trembling. Mulheisen turned to her husband.

"Did you hear anything, sir? Did you hear the bell?"

"I was in the bathroom," Mr. Mercer said. "I didn't hear the bell. But I did hear a scream. I thought perhaps Edna had fallen. I came downstairs as soon as I could."

"When you were in the greenhouse, Mrs. Mercer, did you hear any sounds before the bell rang? Like gunshots?"

Mrs. Mercer shook her head.

Mulheisen nodded reassuringly. "I see. So Mrs. Clippert was at the door. Did she walk in by herself? Did you help her?"

"No, I didn't touch her. I was afraid. I backed away from the door, I believe, and she—she seemed to stagger. I could see she was hurt badly, and then I recognized that it was Jane." Mrs. Mercer sobbed. She took off her glasses and patted her eyes with a handkerchief. After a moment she got control of herself and went on. "She took a couple of steps toward me and then she stopped and was swaying and then she spoke and then she just slumped and fell backwards and she hit the floor. Yes, she hit the floor very hard. And I screamed and then I guess I fainted."

"Just a moment, Mrs. Mercer," Mulheisen said. "You say she spoke? What did she say?"

"I hardly know," Mrs. Mercer said. "I'm not sure. She didn't speak very clearly."

"What do you think she said?" Mulheisen asked. His tone was a bit less solicitous now, more demanding.

"I'm not sure. She said—well, it was two things, actually. The first thing was 'not drunk,' I think."

"Not drunk?" Mulheisen said.

"Yes. And then she said something that sounded like 'black blood,' or it could have been 'black love.' I'm pretty sure about the 'black' part, but not the other word."

Buchanan will flip, Mulheisen thought. If there is a racial angle to this he'll be expecting a riot.

"Let's go on to some other things," Mulheisen said. "What kind of person was Jane Clippert? What kind of life did she lead?"

"Janey was a wonderful girl," Mr. Mercer put in. His wife nodded in agreement. "She was a beautiful girl and became a fine woman. Her father tried to spoil her, but she couldn't be spoiled. He sent her to schools in Europe. She used to send us postcards from Switzerland."

"Mr. Bodnar thought the world of her," Mrs. Mercer said. "She was smart as a whip and sweet, very well-behaved. She wasn't wild at all, like some of these young people you see on television."

"Did they have any children?" Mulheisen asked.

"No, they didn't," Mrs. Mercer said. "I don't know why. I never asked."

Mulheisen hadn't noticed any pictures of children around. He suspected that the Mercers hadn't had any children either. Perhaps they had idealized Jane as a child that they hadn't had. He wondered if they really knew much about her. Well, there would be other sources.

"I suppose the Clipperts were very wealthy," Mulheisen said. "Did Jane inherit a lot of money from her father?"

"Now that's a funny thing," Mr. Mercer said. "I was surprised that Arthur didn't go into Bodnar's company, since Axel didn't have any sons. The natural thing would have been for Arthur to take over when the old man retired. But I guess Arthur wanted to go his own way. The company is still going strong, of course, but I don't believe that the Clipperts had any financial interest in it."

"Well, Jane must have inherited something," Mulheisen said.

"Yes, and you know what old Axel did? He left her a trust

fund so that she got a certain amount each year and then when she turned thirty she would get all of it."

"That seems odd," Mulheisen said. "Thirty is kind of an advanced age for that sort of thing, especially if your only child is happily married to a respectable young lawyer. Do you suppose that Bodnar didn't trust Clippert?"

"I don't know about that," Mr. Mercer said. "I think it was just one of Axel's peculiarities."

"So she inherited when she turned thirty," Mulheisen said. "How old was Jane?"

"I'm not sure," Mrs. Mercer said, "but I think this next April she would be just thirty. April seventeenth."

Mulheisen was thoughtful. "So, if she wasn't old enough to inherit before she dies, who gets the money?"

"I'm sure I don't know," Mr. Mercer said. "Perhaps a lawyer could tell you."

Five

When Mulheisen came downstairs the body was gone. So were Buchanan and Johnson. Mulheisen went over to the Clippert house. He avoided the reporters by cutting across the lawn. His feet sank into the snow and he got snow in his shoes.

The Clippert place was crawling with lab men. They had a lot to work with. The walls had bloody handprints on them. A photographer was taking a picture of a crumpled peignoir that lay on the living-room floor. But it was much, much worse upstairs. It looked like a slaughterhouse. In the bedroom there was even blood on the ceiling.

Inspector Laddy McClain was in there. He was a giant man, standing six-six. He waved Mulheisen into the room. "What a mess, eh, Mul?" he said.

Mulheisen looked around, amazed. "She walked out of here?" he said. "It looks like the Manson family had a party."

"There's a whole pile of stuff, TV's and paintings, piled by the kitchen door," McClain said.

"Burglary?" Mulheisen said.

"Could be," McClain said.

"Any witnesses?" Mulheisen asked. "What about that security patrol?"

"No witnesses, so far. The security patrol passed by here about eight-fifteen. They didn't see anything unusual. I put some of your precinct boys out on the street, door-to-door, talking to neighbors."

"Funny time for a house job," Mulheisen said.

McClain rocked on his heels, hands in pockets. "They must have had the place pretty well cased," he said. "Except, how come they didn't know that somebody was home?"

"You think that maybe they weren't expecting her to be here?"

McClain shrugged. "Hard to say."

"Maybe they wanted her to be here," Mulheisen said. "There are some bad men in this neighborhood. She must have been a pretty sexy-looking broad."

"Then how come they left the loot?"

"Maybe it got rougher than they had planned, so they panicked and ran."

McClain shook his head. "I don't know," he said. "But just look at all the blood, will you. Mul, I want you to work on this."

"Buchanan won't like it."

"Screw Buchanan. I'll take care of him. Anyway, that's not quite what I had in mind. Officially, and in fact, Homicide will handle the case. I'll be handling it personally. I'll handle the press and the prosecutor's office. What I want is two lines of investigation. The routine, standard approach plus your private investigation. This is going to be a hot case."

"Fine," Mulheisen said. "Where's Clippert, by the way?"

"His office says he flew to New York this morning. United confirms that he was on their eight-fifty flight."

"That lets him off the hook, then," Mulheisen said. He fished a Dunhill Corona out of his jacket pocket. He clipped the end off with a little device and lit the cigar. McClain looked at him reproachfully. Mulheisen got out another one and handed it to him.

"I'll get Clippert back here right away," McClain said.

Mulheisen told him about the inheritance problem.

"Interesting," McClain said. "Brings up the notion of a contract killing, eh?"

"If Clippert inherits," Mulheisen said.

"Well, it's too early to think about. Thanks for the cigar, Mul. I'll go see the press boys now and then head back downtown. We should start getting the preliminary stuff this afternoon. Give me a call."

Mulheisen looked into the bathroom. Three lab technicians were bailing bloody water out of the tub. They carefully poured the water through paper filters into labeled jars. A young man with heavy dark-rimmed glasses looked up and pushed the glasses back up on his nose with one finger. "Hi, Mul," he said.

"How's it going, Frank?"

"Too damn much evidence, Mul. Enough to keep us busy for weeks. And then what'll it amount to?" He gestured at the number of labeled jars, at a cardboard box that was full of small plastic bags that were also labeled and apparently held evidence. "Probably a lot of useless information. But we'll analyze it all. It looks like a hell of a lot of blood in this tub."

"So she must have been attacked in the tub, Frank."

"I'd say so," Frank said. "And from the amount of dirt we've already filtered she would either have had to be the filthiest woman on record, or else someone was in there with her."

Mulheisen considered that one. He thought of Mrs. Mercer's recollection of Jane Clippert's last words. "Black blood," or "black love." Could Mrs. Clippert have been in the tub with someone at eight in the morning, with a lover, perhaps? A black lover? Why not? It was no stranger an idea than that she had been killed.

"I think she probably got out of the tub," Frank said, "and went into the bedroom. Somebody shot at her at least four times in there. The bullets are in the bed and the wall. If he had a six-shooter, the other two should be in the body."

"It could have happened in reverse order, couldn't it?" Mulheisen said. "Say they messed her up in there, then ran a bath and threw her in, maybe tried to drown her. They tried everything else."

"I doubt it," Frank said. "For one thing, there's fancy bath crystals and oils in the water, as if someone prepared the bath carefully."

"Here's something, Frank," one of the other technicians said. He held out a filter on which there was sand and dirt and a piece of wood or plastic about the size of a silver dollar. Frank picked the piece up with a pair of tweezers and held it up for Mulheisen to see.

"Know what that is, Mul?"

"That? That is . . . ah . . . well, let's see. What do you think, Frank?"

Frank smiled and pushed his glasses back onto the bridge of his nose. "Sergeant, in my professional opinion this here is a piece broken off a pistol grip." He dropped the fragment into a plastic bag and sealed it. The bag was labeled and initialed. "Know the make of the gun, Mul?"

Mulheisen looked at him sourly. "No," he said.

"It isn't an automatic," Frank said. "There's no empty cartridges lying around. Of course, they could have picked up their empties, but it doesn't look like they were that careful. And then this shape isn't rectangular enough for an automatic grip. No, I'd say it was a revolver, probably an H & R .32, say. Looks like the kind of material they use for grips, something they call cycolac."

"I'm impressed," Mulheisen said. "How about latents?"

A Tennessee drawl that belonged to a long, raw face said, "Feller was wearing gloves. Got blood smudges all over, whole handprints, but no fingerprints."

Mulheisen went back into the bedroom. He began to look through the desk drawers. There were several pictures of the murdered woman, a couple of them in which she wore a bikini. One of the technicians glanced over his shoulder at the pictures. "Wow," he said.

"Yeah," Mulheisen said.

There were a few letters, presumably from friends. Most of them seemed to be from people in distant cities like San Francisco, New York or London. One, however, was from a woman in Grosse Pointe. Why, Mulheisen wondered, would someone in a Detroit suburb write a letter to someone in Detroit?

It was a social note, on engraved stationery, dated December 10—last week.

Dear Jane,

I haven't been able to get you on the phone, dear, but I thought you would like to know that Lou will be home next week, the 16th.

Why don't you call? Perhaps you could have lunch.

Affectionately,

Margaret

The engraved address said "Mrs. Margaret Drake Spencer, Lakeside Drive, Grosse Pointe."

There was an address book on the desk. Mulheisen flipped it open to the "S" section. The address and telephone number of Lou Spencer was written in a woman's handwriting.

Who was Lou Spencer? he wondered. An old friend? Or an old lover? Today was the seventeenth.

"What time is it?" he asked a lab man.

"Going on eleven," the man said.

Mulheisen thought it was unlikely that he would learn anything from the Spencers. But it was early and he had to start somewhere. He had to start learning about a beautiful heiress, said to be carefree and gay, a perfect daughter and wife, who now lay under a bright overhead light in the Wayne County Morgue while men she had never known peeled back her skin and probed her body with delicate instruments.

Six

Lou Spencer was not what Mulheisen had expected. She was not beautiful, but her figure compared favorably with Jane Clippert's. She was twenty-nine years old, five-five, and had a way of smiling that made her seem to squint.

The Spencer place was pretty impressive, as well. About two hundred thousand dollars' worth of Colonial splendor that looked out on Lake St. Clair across a lawn that was larger than the combined flight decks of several U.S.S. *Forrestal*s. A very pretty black maid put Mulheisen in a long and elegant room to wait for the Spencers. There were tall windows with pale draperies. The fireplace was tall and ornate and there was a very clean fire of logs on the grate.

Lou Spencer was a voluble and cooperative informant. She seemed genuinely shocked by the death of her friend, but it was not possible for her to keep her normal good spirits from surfacing. "Most of the time I just can't believe it," she said, "and then I convince myself and I'm outraged."

"When was the last time you saw Jane Clippert?" Mulheisen asked.

"I talked to her just yesterday, when I got in," she said. "But the last time I saw her was in September, in New York. We went to school together—Country Day, then later in Switzerland. She went on to Vassar and I went to Berkeley. Since then I've lived a rather different life than hers, but we always kept in touch and saw one another when we were in town together."

"Lou and Jane were always the dearest of friends," said Margaret Spencer, Lou's mother. Mrs. Spencer sat in a chair by the window. "But they were quite different personalities. Jane is—was —not so serious as Lou."

"What my mother means, Sergeant," the girl said with a smile, "is that I spend far too much time doing things like sociological research, instead of marrying and settling down. I suppose this isn't helping you much."

"Oh, I don't know," Mulheisen said. "I'd just like to get some kind of picture of Mrs. Clippert. I need to know how this thing could have happened to her."

"Is there a certain kind of person who gets murdered, Sergeant? I didn't know that."

Mulheisen bared his teeth. It could have been a smile or a grimace. "It's pretty early to make assumptions, Miss Spencer, but at first glance it appears that she was attacked by a person or persons who were interrupted in the course of a burglary."

"Why, it's practically an accident then!"

"It was hardly an accident that her assailants were in the house," Mulheisen said. "I mean, she was a wealthy woman and an attractive one. Those are things that might, uh, interest certain types of people. But maybe there were other qualities or aspects to her life that would put a different slant on what happened this morning."

"That's not very clear," the woman said mildly.

"Harumph!" Mulheisen cleared his throat, thinking he sounded like Major Hoople. Stop beating around the bush, he told himself. "Do you think she might have had . . . a lover?"

"What?" exclaimed Mrs. Spencer, shocked.

Lou Spencer was thoughtful. "I'm not sure," she said.

"Lou! The idea!" snapped her mother.

The girl ignored her. "I think Jane had changed quite a bit in the past couple years. She struck me as being more withdrawn, quieter. There was a time, though, when she certainly did have lovers. I thought she was rather a sensual woman, Sergeant."

"Really? Do you happen to know who her, uh, lover might have been?"

"I didn't say she had one—recently, that is. But a woman who looks like Jane always has men hanging around her. Especially if they are lonely, and more especially if they are rich. You know the cliché of busy men's wives." She caught herself. "Well, I really don't know much about her private life, not lately."

"Tell me about the past, then," Mulheisen suggested.

"I think the Sergeant might enjoy a drink, Mother. Whiskey, perhaps?"

"Ah, sure," Mulheisen said. "Bourbon is fine, with a little ice and water."

Mrs. Spencer knew her cue and left. Lou began to drift slowly about the room, touching things. Mulheisen watched her with interest. She was an attractive woman, he thought.

"I can't imagine what Jane did in that big house all day," she said. "She used to read some, the latest novels. She was a good athlete, terrific at tennis."

"But in the winter . . ." Mulheisen prompted.

"They used to go south, Florida or the West Indies. They have a lovely place up north, though. Not too far from Boyne Mountain, I think. They may have gone there to ski. She was a very good skier in school, in Switzerland. She had her first love affair on the slopes, so to speak. A skiing instructor, naturally. It's appallingly common. He was an older man. At least, that's how we thought of him. Perhaps he was only thirty, but we were just teen-agers."

"What was his name?" Mulheisen said.

"You can't be serious," she said. "That was an eternity ago. He was German. I imagine he's still there. It was all over within a few weeks, despite Jane's insistence that she was in love forever and that she would run away to Italy with him. Anyway, that's how she lost her cherry."

"My, my," Mulheisen muttered. His mocking tone did not seem to affect the woman's flippant manner. In fact, he could have sworn that her smile was mocking him. He thought that she must think him terribly stuffy.

"Let's see," she went on, "after Dieter there was a suave Continental type, 'a real gentleman,' she called him. She met him in Zurich. An older man indeed. I don't think you'll want his name either. And there was another older man, in London. He even came over to Lausanne to see her. A creepy fellow, lusting after young girls. Just the Humbert Humbert type."

"What was his name?" Mulheisen said. He took out a note-book and pen.

"I haven't the faintest notion," Lou Spencer said. She stood by the fireplace, caressing a glass bell that covered an intricate clockwork of gears and balls.

"So she liked older men," Mulheisen said.

"I never thought of it that way, until this moment, but I suppose that's true. Of course, it's easy to make too much of incidental details. Her husband, for instance, is ten years older than she. Perhaps it all has something to do with her father. He was quite a dynamic character who must have had a tremendous impression on her, especially since her mother died when Jane was just an infant."

"Did you ever meet her father?"

"Occasionally. He was very busy. He didn't spend much time with Jane. Rather paradoxical, perhaps, to have this powerful father figure that alternately ignores you and then dotes on you. It must be unsettling."

"Well, what about other men?" Mulheisen said. "Were there many, over the years?"

Lou Spencer looked rather concerned. "I don't know if I should tell you this. It seems scandalous, even to me. And danger-ous, too."

Mulheisen was interested. "What is it?"

"She told me she used to go into strange bars and pick up men. Total strangers. They'd go to a hotel. It seemed to me like she was taking a terrible chance. I mean, not only VD, but how can you tell what some guy sitting in a bar might do? She laughed at me. She said it was great fun. She really enjoyed the power she had over men."

"When did she do this? Where?"

"It was when she was at Vassar that she started. She would

go to New York to stay with some relative. I think she was twenty-two or -three at the time. And then later, she said she had done it in Detroit, as well as almost every large city she was ever in."

"Do you think she was still doing it?"

"No. No, I'm certain she didn't, not after she was married. I never knew anything about it, you see, until just a year or so ago. I have to confess, I was shocked. But she just laughed. She said it was a long time ago, before she married Arthur."

"Maybe lately she had a more steady boyfriend," Mulheisen said.

"I don't think so. She didn't seem so interested in sex in the last year or so. I don't think she was sleeping with anyone."

"Including her husband?"

Lou shrugged. "How do I know? I shouldn't be saying all these things. It's just hearsay and speculation."

"What kind of life did she lead?" Mulheisen wanted to know.

"A rich woman's life. Go shopping, go to the country club, go to dinner, go to South America. I don't know what she did. I don't think she had many friends."

"Why is that?"

"Most of the women who would have been her friends are married. If you were a married woman, would you want someone who looked like Jane hanging around? Of course," she added, "if Jane had chosen to be around, I'm sure she would have had more friends. She was a very sweet, thoughtful person." The woman bit her lip, suddenly, thinking about her friend. She turned her back to Mulheisen and stood against the fireplace.

"Where do you live, Miss Spencer?" Mulheisen asked. "New York?"

"That's right," she said, facing him again. "I'm a sociological researcher for a large organization there."

"And when Jane was in town, she'd certainly stop and see you."

"That's right."

"How about when Arthur Clippert was in town?" Mulheisen said.

"I don't know what you mean," she said.

"Well, I mean, if Clippert happened to come to town, alone, would he ever call you?"

"Why should he?" she said.

"Well, you were a friend of his wife's. You said she had seemed changed in the last few months. Maybe he would have noticed it too. Maybe he would be worried. What could be more natural than to turn to an old friend of your wife's if you are worried about her."

Lou Spencer looked skeptical.

"Or maybe he just wanted to take somebody to dinner," Mulheisen suggested.

The woman looked at him casually and said, "No."

Mrs. Spencer returned, followed by the maid who wheeled a trolley on which were bottles and ice. The maid poured a bourbon and water for Mulheisen and gave Mrs. Spencer a martini from a shaker. Lou had nothing. The maid left.

"Mrs. Spencer," Mulheisen said, "did you see much of Mrs. Clippert?"

"Why, no, Sergeant. Not lately. She used to be active in the Institute of Arts, but not recently."

"How about Mr. Clippert? Ever see him around?"

"Occasionally, at a restaurant or something."

"With his wife?"

"Well—not usually, no. He's usually with a party of people. Men, mostly. I suppose it's business."

"Ever see him with a woman other than his wife?" Mulheisen said.

"I beg your pardon!" She looked at Mulheisen frostily.

"Oh, Mother," Lou said, laughing, "no need to be so uptight. Arthur's a big, handsome man. I suppose it happens sometimes."

Mrs. Spencer looked very upset. She left the room. Lou turned to Mulheisen, shaking her head. "I shouldn't do that. It's too easy."

"Children always break their mother's hearts," Mulheisen said.

"Is that so?" Lou said. "Did you break your mother's heart?"

"Not just my mother's," he said.

Lou Spencer laughed aloud.

"You seem to have recovered from your shock," Mulheisen observed.

Lou's face reddened. "It's your fault," she said.

"Mine?"

"Yes." She walked toward his chair and settled onto a damask-covered stool near his feet. It was a low stool and her dress was short. It was easier for Mulheisen to look between her legs than not to. He struggled.

She smirked at his embarrassment. "Are you always so stuffy?" she asked.

"I don't think of it as stuffy," he said.

"What do you think of it as?"

"A job. I don't consider it a game."

"Oh, sometimes you must," she said. "Don't you occasionally put people on? Don't you play roles—the tough cop, the kindly cop?"

Mulheisen smiled. "Sometimes," he said.

"I've heard the role of detective described as a peculiarly interesting and relevant one in terms of modern mythology," she said.

"Who says?"

"Usually it's a tall boy with narrow shoulders and wide hips," she said, "and he teaches at the New School."

Mulheisen sipped his bourbon. "I suppose a young girl hears all sorts of things these days."

"You would be surprised what a young girl hears," she said.

"I don't think so," he said. "My job isn't glamorous, you see, despite what the boys from the New School will tell you. There is a certain sordid reality to it."

"Still, it must be interesting," she said. "Do you enjoy it?"

"Sometimes. It wasn't much fun this morning."

Lou did not flinch. "Are you scolding me, Sergeant?"

"Have you been bad?"

"Lately?"

"Usually."

"Not in an indictable way, I think," she said. "There are all kinds of bad girls, though. Jane could be a bad girl at times."

"How about yourself?"

"Janey and I were friends. We had a lot in common."

"How about older men?" Mulheisen asked.

"You mean as opposed to young men with wide hips?"

"That's right."

"Are you going to ask me to dinner, Sergeant?"

Mulheisen sat back in his chair and thought about that one. He had no business asking a woman like Lou Spencer to dinner. His type was more the older and affectionate divorcee who hung out in downtown bars. On the other hand, even a beauty like Jane Clippert had been an occasional bar cruiser. He stood up and drained off his bourbon.

"Have you ever been married, Miss Spencer?"

"No," she said. She looked up at him from the low stool. "Why not?"

"None of your business," she said. "How about yourself?"

"No," he said.

"Are you queer, or something?"

"Maybe I will ask you to dinner, Miss Spencer."

She smiled. "My name is Lou. And you are . . . ?"

"Mul."

"When do we eat, Mul?"

"I'll let you know," he said, and walked out of the room. The maid waited in the foyer with his coat.

"How do you get along with these people?" he asked her. He regretted the question the minute he spoke it. The maid didn't answer. She helped him into his coat.

Seven

On the afternoon of December seventeenth, another heavy, gloomy snow fell on Detroit and was ground into gray mush by thousands of tires. The mounted cops of the city's one remaining mounted division clopped carefully up Woodward Avenue toward the stables on Bethune Street. The tops of the Penobscot Building, the Fisher Building and the David Stott were lost in the low overcast.

An old Polish woman in Hamtramck, a city completely enclosed by Detroit, was knocked down in an alley. Her grocery cart was dumped and the bread and eggs stomped. She lay in fear while the boys ransacked her purse. They threw it at her and ran away. She felt lucky.

On the west side, the driver of a semi waited for several minutes on McNichols for a chance to turn onto Livernois. Just when it looked like he would make it at last, a young man in a Corvette cut in front of him and stopped for the traffic light. The trucker leaned out his window and shouted abuse at the Corvette. The young man rolled down his window and made an obscene gesture. That was it for the trucker. He climbed down out of his rig. The young man got a pistol out of his glove compartment. The trucker ran back to his cab for his own pistol. The young man leaped from his car and raced across the sluggish traffic of Livernois with the truck driver in hot pursuit.

A squad car skidded to a halt and an officer got out and ran after the two armed citizens, his own .38 in his hand. Officer Duncan, driver of the squad car, noticed another man, apparently a bystander, run after the other three. Officer Duncan radioed for help.

The Big Four were cruising on Seven Mile Road when they heard the call: "Man with a gun, McNichols and Livernois, officer needs assistance." The uniformed driver of the Big Four's Chrysler put his foot down.

Dennis Noell was the honcho of this crew. He was six-five, two hundred forty pounds and had a nose like the prow of a ship. The whole squad was large and intimidating and they carried an armament of axe handles, tommy guns, a Stoner rifle, sawed-off shotguns, and .44 Magnums on their hips. Noell had the Stoner rifle.

They pulled off Livernois just before McNichols when Noell spotted an officer, gun in hand, running down an alley. Noell didn't see the first two men, but he saw the fourth. That man was following the officer and he had a gun.

"What the fuck?" Noell said. He went after the man. When he hit the alley the cop was gone but the man was running. "Stop!" Noell shouted.

The man stopped and turned. He looked back at Noell. "Put it down," Noell yelled. He held the Stoner to his shoulder.

The man fired a shot at Noell. That was a mistake.

Noell squeezed the trigger on the Stoner. The automatic rifle had a 30-shot clip of 5.56-millimeter cartridges in it. In just over two seconds the clip was empty. A hail of very high-speed, unstable bullets flew down the alley and cut the gunman to pieces.

The young man lost his pursuers, returned to Livernois and escaped in the Corvette. No one got the license number. The truckdriver was not so lucky. Several officers were waiting for him at his rig. Fortunately, he had a valid permit for his .32 automatic. He was cited for blocking traffic and menacing the public safety.

Officer Duncan was trying to explain to Noell what had happened. "Who is this one?" Noell asked, pointing with the Stoner in one large hand at the crumpled corpse.

"I don't know," Duncan said, shaking his head. "I never saw him before."

Mulheisen was sitting in McClain's office at Headquarters. Headquarters was busy. The broad hallways smelled of wet wool. Few people looked happy, including the cops. The police asked parents and sons to step into their offices for a minute; they leaned over counters and asked questions; they walked down the hallways with files in hand, carrying plastic-foam cups of coffee; they said "Hiya, Irv," and Irv said, " 'Lo, Bob, Jim."

McClain had his giant feet on his desk. The desk was covered with memos and files and letters. The In-Out baskets were jammed. He was listening to Mulheisen tell about his interview with Lou Spencer. "Jesus," he said, when Mulheisen had finished, "she sounds like a cross between a saint and a nympho."

"I didn't get that impression," Mulheisen said. "You're just old-fashioned."

"Bullshit! Any broad who goes into strange bars cruising is a tramp."

Mulheisen shook his head. "The Spencer gal seemed to think it was more of a youthful fling, maybe like a young stud who discovers he can score with women so he goes wild for a while. An ego thing. It's like Lou said, she enjoyed her power over men."

"Lou, is it? Better watch yourself, Fang." He laughed and sat up, dropping his feet to the floor with a crash. "Okay," he said, "I'll leave that up to you. I got everything else straightened out. Don't worry about Buchanan. He doesn't know anything and doesn't need to know anything. I'm fronting the whole investigation. Just like always. I talk to the press, I talk to the prosecutor, I talk to the commissioner, the mayor, whoever. You go do your job, but let me know how things are going.

"Now, about this sainted tramp, despite what you say I think I'll have my boys check out her neighbors on strange men coming at odd hours, that sort of thing. And we'll ask around in the bars, see if she was up to her old tricks. I'll let you know how that comes out. You didn't find out what bars she might hang out in, did you?"

Mulheisen shook his head. "Lad, that's a waste of time."

"So? We'll try it anyway. Listen, Mul, it's important that we score an early bust on this. Clippert is big stuff. And a lot of strange people are interested in what's going on."

"What do you mean?"

"I got calls today from the U.S. Attorney's office, from the FBI, from the SEC, from the Michigan Insurance Commission—"

"What? What's all this?"

"Mul, you ever heard of Arthur Clippert before?"

Mulheisen shook his head.

"I'm disappointed," McClain said. "I thought you were an intelligent man, the kind of guy who reads the paper from front to back every day. At least you read the sports pages, don't you? You ever hear of the Flying Clipper?"

"Oh, sure," Mulheisen said. "So that's him. Yeah, halfback for Michigan. All-American."

"Right," McClain said. "But you know who else he is? Here, read this." He handed Mulheisen the morning *Free Press* folded open to the story on the Fidelity Funding scandal. Mulheisen read the article.

"Very complicated swindle they pulled over there," McClain said. "It involved a lot of computer diddling, a lot of fast talking and a lot of smart planning. The federal grand jury has indicted a whole shitpot of them, but they haven't been able to touch Clippert yet, even though the U.S. Attorney hinted to me that the Flying Clipper was the biggest fish of them all."

"What makes him so golden?" Mulheisen asked.

"I'm glad you asked," McClain said. "You know what the take was over there? No? The feds don't know either. They haven't been able to untangle the computer yet. But so far, they think it might go to twenty million dollars."

"Dollars?"

"Moola, mazooma, gelt, shekels, bucks. Twenty million. And no one—I repeat, no one—will say a word against the chief counsel of the corporation, the honorable All-American. The federal attorney says, but not out loud, that the reason no one will implicate Clippert is because Clippert is the bagman."

"So," Mulheisen said, "a number of people are looking at jail terms and the only guy who can bankroll their defense is Clippert, and nobody wants to annoy his banker."

"Plus," McClain said, "they know they won't be in the can forever and when they come out—in six months, eighteen months, five years, whatever—the twenty big ones will still be there and their faithful banker will be making discreet deposits in discreet accounts—"

"If he's still around," Mulheisen said.

"Oh, he'll be around. It's a two-way street. If he doesn't come through for his clients they could have him inside so fast the snow wouldn't melt on his galoshes. But for now, they're like a deaf-and-dumb choir. And don't think the feds haven't been on them. They've got some promising candidates, about twenty of them. They've got executives, secretaries, a computer programmer—he was the genius, I guess. The feds have offered immunity, reduced sentences, everything. The grand jury is going nuts. Not a sound from the choir."

Mulheisen lit a cigar.

"That the only one of them things you got?" McClain asked.

Mulheisen dug out another one.

"But we still have a murder, Lad," Mulheisen said. "What's the connection between Fidelity Funding and the murder? Or are you still thinking it was a simple burglary that went haywire?"

"Twenty million dollars is a very strong motive for murder, Mul. Say you stage a fake burglary and then score Clippert's old lady . . ."

"But why, Lad?"

McClain shrugged. "Who knows, at this point? Maybe somebody knows that Clippert is trying to pull a fast one, skip country or something. Maybe it's a shakedown by the Mob. The Mob hears about an unattached twenty million floating around, they'll get on it quick, like Tom Mix on Tony."

"And what if Clippert is innocent in the Fidelity Funding case?"

Laddy McClain's face was contorted in scorn. "Shit. And double shit." He laid his hands palms down on the littered desk and puffed out a billow of cigar smoke. "Here's what we got," he said.

"We got a corpse, a ton of unfinished lab work, no autopsy yet, and no witnesses. But we think it was just one guy did it."

"How do you figure that?" Mulheisen asked.

"Footprints in the snow. A single set of them in fresh snow leading out the back door of the garage, across the yard and down the alley. He fell down at least once and there was blood. He was headed toward Kercheval. The boys are canvassing up there. There's a drugstore, a restaurant, a couple of record shops. Somebody must have seen something. He had to hail a cab, or take a bus, or maybe he had a car there."

"Or maybe he lived around there," Mulheisen said.

"That too," McClain said.

"By the way, where is Clippert?" Mulheisen asked.

McClain looked at his watch. "He's home," he said, "waiting for us."

Eight

There was still blood on the wall of the living room, where Jane Clippert had staggered through en route to the Mercers'. But the lights had been turned low in that room and there was little evidence of the tragedy that had taken place that morning. They went into the study, a large and handsome room near the rear of the house. The walls were lined with bookcases. A fire burned in a brick fireplace that had a raised hearth.

Arthur Clippert looked only slightly weakened by grief and shock. He sat in a large chair, smoking a briar pipe, a balloon glass of brandy on a table at his side. The two detectives also held drinks. McClain was sprawled on a black leather couch, but Mulheisen preferred to lean against a bookcase, facing Clippert's chair.

"You don't have a regular maid," Mulheisen said.

"No, just a cleaning lady . . . well, more like a general house-keeper. She cooks sometimes and does things on special occasions. But today was one of her regular days off, unfortunately. If only she'd been here!"

McClain asked for her name and some particulars. Clippert went on to assure him that she was completely trustworthy.

"Your wife ever receive any threatening phone calls?" Mulheisen asked. "Or mention any suspicious characters hanging about? Anything unusual at all like that, lately?"

Clippert puffed on his pipe and frowned. "No, nothing like that. You don't suspect . . . it was some kind of freak? Some sex . . . fiend?"

"We haven't gotten complete lab reports, yet," McClain said, "but initial indications are that there was no sexual assault or anything of that kind. We're not thinking anything at all at this point, Mr. Clippert. We're just covering all the bases."

Clippert picked up his brandy glass and stared down into it. "She was a hell of a woman, gentlemen. One hell of a woman."

His words made Mulheisen uneasy. They had already established that Clippert had left his home well before eight, in order to make the eight-fifty flight to New York. A preliminary report from the pathologists posed some difficulties, in that while the time of death was accurately established as eight fifty-five, it appeared that the fatal wounds had been inflicted more than just a few moments earlier. There was a significant amount of congealing and healing already in progress at the time of death. Obviously, it was possible that Clippert could have left his wife for dead and gone on to the airport. Neither Mulheisen nor McClain believed that that had happened.

"She wasn't just a woman of uncommon beauty," Clippert said, "but a woman of integrity and courage. She had a kind of inner beauty."

Mulheisen raised an eyebrow and glanced over at McClain.

"What kind of life did she lead, Mr. Clippert?" Mulheisen asked.

"It was a happy life, I'd say. Basically a life of leisure, of course. She had many friends, most of them the wives of my friends. I could give you a list. She was not indolent, however. She involved herself in various community projects. She was a sports-woman. We traveled a good deal. In the winter, naturally, she was home more. She liked to read. And she liked to ski. We have a place up north, not far from Boyne Mountain. It's really more of a summer place, belonged to her father, but we used to go there in winter as well, to ski. Sometimes we went out west, to Aspen. We were . . . well, we had planned to go skiing in Utah next month, at Alta. She was looking forward to that."

"That reminds me," Mulheisen said, "ah, some of my questions may seem a little, ah, indelicate, but they have to be asked."

"I understand," Clippert said. He smiled encouragingly. "I want you to be able to do the best job you can in catching these —these vermin. So ask ahead."

"Well, it's about her inheritance," Mulheisen said.

"Oh, yes. As a lawyer, of course, I am quite familiar with these matters. Jane had made a will. Except for some minor bequests I am her sole heir—as she was in mine. She was a wealthy woman. Not a millionairess, but wealthy. In another year or so she would have become quite wealthy, thanks to the provisions of her father's will. But that is out, now. It's my understanding that her prospective fortune will revert to a kind of charity."

"What charity?" Mulheisen asked.

Clippert smiled grimly. "My wife's father was perhaps a bit eccentric," he said. "He fancied himself a sportsman. Therefore the bulk of the fortune goes to Ducks Unlimited."

"Ducks Unlimited?" McClain said. "What the hell . . .?"

"It's a nonprofit organization devoted to the conservation and welfare of migratory waterfowl, I believe," Clippert said.

There was a moment of silence, then Mulheisen said, "Well, I have to go on with the, ah, difficult questions. Would you characterize your marriage as a happy one, Mr. Clippert?"

Clippert set his pipe down and picked up the brandy glass again. He swirled the brandy, then sipped. He looked up at Mulheisen and said, "Yes, it was, Sergeant. But let me ask you a question. Are you married?"

"No," Mulheisen said.

"Every marriage has problems, Sergeant," he said. "Sure, we had problems. But we had, I think, an unusually open and very strong personal relationship. We talked things out. It wasn't always easy. I suppose you're aware that I've had a rather difficult time lately?"

"How's that?" Mulheisen asked.

"You haven't heard about Fidelity Funding? I thought everybody had by now, thanks to the media. It's a corporation for which

I was once counsel. Due to a rather spectacular bankruptcy, the corporation and many of the people most prominently connected with it have come under considerable investigation. There's nothing to the allegations, I assure you, at least not as far as I am involved. But, there it is. I don't blame the authorities. It's their function to monitor and regulate this sort of thing. Just as it is your function to find and prosecute the filthy scum who did this terrible thing to my wife.

"But let me tell you gentlemen, throughout all this difficulty Jane was a tower of strength to me, and it won't be easier now that she's . . . she's gone. So ask your questions. It's just tough for me, that's all. Well, I think I can take it."

"I'm sure you can, sir," McClain said blandly.

"Was your wife ever involved with any other men, Mr. Clippert?" Mulheisen asked quietly.

It was obvious that Clippert was fighting to maintain his calm. His face flushed and he glanced over at McClain. He drank off the remaining brandy in his glass.

"I think I understand the motive for that question, Sergeant," he said. "But there is only one answer I can, in conscience, give: my wife was a faithful wife."

In the car, Mulheisen said to McClain, "A real smoothie, that one."

"Pretty smooth yourself," McClain grunted. "For a minute I thought he was gonna dent those fangs of yours. But you're right. He's too damn smooth."

"What do you think," Mulheisen said, "maybe I ought to have Ayeh keep an eye on him." McClain agreed.

On his way home, Mulheisen stopped at the precinct and caught Ayeh before he left. "Just watch the place," he told the young detective. "When he goes to bed, or it looks like he's in for the night, you can knock off. I'll try to get you some relief, so you can do it in easy shifts."

Mulheisen's way home took him by the Spencer place on Lakeside Drive. He thought about Lou Spencer. He wondered if he ought to call her. She had a nice build, all right, he told himself.

There was another note waiting for him on the refrigerator door, informing him that there was chicken salad, ham and deviled eggs, and that his mother had gone to a meeting and would be home late.

He made himself a sandwich and opened a bottle of beer. The Detroit *News* had a front-page story on what they called the "Indian Village Murder." The reporter had quickly made a connection with the Fidelity Funding scandal, but not in any direct or causatory way. The press seemed to accept the official line of Inspector McClain that the crime appeared to be the work of a housebreaker who had been caught in the act. There was an attempt to inject a sex angle, since the victim was beautiful and had been found nude. The paper carefully avoided any notion of a racial aspect. Detroit had had enough of race trouble.

Also in the paper was a bizarre story about citizens and cops pursuing one another with drawn guns. It had ended badly for one of the participants.

Mulheisen went up to his room and sprawled across his bed with a half-finished book, Morison's *Admiral of the Ocean Sea,* a biography of Columbus. He fell asleep at the point where the Great Discoverer had left Isabella's court with his final rejection of the proposed voyage to the East, only to be called back before he had gone five miles down the road.

Mulheisen was on muleback in deep snow, pursuing a figure in black. The snow was spotted with blood. And then he himself was pursued. Looking over his shoulder he could see that it was a woman, but she had no face. And then the face itself became detached and loomed closer. He could almost recognize it.

His mother stood over him, shaking him.

"What the hell . . .?" he said, rubbing his eyes. He lay on the bed fully clothed. His mother had already changed into a flannel nightgown.

"You were talking in your sleep," she said.

"Oh yeah? What did I say?"

"Something about a black glove," she said, "and then a woman. Who is the woman?"

"I don't know any women. Not any women you want to know about," he said. "Get out of here and let me undress."

She came back when he was ready for bed. She sat down on the bed, a slim woman of sixty-five, with long teeth.

"See lots of birds?" her son asked.

"Not many," she said. "A handful of chickadees, and oh, yes, a purple finch. It was much too cold."

"So, what do you do it for?"

"It's absurd, I suppose. But that's bird watching for you. It gets obsessive. Every little flicker of a shadow past the window gets you running around with binoculars. You just can't bear not to know what species it might be. Why, it might be a purple finch, or even a Northern shrike. It was nice seeing the purple finch today, even if I almost froze. Something new for my Life List."

"Ma, you're nuts."

"Thanks," she said. "But not really. I've been thinking . . ."

"What?" he said.

She laid a bony finger along her bony jaw and looked like a parody of Thought. "Do you suppose," she said, "that you could get along by yourself here for a week or so?"

"Now what? You going on a survival hike?"

She hurried on. "No, I've been looking at those TV commercials, the one where they show a big jet taking off into the sun and a voice says, 'It's ten o'clock, folks, and another Delta Fan-Jet is on its way to Miami.' They have a flight every hour, Mul." She was suddenly protesting. "It's just too darn cold to be bird watching in Michigan. I understand that they also have birds in Miami."

Mulheisen laughed aloud. "What have I been saying?"

But she wasn't listening to him. She was detailing how she could arrange for him to have dinner every night of the week with a different old friend of hers, and someone would come in to clean . . .

"Ma, it's all right. I'm nearly forty years old. I can hack it on my own. Go to Florida. Go tomorrow."

"I was thinking about leaving tomorrow," she said. "But then, oh, Mul, it would be the first time we didn't have Christmas together, except when you were in the Air Force. And I haven't put up any decorations yet. I haven't even bought your present. I'd better wait until after Christmas."

"You can't," he said.

"Why not?"

"Cause that's my present to you. A ticket to Miami."

"You won't have any orgies here, will you?"

Nine

The Tuttle Hotel wasn't fancy. They didn't mind if you had forgotten your luggage. To some the rooms might seem cheap and shabby, but they were private. There was a lock on the door. There was a bed with steel springs and the steam heat hissed too liberally from the radiator. All of these were qualities that Elroy prized.

Elroy took off the long overcoat that Byron had given him, then shed the bloodied black jacket. From the jacket he took the crumpled cash, the pieces of jewelry, and tossed it all onto the bed. He should have given them to Byron but he had forgotten. And Byron had been so furious with him for bungling the job that he had forgotten to ask about money and jewels.

But that was this morning, a long time ago. Elroy felt better now, though quite exhausted. Byron had calmed down, too. The main thing was, he was safe. He looked about the room. This was real comfort, he told himself. He thought of some of his old associates. They would be lying in abandoned buildings, wrapped in newspapers. One of them might have a pint of "golden," or they might have pooled their pennies for a "fif' of tokay." They would tell each other, "The hawk is out tonight."

But not for me, Elroy thought. No hawk tonight. Tonight he was safe and warm.

This room even had a bath. An old bathtub on ornate feet, with little packages of soap and thin towels. Elroy took a long and steamy bath. Afterwards, he rinsed out his stiff and blood-crusted trousers and hung them up to dry. Then he sank down onto the stool for a long and leisurely time.

Elroy rang for room service, and fifteen minutes later a cheerful young black man showed up wearing a dirty bellhop uniform. When he smiled there was a gap in his front teeth and he clearly expected Elroy to ask for a whore. Instead, Elroy requested a bottle of whiskey and gave him ten dollars. A half-hour later the bellhop returned with a fifth of Four Roses. He offered no change from the ten. Elroy knew how much the bottle had cost, but said nothing. It was a pleasure to spend money again.

He emptied the huge pockets of the overcoat onto the bed. There was a pile of money and a .32 revolver with a chip missing from the grip. He opened the bottle of whiskey and counted the money with pleasure. Ten thousand dollars. It made him feel wonderful. It made up entirely for the terrors and exhaustion of his day's work. In fact, he'd go through it all again, if he had to.

And Byron! Imagine Byron not wanting to give him his share right away. "It'll be safer for you, Ellie," he'd said. "The cops pick you up now, with this kind of bread on you, you've had it."

"I want it now," Elroy had insisted. He was glad he had insisted. He counted the money several times and thought of the fun he was going to have in Florida. Leaving tomorrow. He wished he had gone today, but Byron had talked him out of that. "We'll have to get you some clothes." Byron was too careful.

Elroy drank the whole bottle before he went to bed. He didn't want any dreams.

He woke early, conscious of some bad dreams. His head was pounding. He was hot and stuffed up, his lips puffy, his tongue swollen. All he could do was groan and repress the bad dreams. The scratches on his face stung. Immediately he thought of Byron. He called the desk for the time and to see if there were any messages. There weren't and it was just seven. He ordered a newspaper.

The *Free Press* was full of the Indian Village murder. Elroy read all the articles twice. There was nothing remotely connecting him and, oddly enough, this made him feel resentful. He was surprised to learn just who Arthur Clippert was. Then he began to worry about Byron.

Elroy was nervous about Byron this morning. Yesterday Byron had been furious when Elroy had come panting up the alley and piled into the cab, covered with blood, soaking wet. They had driven all around the city with Byron ignoring his dispatcher's calls while Elroy told over and over exactly what had happened. Elroy almost fainted when Byron said he was going to drive by and see if the cops were there yet. He pleaded and pleaded, but it was no use. They passed safely, a block away, and looked down the street where all the cop cars were parked.

Later, Byron had gone to a pawnshop and gotten the long, heavy overcoat for him and then they had driven to Belle Isle and had lunch at the Casino. Nobody noticed him in the long coat. They argued about the money and finally Byron gave it to him and brought him to the Tuttle. He was to be ready by ten o'clock. Byron would bring new clothes and he would be flying to Florida by eleven.

Elroy was suddenly afraid. Why didn't Byron want to give him the money yesterday? Why did he have to hide here, waiting for Byron to come and get him? The trouble was, of course, that he was totally dependent on Byron. If something happened to Byron, Elroy would be in bad shape. And Byron had always been a pal to him. He could count on Byron, all right.

He had to have an Alka-Seltzer, or something, some coffee, maybe. He put on the dry pants, still a little stiff, and went out wearing the overcoat. He took everything with him except for the bloodied jacket.

There was a drugstore on the corner of Woodward and Sibley that had a lunch counter. He had an Alka-Seltzer and a couple cups of coffee with two donuts. The coffee made him feel much better. He bought a copy of *Playboy,* one of *Penthouse,* and a carton of Camels.

He went down the street to a pawnshop and purchased a zippered bag that said Pan-Am on it. He put the magazines and cigarettes in the bag, then went to a clothing store, where he purchased socks and underwear.

It was a little after nine as he approached the Tuttle Hotel. A

Dixieland cab was parked in front. Elroy hesitated. Then he ducked into the alley. An icy wind blew down the alley and he buttoned up the overcoat, turning up the collar. He could feel the reassuring weight of the .32 in his pocket.

He walked quickly to Cass Avenue carrying the bag first with one hand, then when that hand got cold, switching to the other. He came out onto Grand Circus Park and angled on up toward Cadillac Boulevard, where the airlines had their downtown offices. BOAC, KLM Dutch, American, Air France. He jostled against the Christmas shoppers and began to feel more secure.

At Delta Air Lines there was a poster of palm trees and girls in bikinis, waving. He went in.

"May I help you, sir?" asked a young woman who wore a name tag on her left breast. Ann Tyler. Elroy was unshaven and seedy looking, his hair askew from wind and no combing. Miss Tyler looked skeptical, but she was trained to be polite.

Elroy hauled out several packets of cash and said, "I want to go to Miami, right away."

"First class or tourist, sir?"

"What's the difference?"

Miss Tyler explained the difference and pointed out that there were flights leaving Detroit hourly. He could be in Miami within a few hours. Elroy took first class.

"You'll have to hurry, sir, to catch the ten o'clock flight," Miss Tyler said. "I'll call the desk at the airport. You'll have to take a cab. Is there any luggage?"

"Just this little bag," Elroy said.

"That's all right, then. And if you don't make the ten o'clock, you can take the eleven."

Elroy snatched his ticket and change and bolted out the door. There were dozens of cabs sliding up and down the boulevard and one immediately pulled up before him. Elroy jumped in the open door.

The cab pulled away quickly. The driver didn't ask where they were going. Elroy looked up at the driver's permit card, issued by the police department. It carried a photograph of the driver.

Elroy sat frozen in the rear seat. When they stopped for a light, Byron turned slightly and said, "Let's see your ticket, Ellie."

His pitted face was calm and his voice mild. He didn't seem to be angry with Elroy at all.

He took the ticket from Elroy's frozen fingers. "Delta, hunh? That'll be the main terminal. Miami. Be nice in Miami, Ellie, you'll love it." The light changed and the cab moved away. It turned down an entrance ramp onto John C. Lodge Expressway. Byron did not return the ticket.

"Be nice to get away from all this snow and crap," Byron said. He lit a cigarette and steered swiftly through the expressway traffic. They maneuvered onto westbound Edsel Ford and headed out toward the airport. "Be there in a few minutes, Ellie, but I can't guarantee this ten o'clock flight."

Elroy slumped down in the back seat.

They rolled out of town past the bleak scenery of warehouses, fuel storage tanks, assembly plants. Soon there were bare trees and the median strip grew broader until it almost hid the westbound lane from the eastbound.

The taxicab shot by an exit ramp where a sign pointed to Metropolitan Airport. Byron cursed. "Goddamn. There goes your ten o'clock flight. Now I have to go all the way to the next exit and come back. Or do I? I guess I can take this service ramp."

Elroy sat silently. "Oh well," Byron said, "there's another flight at eleven. That'll be better, anyway. Give us time for a drink in the bar, eh, Ellie?"

The car turned onto a quiet road and soon they were driving along a gravel surface that ran along the perimeter of the airfield. There were no cars on the road, no houses. Jet airplanes took off and landed. There was a great deal of paper blowing around. The paper stuck against a low wire fence that bounded the airfield, or tumbled and skidded across the thin snow, catching in scrub brush.

"Is this the way to the airport?" Elroy forced out, almost in a whisper.

Byron slowed the car. "I think so," he said. "There ought to be a way to get around to the other side." He looked across the field at the distant terminal buildings and hangars. "No, maybe you're right, Ellie. I guess I screwed up."

They cruised slowly, looking for a likely place to turn around. When they came to a little dirt track that led off through the scrub brush, Byron turned onto it and drove in off the perimeter road about thirty feet and stopped. Byron got out. He opened the back door and beckoned to Elroy.

Elroy's face was paler than the dirty snow. He trembled in the heavy overcoat. "No," he said.

"C'mon, Ellie," Byron said. The big pitted face loomed in the doorway. He wore a brown wool workman's cap with a union badge on it. "We're going to walk."

"Walk?" That didn't sound right to Elroy. His mind was flooded with panic and confusion. He was so abjectly fearful that he could not be certain of Byron's intent. He wanted to believe the best, that they were going to walk to the airport. "Something's wrong with the car?" he suggested plaintively.

"That's right," Byron said. "Out of gas." He stood in the snow and weeds next to the door, looking in at Elroy. Elroy sat primly on the seat, not daring to get out.

"But I'm going," he said. "I'm going to Miami."

"You should have gone then, Ellie. C'mon." The big man reached in and dragged the smaller man across the seat and out the door. Elroy was so shaky that Byron had to hold him up. He walked him around the car and down the little lane, back through the brush and away from the perimeter road.

"I'll go to Miami, Byron," Elroy rasped, "I'll go there and there won't be no trouble, honest." He suddenly broke down and collapsed against the larger man, sobbing. Byron continued to move him along with his arm around him, almost as if comforting him. "Oh, God," Elroy sobbed, "Oh, I can't help it. I can't help it. Help me, Byron."

"It's all right, Ellie," the big man said in a gentle voice, carrying the smaller man. "I'll help you. Just a little ways further, here."

Elroy fell to the ground on his knees, his hands on the grimy soiled snow. Tears ran down his thin cheeks into the stubble of his beard. "Oh God, Byron, don't do it," he begged. The tears were cold on his cheeks in the harsh wind.

Byron stood over him and looked somber. He puffed out his cheeks and breathed heavily. The wind made tears in his eyes.

"I'll give you the money back," Elroy said.

Byron's brow knitted. He was a cold-looking man, but there was an aspect of understanding and reasonableness in his craggy face. He looked sympathetic. He took a moment to consider, looking away from the pleading, whining figure at his feet.

At last he sighed and said, "All right. Let's have it then."

Elroy scrambled to his feet and felt inside the overcoat pockets. He withdrew packets of bills and handed them to Byron.

Byron leafed through the stack. He looked back at Elroy, thoughtfully. "But if I take this," he said, "you won't have any money, for when you get to Miami."

"I don't need it, Byron," Elroy said quickly, hopefully. Then he noticed that Byron had a very large pistol in his hand.

Elroy was calm, suddenly. He felt very distant from himself in a curious way. He thought about the little room where he had spent last night, about the hot tub bath and counting the money. It seemed to him to have been one of the most enjoyable evenings of his life. And now, for some reason, it was difficult for him to keep his mind on the present moment. He shook his head as if to wake himself.

The difference between being safe in the room at the Tuttle and being out here on this bitter cold plain, where jets roared in the distance, seemed at once incredible and minor. He could just as easily be back at the Tuttle as out here. If only he could think how it was done. Or, he could be over there, across the field in that large glass-and-concrete passenger terminal. Obviously, some insignificant factor, some tiny secret, escaped him and kept him from being safe over there instead of here . . .

"I have more," he said.

Byron looked at him closely. "Where?"

He knew he should have said that it was back at the Tuttle, but instead, he said, "Right here." He reached into his coat and drew out the .32.

Click. Click. Empty.

BAWHOOM! The blast from Byron's .44 was incredibly loud. It knocked Elroy spinning, back into briars that tore at his thin pants and scratched his legs. The second shot lifted him off the ground and he landed rolling. He no longer had his empty pistol.

He thought about the room at the Tuttle, about his full carton of Camels, about the unread *Playboy.* Doggedly, instinctively, he tried to get back on his feet.

The third shot slammed him onto his back into a shallow ditch. He lay there, trying to clear his vision. He looked up and saw nothing. The sky was a gray overcast so solid and of such a texture that there were no features to it, no seams. It looked like there was nothing there. For a great second he lay on his back, as alive as he had ever been. Then he arched his back, as if to breathe. And then he wasn't there at all.

Byron looked around him. There were no cars on the perimeter road, nobody in sight over the flat fields, nothing but crows flapping toward a patch of woods. The airliners landed and took off. A brightly colored pickup truck drove toward the GCA shack a mile away. The wind swept debris against the fence.

Byron began to strip Elroy naked in the snow. Methodically he removed the overcoat, shoes, socks, pants, underwear. He took the remaining money and the jewelry and put them in the pockets of his leather jacket. He went back to the car and got the little Pan-Am bag. He put all of Elroy's things in the bag.

The little man now lay completely naked, his eyes staring at the gray sky, his mouth open. It began to snow, just a few thin flakes that fell into the open mouth and melted. There were three dark holes in the chest and stomach. Byron knelt beside the body and formed the limp right hand into a fist. He laid the .44 Magnum next to the fingers and pulled the trigger. The fingers flew away. He did the same to the left hand. With his remaining bullet he shot away the lower half of Elroy's face.

He picked up the overcoat and the airline bag and walked back to the cab. He drove off toward the airport.

Ten

The room was white and brightly lit. There were no shadows and the walls were marred by black smears.

It was a rectangular room with a high ceiling. The only door was short, a door for midgets. It was held shut by a magnet and had a shallow depression for a handhold, allowing it to be pulled open from the inside. There was a slit in the door, through which those on the outside could peer to see if the room was occupied.

In addition, there was a gallery that looked onto the room from ten feet up. It was screened with heavy wire.

"Takes longer and longer to get warmed up, these days," Arthur Clippert yelled. His voice echoed and boomed, distorted by the horrible acoustics of the court and partially drowned by the rubbery *barong* of balls hitting the wall.

"What?" said the younger man, loudly.

Clippert repeated his remark and the young man nodded. It was not clear if he really understood. Clippert continued to cuff and chase an energetically rebounding black ball. He noted with satisfaction the spread of dark sweat on his thin leather gloves. The younger man seemed quite warmed up and even anxious to start. Clippert ignored him. He whipped the little ball around the court with graceful ease and power, setting up rebound shots, leaping for high shots, getting more and more limber. At last he felt ready.

The air was scented with the odor of the two men already. "Low man on the wall?" Clippert said to his younger opponent. The words blurred, but the other nodded. Clippert braced his right foot against the base of the rear wall, stepped forward and delivered a smooth, sweeping sidearm pitch. The ball struck the front wall just a fraction of an inch above the floor and sizzled back toward them.

"Damn," the younger man said. He didn't really try to beat the throw, making a perfunctory toss that bounded off the front wall at least a foot higher than Clippert's had. "You're up," the young man said.

Clippert went to the serving lane that was painted in red on the smooth floor. He dropped the ball with his left hand and as it bounced his right hand came through and whipped it against the forward wall. It was a high shot, seemingly lazy, that hit on the left, but it came out with power and glanced off the left wall, hit just short of the rear wall and rebounded with a short quick pitch.

The young man was ready and relayed the shot forward. Clippert took the shot on the rebound and drove high again, to keep his opponent in the rear court. This time his shot came back high and the young man had to return it high.

Clippert waited calmly for the rebound. He was bent low, facing the back wall with one hand stretched out behind him and the other on his knee for balance and to insure that he would be down low enough. He timed his swing perfectly, cupping the ball an inch from the floor and following through with a skimming, powerful sweep.

The ball never got an inch off the floor and smacked into the forward wall just above the point where it met the floor. It did not rebound so much as simply roll back out. There was no chance for a return.

"One-oh!" Arthur shouted. He returned to the serving lane, bouncing the ball as he went.

An hour later they were stripping off their sweaty gear in front of their lockers. "Your problem," Clippert told the young man, "is you just don't have a killer shot. You have a good left hand, you've got reach and range, good legs"—he glanced down ruefully at his own exhausted forty-year-old legs—"you've got a great sense of where the ball is going to be, good hand-eye coordination, but where's the old kill shot? Hunh, Bob?"

"Well, you certainly have it, Mr. Clippert," the young man said. He flushed, uncertainly. "I, uh, no offense, sir," he stammered.

Arthur wadded up his damp socks and tossed them into the locker. He banged the door shut and smiled grimly at the young man. "That's all right, Bob. You'd be surprised how these days the most innocent words take on added meaning. It confronts a man at every turn."

The two walked toward the showers, naked except for towels over their shoulders. "You seem to be bearing up awfully well," the young man said. "Everyone at the office thinks so."

"Do they?" Clippert seemed pleased. He stood under the roaring hot shower, allowing the stinging rain to soothe away the aches. "Well, you know what they say," he shouted. "When the going gets tough, the tough get going."

A half-hour later the two men stood fully dressed in the bitter cold wind outside the Club. Their hair was still damp and seemed likely to freeze if they continued to stand there. Clippert winced and turned up his collar.

"Are you coming back to the office, Mr. Clippert? I can give you a lift."

"No, thanks, Bob. I have my car. Anyway, I won't be in the office this afternoon. Tell Miss Carpenter that I'll give her a call with instructions."

"Certainly, Mr. Clippert. When would you like to play again?"

Clippert looked at the young man and took him by the shoulder, affectionately. He was a good-looking fellow and reminded Arthur of himself at twenty-five. The boy was a real asset to the firm, Arthur thought. A damn good record in law school, and besides, a varsity football player at Arthur's old university. Not an All-American, as Arthur had been twenty years earlier, but Arthur conceded that it had been easier in his time. It had been a time of amateur sport. Today, everyone was a pro.

62

"Come on, I'll buy you a drink, Avery," Clippert said. They walked down Cass Avenue, hunched up in their overcoats. The first place they came to was a quiet neighborhood bar, but Arthur stopped in the vestibule. The place looked too dingy to him. They went back out and walked an extra block down to a cocktail lounge on Grand Circus Park.

"It's been rougher than you can perhaps imagine, Avery," Clippert said. They had not removed their overcoats, but merely unbuttoned them and stood at the bar, sipping bourbon and water.

"Just the constant harassment of the federal authorities and the threat of indictment would be bad enough. But I can handle that. This thing with my wife, though . . . it's not just her tragic loss, but now I no longer have anyone to turn to for support and . . . well, comfort." He shuddered, either from the memory of her brutal death or from the strongly mixed whiskey.

He remembered something. "Incidentally, you can tell the kids at the office that we'll be closed on the day of the funeral."

"When will that be, Mr. Clippert?" Avery asked.

"I'm not sure. As soon as the coroner's inquest is finished and the body is released. A few days.

"It's curious," he went on, "but the death of my wife seems to have worked against me. At least in the minds of some people. There seems to be an inevitable suspicion and prejudice that develops against the husband of a woman who dies . . . like Jane did. As if I killed her! Or at least, that I wasn't there to protect her."

"But that's ridiculous," Avery protested.

"I know, I know." Clippert waved a hand. "I try not to think about it. God knows, I wish I had been there. It's a heartbreaking thing. But do you know the really funny thing? Some of the fellows in the business community who used to be my great good friends now seem distinctly cool toward me. I don't think it's the possibility of the indictment. They wouldn't let that bother them, if it was just that. Do you understand what I'm saying?"

Avery nodded seriously.

"If it was just that . . . hell, those guys know that an indictment is only an indictment. It isn't a conviction. And I haven't even been indicted!"

"I don't think you will, now, do you, sir?" Avery said. "I

mean, if they had anything against you, wouldn't they have indicted by now?"

"I don't know, Avery. But God knows, I had no part in that mess at Fidelity Funding. I had no idea what was going on. I believe those people deliberately used my position and reputation for integrity as part of their front."

The young man was embarrassed, but he responded earnestly, "I believe you, Mr. Clippert. We all do."

"Thank you, Avery. Thank you. And I wish you would thank everyone at the office for me." Clippert drank his whiskey and made a circular "fill-'em-up" motion to the bartender. "The police were over last night," he said.

"Oh," Avery said.

"Oh, they were polite enough, I guess," Clippert said, "but I could tell they were just itching to tear into me, especially the one guy. He's some kind of hotshot detective, I guess. He was suspicious, I could tell."

"Suspicious of what, for crying out loud?" Avery said with youthful indignation.

"It's their job," Clippert said. "But it doesn't make things any easier. I'm so sick of cops and investigators, and—" He stopped himself, realizing that he must sound as if he was ranting. "Things are piling up, Bob. I have to fight. It's the only way I know."

"If there's anything I can do," the young man said.

"No, this is my fight. I don't have anybody blocking for me this time."

They walked to the parking lot. As they separated, Clippert slapped Avery on the back and said, "Didn't mean to unburden myself on you like that, Bob, but thanks for listening. Take care. See you tomorrow, probably."

He started for his car, then turned and called back, "And work on that kill shot, boy."

Avery grinned and waved. Back at the office he told everyone what a hell of a guy the old man was. "When the going gets tough," he said, "the tough get going."

Arthur Clippert was in a phone booth, crowded up with his heavy coat, his breath steaming the windows. There was some

64

change on the shelf before him. He dialed several numbers, occasionally talking to someone, but most often hanging up after several unanswered rings. He finally left the booth, disappointed.

"Gone," he said under his breath. "But where? And is that good or bad?"

Eleven

The coroner's jury ruled the death of Jane Marie Clippert a homicide by a person or persons unknown. Although the Wayne County prosecutor's office had an impressive quantity of information and evidence, they had nothing to show a grand jury that would point to a specific individual as the perpetrator of the crime.

On December nineteenth, Mulheisen sat in his little office mulling over his copies of the pathology reports on Jane Clippert and the results of laboratory tests on various items found at the scene of the crime. The findings were that Jane Clippert had died of massive internal hemorrhage, due to a knife thrust into the chest cavity. The knife had punctured the left lobe of the lung but had miraculously missed all other organs.

The victim had suffered two bullet wounds, but neither of these were sufficient in themselves to cause death, nor would the severe concussions and broken facial bones have caused death. The pathologist noted that the subject was in excellent health, had not been raped and had never been pregnant. In fact, pregnancy would have been extremely unlikely or even impossible, due to curiously undeveloped ovaries. Probably the subject had irregular or difficult menstrual periods, the report said, and her condition might have been potentially dangerous, even precancerous, but it had obviously posed no problems to her yet.

No problem, Mulheisen thought, obviously.

Someone knocked at his door. It was a tall, slender man of thirty, wearing a heavy wool suit and vest, topcoat over arm, carrying a briefcase. He was a very serious looking young man with spectacles and thick auburn hair that was cut rather long.

"Sairjeant Moulhaysen?" The brogue was Scots and thicker than honey butter.

Mulheisen was tempted to answer, "Aye," but instead he said, "That's right. What can I do for you?"

"Inspectorr McClain has sent me. It's aboot the Clipperrt case." He handed Mulheisen a business card that read, "Alec McKenzie, The Underwriters Life Assurance Company of Canada."

" 'Twas aboot a life insurance policy," Mr. McKenzie said. "Sairjeant, have ye any evidence that would indicate that Mister Arrthurr Clipperrt was involved in the death of his wife?"

"Not a thing," Mulheisen said.

"Soospicions, then?"

"I'm suspicious of everyone, including the husband," Mulheisen said, "but not one item of evidence points to him, at present."

The man sighed. "In that case, I'm afraid we no longer have any rrright to withhold the benefit."

"What benefit?"

"The life insurance benefit. Mrs. Clipperrt named her hoosband the beneficiary of her life insurrance policy."

"How much?"

"One million dollars, Sairjeant. The company prrides itself on prrompt settlement of claims."

"One million," Mulheisen said. "Now I find that suspicious."

"Do you? Ach, but we canna," the Scotsman said. " 'Tis air business, you see. We must pay. Which is not to say that we won't continue to investigate."

"Who took out this policy?"

"Mrs. Clipperrt, aboot five yairs ago."

"Wouldn't the premium on such a policy be prohibitive?"

"The premium was near eighteen thousand dollars, annually. You see, Mrs. Clipperrt stood to inherrit more than a million dollars on her thirrtieth birrthday," McKenzie said. "She was only twenty-five. The premium would have come to ninety thousand dollars. It's nought so foolish in her."

"Of course, if she died the loss would have been her husband's," Mulheisen pointed out. "I imagine that when you insure someone for such a large amount, you investigate pretty thoroughly?"

"Aye. I have here a copy of the investigative reporrt. You'rre welcome to it." He took a manila folder out of the briefcase and slid it across the desk. "We want to cooperate with the police in everry way."

"I'm sure," Mulheisen said, dryly.

McKenzie rose from his straight-backed chair. "I must be off. I have an appointment with Misterr Clipperrt."

"Do you have the check with you?" Mulheisen asked.

"Aye."

"Uh, could I see it? I've never seen a million bucks before."

"Surely." McKenzie extracted an envelope from the briefcase and handed it to Mulheisen. Inside was a draft on the Chase Manhattan Bank for a million dollars. It looked like an ordinary bank draft, made out by a check-writing machine and signed by three officers of the Underwriters Life Assurance Company of Canada. One of the signatures was that of Alec McKenzie.

"Ye might say we're forrtunate, I suppose," Mr. McKenzie said, retrieving the check, "since she didna die by accident. There's double indemnity for that. Pairsonally, I didna approve of that, but we took it into account, of course, when we calculated the premium."

"Double indemnity?" Mulheisen said. "If she died by accident the policy would have paid two million?"

"Aye," the man said gloomily, and left.

The investigation report was quite thorough. It even included reports from Europe. A Swiss investigator had interviewed Jane Clippert's teachers and acquaintances. A British investigator had queried friends in London. There was nothing exceptional in her past. It was noted that she rode horses and skied, and someone had penciled in a remark that said, "Note policy provisions." That suggested to Mulheisen that the company had defended themselves against equestrian and skiing accidents.

Other investigators said that she was a very light drinker, a good driver, and did not to their knowledge use narcotics or barbiturates. There was a complete medical history, including a lot of talk about her menstrual problems and whether or not her ovaries were going to cause trouble before she was thirty. Presumably, the company had decided to take a chance. Her family doctor felt that she was a remarkably alert, vivacious young woman with hardly any vices, except cigarette smoking, which was not notably excessive. She did not seem depressed, and he had never prescribed sleeping pills or anything of that kind for her.

Of course, this report was five years old, Mulheisen reminded himself.

There was also an investigation of the beneficiary, Arthur Clippert. This was more interesting to Mulheisen.

A successful man rarely has significant gaps in his personal history, and that history is more readily accessible than the average man's. It was easy to establish and describe Clippert's career and life. He was born in St. Ignace, Michigan, a town just across the Straits of Mackinac. His father was a doctor, now deceased. His mother, also deceased, had a private fortune and was a devoted supporter of the Detroit Symphony and the Metropolitan Opera.

Arthur Clippert graduated at the head of his high-school class and accepted a Regent's scholarship to the University of Michigan (supplemented, evidently, by a football scholarship). He was an All-American football player for three years, and All Big-Ten in hockey, baseball and track. He turned down offers to play professional football and baseball from both of the Detroit teams, as well as the Chicago teams.

He graduated among the leaders of his law-school class and immediately entered the Air Force, where he served three years and was discharged as a captain (reserve). He went immediately into a law firm in Detroit that was headed by a former governor of Michigan and included a member who became a federal judge. After three years he left this firm and entered an even more prestigious one. Within another three years he had left that firm and

opened his own. He was a member of the board of several corporations, including the ill-fated Fidelity Funding. This last association
was the only questionable thing in his career.

"Mister Clean," Mulheisen said to himself. He leafed through
the voluminous, meticulous report. He noted the name of the
investigator: Larry Edwards, of Standard Enquiry.

"Nice work, Larry," he said. Then, out of curiosity, he called
Standard Enquiry. Mr. Edwards was no longer with Standard
Enquiry. After a bit of querulous negotiation with a secretary, he
was informed that Mr. Edwards had gone to work for the Detroit
Police Department.

Edwards was a member of the Big Four. He had risen rapidly
to that position. Mulheisen had heard of him. He was called
"Wonny" Edwards. Mulheisen didn't know why they called him
that. He got him on the telephone, at home.

"I liked your report on Clippert," he told him, after explaining
why he had called. "Do you remember anything about the man,
personally?"

"Let's see," Edwards mused. "Rich guy, wasn't he? Insuring
his wife for a bundle?"

"For a million," Mulheisen said. "A tall guy, ex-All-Ameri-
can football player, a lawyer."

"Oh, yeah. The Flying Clipper. Weird."

"How's that?"

"Well, I did a lot of scouting around before I went to see him.
You know, talk to neighbors, old acquaintances, teachers. Everybody tells me what a wonderful guy the Flying Clipper is. So I'm
actually looking forward to meeting the guy. After all, he's a
famous athlete. I saw him on television when he ran a kickoff back
ninety yards against Oregon.

"So I try to make an appointment. Couldn't get one. Always
out of town, out of the country. Well, he's a busy man, and anyway
I had other things to do, but then the company started pressing me
to wind up the investigation. So I really went after him, and finally
I caught him at his summer place, up north. He insists that he can't
see me in Detroit. Too busy. But if I want to drive up, it would be
all right. What the hell, I got mileage and overtime."

"Where was this?" Mulheisen asked.

"An old and very fancy resort area, Jasper Lake. It's about a hundred seventy-five miles straight up the center of the state. Anyway, I get there and it's a real mansion. Only he's modernized the back so he can walk right out to an Olympic-size swimming pool. And what do you think? He's lying on a chaise longue, stark naked."

"You mean you interviewed him while he was naked?"

"Yeah. He was wearing only sunglasses, I remember. Catching a little sun. Not only that, he has this sexy black maid who takes me out there and announces me and he doesn't try to cover up or anything, and she pretends not to notice."

"Where was his wife?"

"I don't remember. I think he said she was out West, or something. We were alone, except that he'd ring for a drink now and then, which the girl would bring. I had a couple of cold beers."

"Do you think he was making it with the girl, the maid?"

"Let me get to that. First I want to tell you what he did. All of a sudden, while I'm talking to him, he jumps up and dives in the pool. After a bit it's obvious that he isn't coming out right away, so I end up walking around the pool talking to him while he swims and dives. Finally he hauls himself out and flops down in the chair again, still buckass naked."

"Did he answer your questions all right?"

"He wasn't friendly, exactly—more kind of annoyed, but determined to get it over with so that the policy would go through.

"Anyway, about balling the maid. She was a number, believe me. But cool as a cucumber. Mr. Clippert is swell, good employer, good pay, so she didn't mind if he went naked, she'd seen men before. He had a cook-housekeeper, too, also black, a real mama. She said Mr. Clippert was wonderful and he didn't mess around with the maid."

"Hmmmph." Mulheisen digested this. "What was your general take on him?"

"Clippert? I thought he was an asshole, frankly. But the trip wasn't a total loss."

"No?"

"Jasper Lake is pretty plush, like I say, and not for the likes of you and me. All real old, elegant joints, plus a few new ones that are built to look old and modern at the same time—you know, stone and glass and heavy shake roofs. But there's a new subdivision, not far from there. Not bad. I looked around the rest of the weekend and I've been back up since. There's some good bass fishing around that area. So, about a year ago, I bought myself a lot up there. I think I'll put a little cabin on it. Take the wife and kids up, get them out of this town all summer."

"Where, on Jasper Lake?"

"No, you can't buy into Jasper Lake. I don't think even Clippert could. His father-in-law left them the house. But there's a public access for fishing, on the northern end. No, the place I bought into is a kind of leisure-homes subdivision, that's what they call them. It's called Black Beaver Lake. Do you fish?"

"Yeah," Mulheisen said.

"You'll have to come up some time," Edwards said, being polite. Obviously he knew who Mulheisen was, although they had never met, as far as Mulheisen could recall.

"Black Beaver Lake, hunh?" Mulheisen said.

"Right. Funny thing, too. The development company at Black Beaver Lake is owned by a friend of Clippert's. I remember because I interviewed the guy for that investigation and then I came across his name on one of their brochures when I was looking for a lot."

"Does this guy live up there?" Mulheisen asked.

"He has a place on Jasper Lake, near Clippert. A summer place. Mostly he lives in Bloomfield Hills. Carl Joyner is his name. You'll see his name in the report."

"Okay," Mulheisen said. "By the way, Clippert was in the Air Force, wasn't he? Do you remember what outfit? It isn't listed."

"It's there," Edwards said. "There's a whole page on that. I had a hell of a time getting the info. I had to go through a buddy of mine at Selfridge."

"Oh, he was stationed at Selfridge?"

"Clippert wasn't, but you know how it is, a guy in a headquarters office can find out anything if he looks long enough."

Mulheisen leafed through the report again until he found the page. "Thanks, Edwards. I appreciate this. If you ever need anything from the Ninth, let me know."

"Sure," Edwards said.

Mulheisen was about to hang up when he impulsively asked, "Why do they call you Wonny?"

"They used to call me One-Shot, and it got shortened."

Twelve

The funeral was held at Trinity Lutheran Church, a Gothic pile on Gratiot Avenue. There were over a hundred mourners, many of them looking warm and comfortable in mink. Clippert sat austerely alone in the front. The casket was black and silver and was closed. Mulheisen spotted Lou Spencer among the mourners and approached her after the ceremony.

She was properly somber, but her expression lightened when she saw Mulheisen. "I haven't heard from you, Sergeant," she said.

"I thought it was 'Mul,' " he said. "I didn't want to rush you off your feet." He looked around at the crowd that had come out of the church. Arthur Clippert was moving among them, accepting condolences and shaking hands. Occasionally he offered his cheek to the peck of what was apparently an old friend of his wife's family.

"Do you know all these people?" he asked Lou.

"Not all of them," she said. "They're mostly lawyers and socialites. Not many politicians. I guess they're afraid of the press associating them with someone who is involved in a scandal."

"So far he hasn't been very involved," Mulheisen said. "See anybody here who was, or might have been, a lover of Jane's?"

Lou looked at him in amazement. "God, you are a pig," she

said, then smiled. "Just like you fascists, trying to make me into a running dog. Get the innocent to do your dirty work."

"Innocent, are you? I'll bear that in mind. By the way, why is there no burial service? I take it we're just supposed to leave."

Lou nodded. "It's rather unusual. I assume it has something to do with the police."

"No," Mulheisen said. "The coroner has released the body. I'll have to check it out. What time is it, anyway?"

She glanced at her wristwatch. "Almost lunchtime," she said.

"Well, we all have to eat, don't we?"

"Life goes on," she said.

"I don't suppose you would care to join me?"

"Did you bring your lunch?" she said. "We could sit in the car."

"No, I was thinking more like Coney Islands, downtown."

She laughed. "Fine. I'll just go say a word to Arthur."

"Say hello for me," Mulheisen said. "I'll be with you in a moment."

Mulheisen went inside to where the coffin still sat before the altar. A group of young men in dark suits were obviously waiting for the crowd to clear before removing the casket to the hearse that waited at the steps of the church. Mulheisen walked over to them and chatted for minute, then left. As he went down the steps of the church toward Lou, his eye caught Arthur Clippert's. Clippert nodded grimly and turned away.

Since she had her own car, Mulheisen arranged to meet Lou at Pinky's, a pleasant little restaurant out on Jefferson, near the Belle Isle Bridge. The restaurant was located in an old house that was reputed to have been a whiskey smuggler's joint back during Prohibition. Then, during World War II, someone had told little Mul that Nazi POW's trying to escape into Canada had been caught in the house. He remembered riding by the place on the Jefferson Avenue streetcar, on his way to the ball game with his father, and thinking with delight, "Right there! Nazis!" It was a notion that still delighted Mulheisen.

The restaurant was unpretentious, the food was good, and it was one of Mulheisen's favorite places. When they were seated in a little room upstairs, Mulheisen told Lou the supposed history of

Pinky's. She laughed and said she had never heard that and doubted it was true.

"I like the part about the Nazi hideout best," he said.

"I'd have thought you would go for the smuggler story," she said, "being an intrepid sleuth, and all that."

"Nah. By the way, how was your conversation with Clippert?"

"Rather sad, actually. He was very calm and cool. I thought he'd be a little broken up, at least. But not Arthur. The man is like polished chrome, one of those brilliant sculptures by Brancusi." She seemed annoyed.

"How's that?"

"Well, he's very beautiful and all that, but when you look closely all you see is your own reflection."

"You had an affair with him, didn't you?" Mulheisen said.

Lou blushed, then she was defensive. "So what if I did? Anyway, it wasn't really an affair. I simply went to bed with him. A single occasion." As she talked on, she dropped her defensive tone and became more speculative. "It's that gorgeous surface. It's very attractive."

"Perhaps women just like to look into mirrors," Mulheisen said wryly.

"Poof. It's not just that. He has a great act. He can seem deeply interested for minutes at a time, I mean interested in *you.*"

"But it's not so, is it?" Mulheisen said.

She shook her head. "No. Not at all. But he fooled me, for a few hours. But before the night was over I was furious with myself. I think he could have had the decency to play out his game, but perhaps I wasn't accomplished enough for him. Just another scalp, I suppose."

"You might have been lucky," Mulheisen observed. "How do you suppose it was with Jane? Not that you were thinking of Jane at the time, obviously."

Lou colored. "You cops are pretty tough on us poor sinners," she said. Then she laughed. "I deserve it, of course. And yes, I did consider myself lucky, thinking about it later. I imagine it could be pretty tough on a woman who loved him, and was able to convince herself that he cared for her."

"Might even be a motive for murder," Mulheisen said, "for the woman, I mean. Not for him, unless . . . unless he was very tired of her and she had some means, some lever to hold him to her."

"What?" she said. "You mean money? He has plenty."

"Plenty as far as I'm concerned," Mulheisen said, "but maybe he wanted a lot more."

"I don't buy that," she said. "Arthur may be a prick, but I don't think he would kill for an inheritance."

"No," Mulheisen said, "especially since I've found out that he will not inherit her anticipated fortune." He told her about the Ducks Unlimited provision of the will.

Lou laughed.

"It's no joke," Mulheisen said. "I suppose he could take the will to court, but now I guess he won't have to. Jane's life was insured for a million dollars."

Lou looked serious. "Uh-oh," she said.

"Yeah," Mulheisen said, and fell silent.

Their lunch came and they talked of lighter things. Mulheisen began to feel very pleased with himself. He had eaten well, he had his second bourbon and water, and he was sitting in the old Nazi hideout with a pretty woman who was also amusing and evidently liked sitting here with him.

"I feel sorry for Arthur," she said suddenly.

"Don't," Mulheisen said. "He's got problems, but he can take care of himself."

"Oh, it isn't just that," she said. "I don't know how much those problems are of his own making. I don't believe, for instance, that he was really involved in that Fidelity Funding scandal—it's not his style. He's more of a loner—"

"The eternal halfback," Mulheisen said, interrupting somewhat peevishly. "Except that the halfback who looks so gorgeous down there, making fools of the downfield tacklers as he scampers for a touchdown, has to have some hard-working blockers before he can step out and strut his stuff. Well, it looks like he has some mighty good blockers now. He's in the backfield and streaking. The only question is, now that he has outrun his blockers, can he make it? And if he does, who gets the six points? Clippert, or the home team?"

"That's just it," she said, "he's all alone. He always has been, or thought he was, I guess. That's what I saw, of course, his coldness and aloofness. I mean, after we . . . Anyway, lots of people are isolated, but most of them know it. They struggle against it. But I'm not sure that Arthur does know it. I think he really believed that he was a one-man show. And Jane was so selfless, once she found the man she wanted, anyway . . . I'm sure she must have buffered him and helped him, and probably didn't let him know it. And he wouldn't notice, of course. But now, he'll have to face it."

"He won't be as alone as you think," Mulheisen said.

"What do you mean?"

"Something different than you do. You're talking about emotional isolation, I take it. That's one thing. There is also physical isolation. And that's one thing he's not going to have much of, whether he knows it or not.

"Incidentally, I found out why there was no burial service. The 'remains,' as the undertaker's boys put it, are to be held in storage until spring, at which time they will be removed to the Clippert estate in Jasper Lake and interred in a, quote, 'suitable memorial,' end quote, which Clippert is planning."

"That seems rather sweet," Lou said.

"Perhaps. I've always been suspicious of monuments, myself. Who do they really honor?"

"You're just suspicious by nature," Lou said. "Maybe that's why you're so good at what you do."

Mulheisen leaned across the table and did his best Bogart imitation. "Baby," he said, "you don't know *how* good."

Thirteen

Joe Service was in town. So far, nobody was aware of it. There were people waiting for him at the airport since noon. It was now 11 P.M. and Joe was downtown. That was the way he worked. Very devious.

The thing was, Joe liked his privacy. But in his business, privacy was a difficult thing to maintain. Too many people were interested in him. They wanted to know where he was all the time. His clients wanted to know more about him; the police were always interested. But so far, nobody knew much except that he got results.

"I don't guarantee," Joe would say, and then he would deliver.

To look at Joe Service you would think, Here is a city boy, born and bred. He was a short man with heavy black hair and thick eyebrows. He was not handsome, but he wasn't plug ugly, either. He smiled a lot, and that helped. Also, he looked intelligent, and that helped, since a lot of people will forgive homeliness for wit. He looked like he came out of the darkest heart of Brooklyn.

Except that he had such a deep tan. The fact was, Joe did come from Brooklyn, but for a long time he had lived in the mountainous West. Lately, he had a little cabin that was closer to Helper, Utah, than any other place. It was little more than a base camp. All he did there was practice with a Colt .38 and hike around the mountains. He drove his pickup truck long distances, to Green River to fish, or up to Idaho to hunt. Occasionally his city breeding would assert itself, and then he would drive into Helper to catch the Denver & Rio Grande to Denver or Salt Lake City. If the cabin fever got real bad, he would take the Amtrak to Reno, or even San Francisco. Joe loved trains.

No matter where he went, once a week he called an answering service in one of three cities—San Francisco, Miami or New York. That was how he heard about a job in Detroit. He was ready to work. He called some contacts in New York and Chicago, to get further information about the nature of this Detroit job. And then he was enthusiastic. So he called Detroit and said he would come.

His original plan was to take the train to Salt Lake and fly directly to Detroit, via Chicago. But when he got to Helper, he changed his mind and caught the train east. He fooled around in Denver for a day and took the Amtrak to Chicago.

In Chicago, he called his clients in Detroit and said he would arrive at Metropolitan Airport around noon. He even went out to O'Hare. But there he got hooked into an old familiar exercise of his and wasted a lot of time. He had a drink at one of the stand-up bars and picked out a face that looked like the straightest, most uninteresting guy there. Then he began to follow the man. All over the airport. To the magazine counter, the bathroom, to another stand-up bar. The man never noticed him, although Joe was not exactly an inconspicuous person. At last Joe followed him into the big restaurant and got seated next to him. In ten minutes he had picked out the man's life story. It was a very boring story and had a lot to do with chemical fertilizers and Grandview, Missouri.

So Joe took the Amtrak to Detroit. Now it was eleven at night, instead of noon, and he was downtown instead of at the airport. His deviousness went so far as to allow him to take a cab fifteen miles out to Metro. Once there, it was easy to pretend that he had just gotten off a flight.

He checked his bag in a coin box and strolled around the terminal. By midnight he had figured out who his contact was. A heavy man in a blue overcoat. Joe walked up to him and said, "I'm Joe Service."

"You're late," the man said. He was surprised that Joe was so short.

"Been here for hours," Joe said. "Came in on another flight, from Milwaukee."

The man shrugged. It was no big deal. He was paid to wait. They went out to a white Continental, which was warm because a driver had been sitting in it since noon. It smelled like a cigar.

On the way to Detroit, the fat man provided Joe with all the information he possessed about Arthur Clippert. He also provided five thousand dollars in cash. A retainer, he said. He also provided a Colt .38 revolver and a box of ammunition. Joe put the money and the weapon in his topcoat pockets.

"We don't expect you to use that," the man said, "and we want it back."

Service nodded. "I'd have brought my own, but these metal detectors . . ."

"That's all right. We'll help you all we can, but basically, we hear you like to work alone. That's fine with us. You just do your number. When and if you find the money, though, we want to know about it right away. We want to be there when you pick it up."

"That may not be possible," Joe said.

"If it ain't possible, okay. But try to make it possible. We didn't bring you in at this expense, rep or no rep, just to get euchred on the payoff. We want to be there." The fat man smiled. "See? We trust you, Joe. But we're careful."

Joe did not smile. "You don't have to trust me. You trust the Big Guy. He knows who I am and so do I. It's how I stay alive." Then he smiled. "I don't guarantee. I just do my best. Now, what do the cops think?"

The white Continental plunged into the concrete ditch of the freeway system. "Screw the cops," the fat man said. "What do they know? All they're worried about is his old lady got taken off. We want to know about the money. Everybody knows the bastard is holding, but how much? And where? He could have stashed it in a hundred banks, but we figure it's not too far away, most of it anyway, cause he has to use it. He might even have it in his house."

"Was that your guys who broke into the house and did the wife?"

"Not us," the fat man said. "We don't know who, yet. Amateurs. All we know is there was two of them and one of them was a cabdriver, maybe. We'd like to know more about them, but don't waste time on it unless you think that's where the money is."

Service nodded. "You people weren't into Fidelity Funding, then?"

"More amateurs," the fat man said. "But they had a sweet deal going. They just didn't know how to keep it going. Too many assholes involved. The word got out. But that computer kid was pretty sharp. We been talking to him. We could use a guy like that. Naw, they blew it, but let's face it, they still managed to rip off the all-time bundle. And they still got it. Question is, for how long?" The fat man spoke authoritatively, like a literary critic who has seen a fascinating but obviously marred work of genius.

"We booked you a room at the Statler, Joe, and we got you a car. We even got you a chauffeur, since you probably don't know your way around town too well. The boss wanted to meet with you, but"—he looked at his watch—"it's late, and you're probably beat. Call this number in the morning." He handed Joe a slip of paper. "We'll set up a meeting."

"Thanks," Joe said.

The Continental pulled off the freeway and turned onto a side street and stopped next to a dark-blue Chevy. The man behind the wheel of the Chevy waved. Joe carried his bag to the back seat of the Chevy. The Continental left.

"You're late," the driver said. He was a young man. The car was full of cigarette smoke.

"You mind not smoking?" Joe said. "It bothers me."

"You don't smoke?" the driver said. He weaved quickly through the snowy streets.

"No. Let's go downtown. I want to check out the local talent. You know a place?"

The driver laughed. "Sure do. We'll go to Johnny's. Ginch up the ying-yang."

"Don't drive so fast," Joe said. "There's no hurry. And stop at a drugstore. I need some Rolaids."

"Rolaids. You got an ulcer, or something?"

"Just a bad stomach. I can't stand that airplane food."

The driver pulled up at a corner drugstore and parked illegally.

"Be right out," Joe said. He walked in the front door and moved directly toward the pharmacist's counter in the rear, then veered out a side entrance onto the side street and walked quickly away. Within a block he found a cab. He rode it to a bar on the other side of downtown and went in for a drink and to check the telephone directory. He made a call, then called another cab. He rode to a place where he could catch a suburban bus.

An hour later he was comfortably lodged in a motel in Royal Oak. He felt fine. The dodging around was good exercise. He had a safe gun, he had five thousand dollars, and he had a distinct absence of heavy breathing over his shoulder. Now he could work. He called the number the fat man had given him. After the angry noises had died down he explained that he was here to do the job. He would do it his way. Period. If they didn't like it, he would go home. Also, the five thousand dollars was a paltry retainer and he would consider it expense money. For the job, he would work on a straight commission—10 percent of whatever he found. If they didn't like it, they should check with the following number in New York City.

There was a lot more noise about that, but finally it was agreed upon.

Joe slept well. In the morning he started calling taxicab companies, asking for work. A lot of the companies needed drivers, but he was able to eliminate those that didn't. It was a start. Now he would have to go and find out why they needed drivers.

He went to breakfast down the street, at a small workingman's joint called Eat. He saw the headlines: GANGLAND SLAYING?

Fourteen

The waning heat of the corpse had been sufficient to cause it to melt down into the old snow so that it could not be easily seen. The crows saw it, however. Two boys were out with their .410 shotguns, looking for rabbits. They had tried to sneak up on the crows but that is always impossible. When the crows flew away, the boys went over to see what the birds had been after. They expected to find a dead dog.

The Wayne County Sheriff's department was first on the scene, but then a lot of other people showed up, including the state police, the coroner's office and the Ecorse police. What the .44 Magnum had started, the activity of the crows had aggravated. It was no longer possible, for instance, to tell what color the eyes might have been. And there were many white stains on the corpse.

It was a patrolman from the Ecorse police who tramped around and suddenly reached down into the snow. He came up with a revolver. Part of the grip was broken off.

"Hey, look at this," he yelled. The gun was passed from hand to hand before a state cop angrily interceded, too late to save fingerprint evidence.

Frank Zeppanuk saw the gun when it came into the forensics lab. He immediately called Mulheisen.

"Must have seemed like a good idea to shoot up the identifying characteristics that way," Frank told Mulheisen when the latter arrived. "It almost worked. I haven't gotten very far on my matchups, but I'm willing to bet you a box of cigars that this guy was the character who was in the tub with Mrs. Clippert. There were two types of blood found, you know, and one of them was Mrs. Clippert's. The fragment from the pistol handle fits perfectly and the hair matches the samples from the tub. The blood match will be done shortly."

"We still don't have a name, though," Mulheisen said. "Homicide is checking the gun registration."

Frank pushed up his dark rimmed glasses with a forefinger. "You notice that the gun is an H & R .32."

"Yes," Mulheisen said, "and I suppose the ballistics match the slugs found in Mrs. Clippert."

"The best match was with the slug that came out of the mattress," Frank said, "but any one of them will do. They all came from this gun."

"Bully for you," Mulheisen said. He gave Frank a cigar and left.

The pistol was registered to Mr. Emil Earle. Mulheisen drove out to Mr. Earle's residence in Redford in the company of McClain and Joe Greene. Mr. Earle was getting ready to leave for his job on the swing shift at Pontiac.

"Yes," Earle said, "I own an H & R .32. Or did. It was stole last fall."

"Why didn't you report its loss?" Joe Greene said.

"I did! And the gun was registered, too. I kept it in my cabin, up north. It was stole last fall along with a buncha other stuff. Some bastard broke in and damn near cleaned the whole joint out."

Mr. Earle showed Mulheisen a map of the area. It was a map printed up by a development corporation showing the layout of numbered lots around a peculiar-looking lake, which consisted of a ten-acre central body out of which a dozen or more perfectly straight "legs" had been dredged. It resembled a child's drawing of the sun.

"Yeah, they went in there with a dragline," confirmed Mr. Earle. "It used to be called Paton's Pond, but the corporation changed the name to Black Beaver Lake. Maybe it ain't like building on a real, natural lake, but the land was cheap and it's right off the freeway. You can get there in a coupla hours. The wife and kids love it and the lake is well stocked with bass. I figure it's an investment, you know?"

The lots were laid out along the legs, or channels, of the lake. Mulheisen could just picture it: an instant holiday village of prefabricated cabins and cottages jammed together like a rusticated version of the suburbs from which these vacationers were fleeing. There would be a thousand kids running along the dusty streets of the community all summer. Teen-aged boys and girls would roam the streets at dusk and drive to neighboring towns at night for movies and beer parties. The wives would lie in the shade and talk to one another, just as they had done in Redford, or Harper Woods, or Royal Oak. The husbands would do a bit of desultory fishing and a lot of beer drinking while they watched the Tigers on television. They professed to want to get out of the city: but they insisted on bringing the city with them.

The officers got a list of other stolen items and the name of the county sheriff there and left. Sheriff Tate was not in. Deputy Barrett was. He told Mulheisen over the phone that he had sent a complete list of goods stolen in several break-ins that had occurred last fall around Black Beaver Lake.

"We figure these things'll be fenced in your larger cities," Deputy Barrett said, "so we sent the lists to Flint, Detroit, Grand Rapids and so forth. One thing you have to realize, of course, is that these people all have insurance. They'll report a lot of things that maybe weren't stolen."

Within an hour, Mulheisen and McClain had several teams on the streets going from hock shop to junk shop to known fences, looking for the goods. Mulheisen's crew was from the Ninth Precinct, a couple of bulldogs named Jensen and Field.

The weather was gray, damp, cold and sloppy. The worst kind of Detroit weather. The streets were filled with Christmas shoppers and shoplifters, pickpockets, molesters, and guys who exposed themselves on parking-ramp staircases. Traffic was mercilessly heavy and there were multiple-car accidents. The hallways of the precincts were crowded with shoplifters and purse snatchers, waiting for interrogation and adding their greasy head stains to the walls. The drunk tanks filled early.

Mulheisen thought of his blue-haired mother lolling in balmy Miami. Soon he would receive the first of the post cards from the dog tracks, the jai alai courts, and the house cards from the Fontainebleau. He also thought of Lou Spencer. There was no time to see her now.

Fifteen

December twenty-first dawned gray, damp, cold and sloppy again. The papers were still talking about the Indian Village murder, despite the fact that there had been over a dozen murders in town since that one. Mulheisen would have preferred staying off the streets where the Christmas hysteria was mounting. But there was work to do. He went over the situation with McClain in the morning.

"The basic case, the murder, is essentially solved," Mulheisen said. "We know that the man who was found in the field by the airport was the same man who was in the house on Seneca Street. He is almost certainly the man who shot Mrs. Clippert. At the same time, the case is wide open. We don't know why he was in the tub with her, if he was working alone, what he was actually doing in the house in the first place, or who he was, even."

"That's a lot you don't know," McClain said.

"If we can get a lead on his identity through the burglary stuff, we'll be well on our way to clearing up that end of it," Mulheisen said.

"If," snorted McClain, his big feet propped up on the desk, on top of a file folder. "What about a connection with our pal the Flying Clipper?"

Mulheisen sucked at his teeth. "There's a curious coincidence," he said, "except that in a murder case there aren't any coincidences. The gun was stolen from a cabin not eight miles from Clippert's summer place. In fact, it was stolen from a so-called holiday development that is owned by a friend of Clippert's. A man named Carl Joyner. I'm going to see him this morning."

"That's a pretty vague connection," McClain said. "How'd you get onto that?"

Mulheisen smiled. "Secret sources."

"Hmmph. Well, we got a possible motive in the insurance policy that can't be ignored, even if it is rather obvious. I don't know if a jury would go for it. If a jury wouldn't go for it, the prosecutor won't. It'd be useful if it's backed up with a lot of other evidence."

Mulheisen ticked off his fingers. "We have a murder weapon, or one of them, coming from an area near the Clipper's summer home, we have a motive, and we have a suspect in Clippert who —thanks to the Fidelity Funding swindle—is criminally suspect. It's not enough, I know, but at least he can no longer pose as the Pure One."

"Mul, don't marry yourself to a single suspect," McClain warned. "You know that can lead to grief."

"I know. I'm fighting it. I'm off to see this guy Joyner."

Mulheisen drove out John Lodge Expressway through vicious traffic. Near Northland Shopping Center he got off the freeway and cruised past the Fidelity Funding Building. It was one of several new office buildings, all rather similar. They were five to ten stories high, of prestressed concrete with lots of glass. They were separated from one another by undeveloped commercial lots and stood on individual islands of their own parking lots. The lots were heaped with snow.

The Fidelity Funding lot was only partially cleared. The few cars parked there were gray U.S. Government Motor Pool vehicles and blue State of Michigan cars. The building looked like an empty honeycomb, with its deepset windows, only a few of which were lit. Unlike the neighboring buildings there was no aluminum Christmas tree in the lobby. Auditors and investigators were its only occupants, still poring over the books and analyzing the computer programs to find out how bad the swindle had been, and how it had been accomplished.

Mulheisen drove on by, all the way out past Bloomfield Hills. Out on the highway he found a model home display that had a huge sign over it, saying "Gitchee-Gumee Estates." The lot was filled with prefabricated model vacation homes of the red cedar and glass-front style. The models were connected by a wooden walkway that ran through the display like a spider web. The business office was in one of the front models, one described by a wooden placard as "The Laurentian, only $15,000, erected on your own lakefront property."

Carl Joyner was an affable fat man with a pink face and white hair. He wore the kind of glasses that changed their tint according to the amount of light. They were pretty clear today and Mulheisen could see his pink-rimmed eyes and white lashes. He was perched on a desk in the front office along with several salesmen in sports coats.

There was a secretary with a short skirt and a beehive hairdo. There was also a bronze enamel coffee urn with plastic-foam cups stacked next to it. There were no customers and the boys were drinking something other than coffee in the plastic cups. Joyner offered Mulheisen some of their beverage, from a blue-velvet-wrapped square bottle of Canadian whiskey.

"Holiday cheers, Sergeant," he said.

Mulheisen smiled and said, "Could we talk privately, Mr. Joyner?"

They went into an inner room, one which in the home would be the master bedroom, but was presently the boss's office.

"Actually, you're lucky to catch me here," Joyner said. "I spend most of my time in my downtown offices. This is only one of several development subsidiaries I'm involved in. I just stopped by to bring the boys a holiday bottle or two and pass out bonus checks."

"What's the name of your parent organization?"

"National Holiday Properties," Joyner said. "It's pretty big. We operate all over, through subsidiaries like this one. Georgia, Florida, Michigan, the far West, you name it. But Gitchee-Gumee is one of our most valuable operations."

Mulheisen listened to this kind of talk for awhile, wishing to put Joyner quite at ease. They sipped the Canadian and Joyner was very friendly. Mulheisen turned the conversation to Clippert.

"A wonderful man," Joyner said enthusiastically. "I've known him for years. This is a terrible thing he's going through. I sure hope he comes out of it all right. I always thought very highly of Art. To me he's the kind of guy who could go all the way, like he used to against Ohio State and UCLA. This is kind of a setback though, isn't it?"

"What is?" Mulheisen asked. "The murder?"

"Well, yes, that too, of course. I meant the Fidelity Funding thing, mainly. The loss of his wife is a terrible, terrible thing. It can't have anything to do with Art though, I'm sure. No, it's the Fidelity Funding thing. If it hadn't been for that, why I believe a lot of people—myself included—were looking forward to seeing Art in the governor's mansion."

"You can't mean it," Mulheisen said.

Joyner looked wise and solemn, or struggled to. "I'm not kidding, Sergeant. Oh, I don't mean next year or the year after. It would mean a term in the state senate first, probably. But ultimately, he's the kind of guy who goes all the way. He's got the young, Kennedy-type looks, the early glamour of the athlete—a great amateur who wouldn't turn pro. He's got brains, money, education, a pretty wi—oops." Joyner was more successful this time in looking solemn. "That part's all changed now, isn't it?" He was thoughtful. "I wonder if even that wouldn't help him, actually. I mean, look at what's-his-name, Percy of Illinois."

"Yes, he's hardly down and out," Mulheisen said wryly. He accepted another dollop of the Canadian.

"True," Joyner said, "but this Fidelity Funding crap is going to be hard to shake. Even if he isn't indicted. The post-Watergate mentality, you know, it's making it pretty tough for folks in the public life. Not that it isn't a good thing, in a way—kind of clears the air and all that."

Joyner looked like a white rabbit as he hunched forward, tucking his plump belly under the edge of the desk. "Now what I'd like to see the boy do is come in with me. This holiday estate business is booming, and recession or no recession, I think it's going to maintain. Folks want to get out of the cities, get away from the niggers, if you know what I mean. You take a thing like this Gitchee-Gumee—that's an Indian name, you know—why, we can't develop these things fast enough. Everybody wants lake property. Are you married, Sergeant?"

"No," Mulheisen said. "And I'm not interested. What I am interested in, though, are all these burglaries at Black Beaver Lake."

"What about them?" Joyner was imperturbable. "I understand there's been no great loss. Besides, the Black Beaver Lake Community Association, which we sponsored, has hired a permanent security staff. Something that should have been done from the start, I guess. But that ought to take care of the nuisance."

"I understand that Clippert has a place near there, at Jasper Lake."

"That's right," Joyner said. "Used to be his father-in-law's place, old Axel Bodnar. Quite a character, Axel was. I have a place up there myself."

"What is it, sort of a community? A fancier version of Black Beaver?"

"No, nothing like it," Joyner said. "You're talking about actual estates when you talk about Jasper. Old houses, a lot of them. All quite private. Oh, we get together now and then, some of us, for a dinner party, swim in each other's pools. But privacy is the big thing, you know."

"Don't you swim in the lake?" Mulheisen wanted to know.

"The lake's kind of cold," Joyner said. "I don't go for that pool stuff much, myself, I burn too easily. But we all have one."

"Ever had any problem with break-ins?"

Joyner waved his hand. "Oh, it happens, from time to time. Usually it's just kids from the farms or the nearby towns. I guess they get a little resentful. A little vandalism, that's all."

"How about when the houses at Black Beaver were hit? Any similar activity at Jasper Lake?"

"Come to think of it, there was," Joyner said. "Can't blame the burglars, either. There's more valuables in my dining room than in a whole block of cottages at Black Beaver. But I was lucky. They didn't hit my place. Hit Art's, though."

"Did they?" Mulheisen's expression was bland, masking his interest. "That's kind of odd, Joyner. Why didn't he report it?"

"Didn't he?" Joyner said, innocently.

"No."

"How would you know?" Joyner asked.

"I asked the sheriff up there, Tate."

"Now why would you do that?"

"Curiosity," Mulheisen said.

"Killed the cat, you know," Joyner said.

Mulheisen smiled, baring his long teeth. "Old sayings like that often have a deep core of truth, they tell me. Maybe that's how they get to be old sayings." He gazed directly into Joyner's pink eyes. "What about Clippert's burglary, Joyner?"

The chubby man seemed uncomfortable, then he shrugged. "Oh well, it was nothing, I'm sure. I don't know why Art didn't report it. But heck, you make it sould like *he* committed a crime, instead of being the victim."

"As a matter of fact," Mulheisen said, "the citizen is enjoined to notify the proper authority in the event of the commission of any crime. If he doesn't it's something like withholding evidence, or interfering with a police officer."

Joyner seemed to get the point. "I suppose you're going to lay this on Art, too, as if he didn't have enough trouble."

"I doubt it. It's really no concern of mine. I'm just curious. But if I can't satisfy my curiosity I'll have to dig deeper, and then the whole business could get out of hand."

Joyner sighed. "Well, what do you want to know?"

"Did Clippert tell you something about the burglary?"

"Yes. Just in passing. He seemed to think it was a funny incident. As I recall, he had gone up to the house after work, one evening in late October. He got there late and caught the burglars at their work."

"Was he alone?"

"Yes, or well—I guess I might as well tell you, his wife wasn't with him. Maybe that's why he didn't report it. He didn't want to get the girl in trouble, or himself, I expect."

"Oh, I think he could probably have kept her out of it," Mulheisen said. "Who was the girl, anyway?"

"He didn't say. Anyhow, he was about to go in the house when he saw a light. He had the girl go back to the car and wait. Then he went in. There were two guys, working different rooms. He took them one by one."

"What do you mean, 'took them'?"

Joyner made a plump fist and stuck out his forefinger. "You know, 'Hands up, podner.'"

"He had a gun."

"That's right. He carries one in the glove compartment of his car. Damn! Now I suppose you'll get on him for that."

"If it's not properly registered," Mulheisen said. "So he had the two men. What happened then?"

"He let them go."

"He let them go? Why?"

"That's the funny part. He said it was because he recognized one of the guys."

"A friend?"

"No, that would be ridiculous, of course. No, he said that he had known one of the guys from something that had happened years back. I think he said it was something from his Air Force days. At first he didn't recognize the guy, he said, but the guy recognized him and reminded him of this other time they had met."

"Did he say who the guy was?"

"No, and he didn't say what the earlier occasion was, either," Joyner said. "I asked him. He was vague about it. 'Oh, just a favor I did once,' he said. Quite a coincidence, isn't it?"

Mulheisen agreed. "He didn't tell you anything else about the men? Didn't describe them at all?"

Joyner shook his head.

Mulheisen sat thinking. Finally, he said, "You've been very helpful, Joyner. This information may be irrelevant to my present investigation, but you never can tell. By the way, did you know Mrs. Clippert very well?"

"Oh, I used to see her with Art, that's all. A very beautiful woman. She was something in a bathing suit, believe me. But kind of stuck-up, you know. I don't believe I ever had a conversation with her."

"How about your wife? What did she think of Jane Clippert?"

"She liked her all right, I guess. But Jane was a lot younger. Just a girl, really."

Mulheisen shrugged. "Well, what I'd like now, Joyner, is for you to write down a complete statement, everything you've just told me, and sign it."

"Aw, come on now, man," Joyner said. "I've been cooperative. I'm a busy man, I have to get back downtown."

"To pass out more Canadian? I'm serious, Joyner. I wasn't kidding about the interfering with an officer's business or withholding evidence. I'm not asking you to come to Headquarters, but I could. Why don't you just get your secretary in here, dictate the statement, she can type it up and you can sign it. I'll wait."

Mulheisen leaned across the desk and helped himself to the Canadian. He took out a cigar and lit it.

Joyner made a face, then called in his secretary. A half-hour later the statement was ready and Mulheisen had a signed copy.

"Thanks a lot, Joyner. You've been very helpful. I'm going to ask you not to say anything about this to Clippert. It's probably not relevant to my investigation anyway. If it does turn out to be relevant, I may ask you for a formal statement to be made in the prosecutor's office. I'll let you know. And thanks for the whiskey. Cheers!"

The irrepressible Joyner even smiled and raised his glass as Mulheisen left. "Merry Christmas!" he called out.

Sixteen

The traffic on the way back into Detroit was not cheering. A heavy snow had begun to fall and it was being ground into a sticky mush that built up under windshield wipers. Cars slithered into intersections like spooky forwards at a face-off at Olympia. The comparison amused Mulheisen at first, then irritated him. It would be a while before he would have the leisure to go to Olympia. He wondered if Lou liked hockey. Living in New York, she was probably a Ranger fan, he thought.

It was early afternoon but as dark as twilight. Mulheisen thought he ought to call on Clippert again. It would be interesting to get his version of the unreported burglary. The idea cheered him. The case was looking up. One of the murder weapons could now be traced to a man, or men, who had at least a passing acquaintance with Clippert. That was very interesting indeed. Almost enough to get a warrant, Mulheisen thought. Just one coincidence too many. But he was in no hurry to pull Clippert in. As long as Ayeh kept him in sight he'd be safe enough.

Mulheisen stopped at Eight Mile Road and called in to the precinct. "Ayeh check in yet?" he asked the desk man.

"This Mul? Yeah. He's downtown at Clippert's club. Evidently his man is playing handball. I got the address."

"Handball? Man oh man, if he isn't Mr. Coolbones. Well, I think I'll just drop down there and talk to him."

The desk man gave him the address and then said, "Oh yeah, your two favorite bird dogs are back. They want to talk to you."

"Put them on," Mulheisen said.

Jensen's voice came on the line. He had a very loud voice. Mulheisen had to hold the receiver slightly away from his ear. "Mulheisen? We found the stuff."

There was silence. Mulheisen waited. Just like Peter Jensen, he thought. Jensen was a meanie. A square-faced man with a brush cut that accentuated a brutal face. He was good at forcing things out of people with his direct, challenging look and blunt questions that only thinly veiled a hint of violence. But then, once he had the information, it was your turn to dig it out.

"Okay, Jensen," Mulheisen sighed, "what stuff are you talking about?"

"The burglary stuff. We found it in a pawnshop in Hamtramck. The stuff from what's-his-name, wait a minute"—Jensen was evidently consulting a notebook—"from a Mr. Emil Earle's cabin at Black Beaver Lake. One portable GE TV . . . wait, I take that back. The TV wasn't there anymore. It was sold, but the pawnshop guy remembered it. And one Kenmore electric steam iron, one General Electric toaster, one Sunbeam electric mixer—"

"Okay, okay, I get the picture," Mulheisen said. "So you found the stuff. How did you know it was Earle's?"

"That was easy. Mr. Earle is one of those identification freaks. He has a Dymo labeler and he put his name and address inside everything where it wouldn't be found unless you took the thing apart. Too bad more people don't do that."

"Yeah, too bad," Mulheisen said. "What about the guys who hocked the stuff? Did you get a description?"

There was a pained silence. Mulheisen realized that he had offended Jensen. Sometimes that seemed like a very easy thing to do, as if the granite façade of Jensen was only a highly sensitive film, perhaps but a micro-millimeter thick.

"We got the descriptions," Jensen said, in a resigned voice. He seemed to be saying, "I know we're just dummies, Bud and me, and that it's the smarty-pants, like you, who really solve crimes, not poor old shitkickers like me and Bud."

"Descriptions? So there were two of them? Good, good. I suppose one was a little skinny guy?"

"That's right," Jensen yelled. "And the other guy was big. Mutt and Jeff. Anyway, that's what the proprietor remembers. The little guy was skinny and looked like a drowned rat. The big guy had a pitted face, like he had smallpox once, and he was a cabdriver."

"How does he know he was a cabdriver?" Mulheisen asked.

"Cause they drove up in a cab. Also, the big guy wore one of them caps that snaps down on the bill and on the cap he had a union badge."

"Maybe the little guy just came there in a cab," Mulheisen suggested.

"Who rides a cab to hock a toaster? Besides, the big guy stood around in the store while the little guy made the deal, but the proprietor remembers that the big guy was listening pretty closely and then they went out together, talking. The proprietor got the feeling that they were buddies."

"Did he notice what company the cab was from?"

"No," Jensen said.

"Well, then, we know what we have to do, don't we?"

"Yah," Jensen said. "We hit the cab companies."

"Give the description and also you might ask if any of their drivers have quit suddenly, in the last few days. How many companies are there, anyway?"

"Maybe a dozen or so."

"Hmmmm." Mulheisen was standing outside and snow was building up on his shoulders. "Okay, here's the program. Get that pawnshop guy in and have someone start him on an Identi-Kit picture of the two guys. In the meantime, you and Field start on the companies that are on the east side. I'm on the northwest side right now, so I'll start on this side of town. Now, put the desk back on the line, will you?"

Mulheisen told the desk sergeant that he wouldn't be seeing Clippert after all. Instead, he'd be canvassing west-side cab companies and he would call in if he found anything. He hung up and checked the Yellow Pages for the addresses of taxicab companies.

It was one-thirty when he started and almost dark by the time he had worked his way down to the Detroit River. He was exhausted by the snow, the traffic, no lunch and the negative headshakes he had received. The last place he went was called Dixieland Cab Company and the offices were located in an old warehouse near the Ambassador Bridge. The visibility was so bad that the big bridge disappeared into fog and snow about a hundred yards out in its arc toward Canada.

There was nobody around but a dispatcher. He was a fat black man with a shiny face and was smoking the biggest, most carbon-encrusted pipe that Mulheisen had ever seen. The bowl of the pipe looked as big as a baby's head.

"Must take strong jaws to hold that stove all day," Mulheisen said.

"Sure do. Sometime I wake up grinding my teeth," the dispatcher said.

"I'm looking for a driver, a tall fellow with a pitted face, wears a brown workman's cap. He may have been missing for the last few days. Since about the eighteenth."

"That's ol' John," the dispatcher said. "He tooken off again."

"Does John take off like this often?" Mulheisen asked.

"Once in a while. He like to go on a little stumble, time to time. Always takes a few days to get him back. Most of the time, though, he drink so damn much gin it seem like it keep him sober. I told him 'bout that gin, I said, 'That shit'll kill you, brother,' but ol' John, that's his water." The fat man took the pipe from beneath his teeth and poked at it with a small metallic device. He puffed happily, sending billows of foul smoke up in the little office.

The radio crackled. "Dixie One, where was that Grand Avenue call?"

"That is *Grant* Avenue," the dispatcher told the microphone. "That's gee-ahruh-ayuh-enn-tee. As in toenail. Numma one-niyun-fo-six." There was some ten-four chatter, and the fat man turned back to Mulheisen.

"John's not a bad guy," he said. "Purty smart boy, only he

kep' off that gin. This time I think he gitten fired, though. Didn' bring back his vehicle. He usually purty good 'bout that.''

"Let's see his employment record," Mulheisen said, showing the badge.

And there it was, complete with a photograph taken by the Detroit Police Department. John Byron Wienoshek, aged forty-three, address: The St. Martin Hotel, Windsor, Ontario. Mulheisen handed the file back to the dispatcher. "I won't need it," he said. "Thanks. Why hasn't your employer reported the missing cab?"

The dispatcher shrugged. "Ain't my business. Mr. Shapiro, I think he like John. Says John is a cultured man, down on his luck. He almost fired him last time he tooken off. But ol' John, he don't give a shit. He always say he lookin' for a job when he found this one." The man chuckled and shook his head as if in admiration. "Quite a character, ol' John. What's our John done?"

"We need to find him," Mulheisen said, "for questioning in a very serious matter. If you hear from him, or anything about him or the missing cab, I want to know immediately. And I have to warn you not to inform Wienoshek that we want him. Just call me at this number, or if I'm not there, call this number." He gave the dispatcher his own and McClain's numbers.

The dispatcher looked at the slip of paper and puffed on his huge pipe. "Yeah, I knowed he was in trouble when that other guy came lookin' for him. Somethin' wrong with that dude."

"Somebody else looking for Wienoshek?" Mulheisen was puzzled. "What did he look like?"

"White dude, about fifty-five, dark hair. Come in here a couple of hours ago. First he said he lookin' for a job, then he ask if anybody quit lately, or didn't show up. I told him 'bout John. After that, no more bullshit about lookin' for a job. He wanted John's address."

"Did you give it to him?"

"Why not? Ain't top secret. Said he was a ol' buddy of John's. He went outa here like his pants on fire."

"A little guy?" Mulheisen couldn't believe it. "A little skinny guy?"

"Naw, he wasn't skinny. Now I think on it, he was kinda well-built fella. Dark, too, like an Eyetalian, or coulda been Jewish.

100

Real heavy eyebrows. First I thinkin' he's a workin' man, but then I see that ain't such a bad suit he wearin'.'"

Mulheisen was very interested. "If this man returns, or if you hear from him, try to get his name and whereabouts, will you? It's very important. I'd like to talk to him."

"Whatever you say, man."

Mulheisen pulled out a cigar. "Here, give your jaws a rest."

"Why, thank you, m'man. Much appreciated." The cigar disappeared into the man's jacket.

Mulheisen stopped to call the Ninth. He left word for Jensen and Field to drop the canvass and the Identi-Kit. It was dark now and still snowing. He called McClain at Homicide and caught him leaving.

"I'll get a bulletin out on Wienoshek right away," McClain said, "and I'll get his complete record. What are you up to?"

"I'm going over to Windsor, check out his residence," Mulheisen said. "I suppose you might as well have somebody check the airport and the bus terminal. If he has left town we're kind of late, but there might be someone who remembers him. And now, listen to this." He gave McClain a quick reprise of his interview with Carl Joyner.

"Aha," McClain said, "sounds like things are cooking out there. Maybe we should pick the Flying Clipper up."

"I don't think so," Mulheisen said. "Arrange for someone to relieve Ayeh, though, will you? He must be dragging ass. We'd better keep a twenty-four-hour surveillance on Clippert from now on."

"I agree," McClain said. "What about this other fellow, the one who's asking about Wienoshek?"

"Can't figure it," Mulheisen said. "Something is up, though. I'll talk to you when I get back from Windsor."

Traffic across the bridge was awful. It was going-home time for the thousands of Canadians who worked and shopped in Detroit. It was 6 P.M. before Mulheisen reached the St. Martin Hotel, a quiet, shabby residential hotel that took its name from the side street it was located on.

The tiny lobby was dimly lit and Mulheisen could smell food cooking. A door opened when he rang the desk bell and a middle-aged bald man came out in suspenders and slippers. There was a noise of plates and children that suggested that it was dinnertime.

Mulheisen was straightforward, explaining that he was from the Detroit police, that he had no authority here, but that he was working on an important investigation. He was sure that the Windsor police would cooperate—if he was forced to call them in. The clerk, Mr. Deavons, didn't argue. He wanted to get back to his dinner.

The first thing he said was that Wienoshek had already had a visitor, two hours earlier. A short, dark man who represented himself as "a friend of John's."

"I told him what I tell you, Byron is not home and hasn't been for several days. I have no idea where he has gone, but I'm sure he'll return. He always does. His room is paid up.

"Byron has lived here since before I came," Deavons went on. "He's very kind to the kiddies, always buys them something for Christmas and the birthday. Very polite to the wife. We don't socialize a good deal, only in passing, because he's an alcoholic, you see, which we don't hold against him as long as he behaves himself here, which he always has, you see.

"This other chap, the short man, I have never seen him before. Byron does not often bring friends here, nor do they often visit him, except for Elroy.

"Elroy? Elroy is a quiet, very pleasant little man," Deavons said. "He was here just last week, visiting with Byron. I believe he has seen hard times. It doesn't do to inquire too closely, is my motto. A man has a right to his privacy. Yes, he's rather a slight chap, dark-haired but not at all like the chap who was here today. Elroy never says much. I don't recall that I ever heard his last name. No, I'm sure I haven't."

Mr. Deavons said that the other man had not gone up to Wienoshek's room, since Byron was clearly not in. He had left. Deavons agreed to take Mulheisen up to the room, casting a wistful glance backward at the sound of dinner being consumed.

When he opened the door to the room, Mr. Deavons started back in shock. The room was a shambles. Every drawer had been turned out, every book opened and tossed aside. The Murphy bed was pulled down and the mattress slashed open. The pillow had been slashed as well and feathers floated about in the draft from the hall door. Furniture was turned over. Coffee, sugar and flour had been dumped on the table. Light fixtures had been removed and left dangling.

Mulheisen advised Deavons to call the police. There was no telephone in the room. As Deavons was going out, Mulheisen asked, "By the way, was Wienoshek a Canadian?"

"No," Deavons answered.

"Why did he live here, then?"

"Why, sir, I should say it was because of his mother. His old mum is a Canadian, you see. She's in a nursing home not far from here."

Seventeen

"Poor little Byron," Frances Wienoshek said, "nothing ever seems to go quite right for him. What trouble is he in now?" Mrs. Wienoshek was a tall and bosomy woman with a pretty face that had crumbled at the edges, softened by time and facial powder. She seemed in good health although she claimed to be much weakened by a gall bladder operation two months earlier. Unlike many of her fellow residents at the Anchorage, who were in bathrobes and watching "Dad's Army" on CBC, Mrs. Wienoshek was fully dressed in a skirt and cardigan sweater and her thick gray hair was carefully done up in coiled braids. She was reading a biography of Mary, Queen of Scots.

"I don't know that he's in any trouble," Mulheisen said, "although he seems to have left his job without notice and failed to return his cab to the company."

"Oh dear. That sounds a bother. I suppose he's drinking again. The holidays are such a trial for Byron. He is by nature a convivial man. But I must say I never fancied his cabdriving. I think he ought to return to University. He took some night courses at Wayne State, you know, and did very well, especially in Literature." She spoke with a trace of a British accent.

"Well, I'd like to talk to him," Mulheisen said. "You must have heard from him."

Mrs. Wienoshek looked very sad. "I'm afraid I haven't, Mr. Mulheisen. Not for several days. But I expect I shall, for we always have Christmas together. But why do you want to talk to him? Is it about the taxicab?"

"No, it's about a friend of his."

"Which friend?" she asked.

"That's just it," Mulheisen said, "we don't know the man's name. The man was found dead in Detroit and, so far, all we have found out about him is that he may have been an acquaintance of your son. Were you familiar with any of your son's friends?"

Mrs. Wienoshek held the book in her lap with a finger in it to mark her place. She pondered. "Byron hadn't many close friends," she said. "He was always rather quiet and retiring— except when he'd been drinking. The only one I've met in recent years is Elroy. He was an old friend of Byron's from the Air Force. I think Byron felt rather sorry for him. He wasn't really the sort of friend one would expect Byron to have. You see, Byron has led a rather checkered career, I suppose, but deep down he's a sensitive, retiring sort. Perhaps he doesn't look it, but he is really quite cultured. We used to go to the opera."

"What about this Elroy?" Mulheisen asked.

"Now, Elroy is a pleasant young chap," Mrs. Wienoshek said, "but he is one of those lads who are always down and out. Not exactly a ne'er-do-well, not exactly, but hardly of Byron's caliber."

"I see," Mulheisen said. "Did you ever hear his last name?"

"Oh yes. It's Elroy Carver. He is just a little fellow, not a big husky chap like Byron."

"About how tall would you say Elroy was?"

"Was?"

Mulheisen nodded. "Was."

"Oh dear." Mrs. Wienoshek's soft face went into mourning. "I do hope poor Elroy hasn't had an accident. Byron will be so upset. He was fond of Elroy. Poor Elroy always looked up to Byron, of course, rather as an older brother."

"I understand," Mulheisen said. "Could you give me a complete description of Carver?"

"He's such a dear little lad. I shouldn't put him at more than five feet five inches, and not more than nine or ten stone."

"Nine or ten stone? Is that his weight?"

She smiled benignly. "So sorry, it's what you would call a hundred twenty-five pounds, perhaps. He has dark hair, a narrow head, and a rather furtive expression, I'm afraid. He does not have good teeth. Byron has lovely teeth."

In the next hour, Mulheisen learned that Frances Wienoshek had been born and raised in Sussex, where she had met and married a visiting Canadian businessman. Shortly after they returned to Nova Scotia, her husband had died. Subsequently she had remarried, to Albert S. Wienoshek, a Toronto mechanic. They had emigrated to Detroit, where Wienoshek worked in the factories and their only son was born. When her second husband died, Mrs. Wienoshek moved back to Canada, but evidently Byron had preferred to be an American.

Among other things, she told Mulheisen that Byron had been in the U.S. Air Force for some fourteen years. "He got into a spot of trouble," she said. "He would never tell me what it was, but I expect that drinking was involved. He always drank too much. He was never violent, however. His father drank a bit, but he was a lovely man."

Mulheisen got away, finally, after receiving assurances from Mrs. Wienoshek that if she heard from her son she would contact Mulheisen immediately. He went back to the St. Martin Hotel where he spent another half-hour mollifying an annoyed Windsor police sergeant who said things like, "You Yanks think you can just go barging around. . . ."

It was ten o'clock before Mulheisen got through the tunnel to Detroit. McClain was still hanging around the Homicide office and he had a complete print-out from the computer on John Byron Wienoshek, including his military record. He left Mulheisen to read it and went to put in a similar request on Elroy Carver.

John Byron Wienoshek had enlisted in the U.S. Air Force in 1951. He had served as a gunner in SAC bombers, had been awarded unit citations in Korea, and then was retrained in 1957, when turret gunners became obsolete. He was trained to be a radio mechanic in AACS. There was a list of bases where he had served.

There was also an increasing incidence of demotions and disciplinary action. Evidently, he had not gotten along too well in AACS. Drinking, perhaps.

Mulheisen was intrigued, since he had been in AACS himself, as a control-tower operator. He had always liked AACS, but there was no doubt that it was a hard drinking outfit. Mulheisen used to think it was the result of the pressure of air-traffic control work.

In 1960 Wienoshek had received a summary court-martial on a charge of destruction of government property. Result: one month in the stockade and loss of rank. Probably wrecked the jeep, Mulheisen thought.

In 1962, back up to the rank of technical sergeant, Wienoshek was given a special court-martial on the more serious charge of attempted burglary. Here Wienoshek seemed to have done better, for he was found innocent. But he continued to have trouble. In 1965 he was in Vietnam, where civilian charges were brought against him for malicious destruction of property and felonious assault. It sounded like an attempted armed robbery to Mulheisen. The Air Force had agreed to court-martial Wienoshek, so civilian charges were dropped. Wienoshek was sent back to the States where he was given another special court-martial and dishonorably discharged.

Wienoshek had not prospered in civilian life. Almost every year since his discharge he had been picked up on one minor charge or another, nothing amounting to more than a misdemeanor, however, and all of them apparently related to drunkenness. But in 1970 he was charged with grand larceny in the disappearance of a valuable painting from the Detroit Institute of the Arts, where Wienoshek had been employed as a custodian. But then the charges were dropped. The report told the story. In exchange for dropping charges against Wienoshek, the painting was returned unharmed. He was allowed to leave his position without prejudice.

Since that time, Wienoshek had been employed by almost every cab company in Detroit and Windsor. There were no more arrests, just an occasional ticket of the sort that all cabdrivers get. Mulheisen couldn't believe that Wienoshek had gone on the wagon, not to hear the Dixieland cab dispatcher talk. It seemed more likely that Wienoshek had been able to occupy himself with other things. Perhaps a lucrative sideline like casual burglary. Once in a while, you drive a man and his wife to the airport, and on the way you learn that nobody will be home for several days.

McClain returned with the print-out on Elroy Carver. Mulheisen groaned. "I'm starving," he said. "I have to have something to eat before I can go on."

"Me too," McClain said. "Let's go downtown to the Coneys. Take the file with us."

Mulheisen had four hot dogs with onions and drenched with heavy chili. He drank two beers. It was reviving. He was able to focus his eyes again, though he knew he would have gas in the night.

They sat at a Formica-top table in the brightly lit Coney Islands and read the reports. There wasn't a lot on Elroy Terrence Carver. He too had served in the Air Force. It became quickly apparent, once one knew where to look, that Carver and Wienoshek must have met at Lockbourne Air Force Base, in Ohio, where both were stationed from 1959 to 1961. Carver had been given a bad conduct discharge from the service in 1963, for mail theft. He had worked in the base post office. He served three years in Leavenworth.

Afterward he returned to his hometown, Detroit, and was arrested several times on vagrancy charges, then a possession of stolen property charge (sentence suspended), a trespassing charge (eight days in the Detroit House of Correction), a breaking and entering charge (dismissed), and in 1972, burglary. He spent two years in the Milan Correctional Institute for that. Back out, there were parole violations that led to another two years. He had been released in June of this year and there was no further record.

"We still have no proof that the corpse is Carver," McClain said.

"He should have a complete medical file from the military," Mulheisen said. "Let's get that to the pathologists and the lab boys. There may be a way to positively identify him . . . blood type, maybe an x-ray of a broken arm, something. I didn't think there was much point in asking Mrs. Wienoshek or Deavons to look at the body."

"No," McClain agreed. "The lab is our best chance."

The big man rubbed his hands together and looked cheerful. "Looks like we're getting closer, Mul. This is good work."

"We could be farther than you think," Mulheisen said. "I have a feeling that Arthur Clippert's military record will show that he knew Wienoshek or Carver during his Air Force tour. I've got that record on file, part of the insurance investigation that Scotchman gave me. It's out at the precinct. I'll check it out on the way home."

"You might have something, Mul. These two birds seem kind of odd to me, though."

"What's odd? Just a couple of boys gone bad."

"Sure, only I can't see Carver killing anybody. Wienoshek, maybe. He has a pretty violent history."

"And so far, everything we have says it was Carver in the house, not Wienoshek. I see what you mean. Of course, then, somebody did a hell of a thorough job on Carver." Mulheisen sipped at his beer and leaned back in the chair. "It suggests no premeditation in the Clippert murder. It was just incidental to the burglary, after all."

"Carver was in there, all right," McClain said, "assuming that he's who the corpse was. It looks like she almost put him down."

Mulheisen nodded. "From everything I've heard about Wienoshek, he sounds like a different caliber man than Carver. A boozer, but evidently he could hold it most of the time. And people seemed to like him. Carver, they hardly noticed."

"What about this other guy who's showing up ahead of you all over town?" McClain said. "Who the hell is that?"

"If he's doing what I'm doing," Mulheisen said, "he must be a detective. A PI."

"Who's the client?" McClain said.

"Clippert? The Mob?"

"The Mob?"

"Sure. Maybe our boys did snatch something at Clippert's house. Like money. Big money."

Mulheisen looked at the clock on the wall. It was after one. He was dead tired. He wasn't going to see the Flying Clipper tonight, that was for sure. The prospect of the long drive out to St. Clair Flats was discouraging, but he had to go out to the east side anyway, to get Clippert's records from the precinct.

Eighteen

He woke up. Someone was there! He sat up in the huge bed and listened. Silence. Or rather, not silence. No, not silence at all. If you started counting you would know that there was no silence. The clock. Snow whispering about the house. The bare limbs of trees creaking. The muffled noise of the city. The house itself made a sound. And there was someone in it besides Arthur Clippert.

For the first time since the death of his wife, he was fully aware of her absence. He was alone. But not quite.

He listened intently, trying not to breathe. Was that a faint step in the kitchen? Did someone bump against the table? A door open, causing a slight draft?

In the dark, his mind's eye pictured the kitchen as he had last seen it. The table heavy and wooden, scarred from a century of cutting and spilling things on it. Jane had bought the table out of an old farmhouse, up north. His supper dishes were still on it. The cleaning woman came only three times a week now. He ate out usually. But tonight on the table were the remains of a too acidic sausage that he had broiled until it had burst. That and the crumbs of a boiled potato, too heavily salted. Jane had liked to cook.

What else was on the table? A fork, half a piece of white bread, butter in a blue dish. And a knife. A very sharp knife, one of a set of French cutlery. A thin, sharp-bladed knife. Not the same one that had been found in Jane's breast. The police had that knife.

He shuddered and his skin was drawn into goose flesh. Forget that, he told himself. It has nothing to do with me.

Another door opening? A faint creak? He couldn't be sure. Just the hint of something brushing against the thick nap of the carpet.

Arthur Clippert eased himself out of bed, naked. He was in the guest room, down the hall from the room he had once shared with Jane. He stepped carefully to the middle of the room and stopped, listening.

He tried to remember where his gun was. Still in the car? No, he had brought it into the house. It was in the linen closet. But did he dare to go there, to get it?

He could hear nothing in the house, except the night sounds. But he was convinced that someone was there. He had to move. He tiptoed across the carpet, into the hallway. He stopped again and listened. Nothing. He went on to the linen closet. Slowly, carefully, he eased the closet door open. He dared not turn on a light. He felt in among the clean sheets and pillowcases, sliding his hand into their smooth coolness until he located the hard lump of the pistol. But then he could not find the naked metal of the pistol and he panicked, pulling out sheets and tangling them around his hand until, at last, the gun was in his hand. Even then he had a bad moment trying to extricate his hand from the tangled linen.

He held the gun up before him in the darkness and could only barely make out its dull gleam. It was a Colt .45 automatic, a relic of his Air Force career.

He stepped carefully along the hallway, his knees making horrible cracks and pops. It was the tension, he knew, but he could not help it. Unless . . . yes, he could go on his hands and knees.

He went down the stairs backward, praying for no squeaky steps and holding the pistol awkwardly. He was naked and chilled.

The clock ticked. Something shifted slightly, a noise like the friction of fabric, perhaps pant legs rubbing together at the thighs. Outside the wind blew harder, the tree limbs rattled and snow was dashed against the windowpanes.

At last he was at the foot of the stairs. To his left was the big

111

living room. He crouched back on his heels, as if to force his glowing white nakedness into the wall. He peered into the shadows of the room, partially lit by the streetlight. It must be three in the morning, he thought, or even four.

It occurred to him then that the gun might not be loaded. He felt the butt. The clip was in.

But another thought came: even if the clip was in, was there a shell in the chamber? Was the safety on? Was the gun cocked and ready to fire? He felt for the safety and flicked it with his thumb. There was a tiny click in the darkness. Could someone hear that? he wondered.

But there was no answering sound from the room.

His scrotum was as tight as a peach pit, and as small. He waited and listened. And then he thought: he had flicked the safety, but did that mean it was now on, or off? He couldn't remember. It had been a century since Master Sergeant Patobny had conducted the course, "Familiarization With Small Arms." For a moment he was distracted by a memory of Master Sergeant Patobny. A stocky man with a fringe of gray-brown hair around a bald dome. He could see the blue Ike jacket, the name tag above the Silver Cross and the campaign ribbons.

He jarred himself back to the present. He knew the distraction of memory was a psychological thing, an attempt of the self to escape present and terrifying reality.

Is this goddamn gun going to fire, or isn't it, he wondered?

He remembered then that he would have to rack the slide back in order to cock the pistol and to inject a round into the chamber. Sgt. Patobny's voice told him that, and also that the safety was now off. So, there was another purpose to the vision of Patobny. But racking the slide, that would make too much noise.

The only way to do it was to slide the thing slowly, easing it past the telltale clicks and minimizing the noise of friction. The trouble was, it was too damn silent in the house. It was as if whoever was there was waiting, holding his breath, listening for the sounds that would tell him where Clippert was crouching.

Click-a-lick-a-lick! It was loud—too damn loud! And he still had to let the slide back. There was nothing for it; he let the slide go slowly back. Slowly!

112

And then he saw him.

He was across the room, standing near the big chair next to the fireplace. An extra darkness, along with a faint glow that must be the face. And there was a slight rustling sound, almost like tinkling.

He sees me! He heard me! Arthur could feel his own too white flesh gleaming in the darkness, his vulnerable nakedness.

He held the .45 in both hands, stretched out in front of him. It has to fire, he thought. Let it fire! If not, I'm dead.

He aimed directly for the thickest, darkest portion of the figure in the corner. He squeezed the trigger.

KABLOWWW!

The noise, the shock and the buck of the .45 knocked Arthur off balance. He fell to his side, firing.

KABLOWM! BLAM! BLA-BLA-BLAMMM!

The room rang with earsplitting noise. There was a crashing, jangling sound. A terrific commotion. Then a ringing silence.

I got him! he thought. He crouched on the floor, looking about him, still blinded by the brilliant flash of the shots.

Nothing.

He straightened up, on his knees, and looked around, open-mouthed and staring, the .45 still in his fist.

Suddenly, the front door crashed open. Clippert gawked, whirling to look behind him. A second later there was a smashing of glass in the front window, just a few feet away, and a hand with a gun poked in.

"Hold it!"

Clippert froze.

"Get up," the voice said, commanding.

Clippert staggered to his feet.

"Drop the gun. Kick it away."

Clippert stubbed his toe on the heavy weapon, but it slid away from him.

"Where's the light switch?"

"The . . . the door," Clippert said.

"All right, move to it slowly, I can see you. Move to it and turn on all the switches there. Move!"

Clippert moved carefully to the switches by the door and

flicked all three of them. The living room, the entry and the little porch flooded with light. Clippert blinked against the unaccustomed light.

"Step out the door," the voice snapped.

"Like this?"

"Move!"

Clippert stepped out into the snow, his hands over his head. He shivered in the brilliant light and peered into the darkness. He had never felt so defenseless.

A man appeared out of the darkness wearing a hat and an overcoat. He was tall and skinny, rawboned. He looked more like a cop than anyone Clippert had ever seen.

"Who are you?" the cop asked.

Coldly, Clippert told him.

Someone screamed and screamed at Mulheisen. And then it was the telephone. He sat up and looked with blurry eyes at the glowing of the bedside clock. After four. He had been asleep for just over an hour.

"Wha?" he said to the phone.

A voice heavily laden with resignation said, "Little bit of a problem here at Clippert's place, Mul."

"Whosis?"

"Maki." Sergeant Maki of the Ninth Precinct was known on the street as Pivot. He looked like a forty-year-old high-school basketball star, but that wasn't why they called him Pivot. He used to have a habit of wheeling on a tough suspect and belting him. This would happen in the early hours of interrogation. It never happened anymore, but the name was still there.

Mulheisen groaned. Maki waited. Finally, Mulheisen said, "What's the problem?"

Maki explained, finishing, "When I heard the shots I rousted the gun, only it turned out to be Clippert himself." Maki glanced over at Clippert, who stood glaring by the fireplace, wearing a red velvet robe and holding a snifter of brandy. That corner of the room was a bit messy—the Christmas tree was sprawled on the floor in a tangle of broken limbs and smashed ornaments, plaster was out of the wall.

"He says he heard a burglar, so he shot the hell out of his Christmas tree," Maki said.

"Any sign of a break-in?" Mulheisen asked.

"Not really," Maki said. "Coulda been, I guess. He says there's no sign of anything taken. You coming down?"

"Why should I?"

Maki stared at Clippert, an unflinching gaze. "Yeah, well, there's some damage here. A broken window, front door kinda messed up. Clippert's pissed."

"To hell with him," Mulheisen said. "Call McClain. Lay on the works, lab, photographer . . ."

"I already did," Maki said. "McClain said to call you. The lab is coming. Also, Clippert's doctor. He's not hurt, but he may need a sedative, or something. He didn't see the burglar, he says. He thought he did. So he shot the tree with this .45 he's got."

"Get the gun," Mulheisen said. "Make sure the lab gets the bullets. Check the registration."

"It's registered," Maki said.

"Anything you can take him on?"

Maki shrugged, then realized that Mulheisen couldn't see a shrug over the telephone. "Discharging a firearm within the city limits, maybe?" he said, his voice ripe with irony.

"Okay," Mulheisen said, "let me talk to him."

Maki held out the telephone. "You," he said.

Clippert was outraged. He downed the brandy in one gulp and snatched the telephone from Maki.

"Who is this?" he demanded.

"This is Mulheisen. Heard you had another burglary, Clippert." Mulheisen's voice was calm and relaxed now. He was lying back in his bed.

"Mulheisen, I have a complaint to make. This officer—"

"Clippert! Did you have a burglar or didn't you?"

"Of course I did! And then I was almost shot by one of your men. Not only that, but I suffered gross indignities and he has been insolent. But what I want to know, Mulheisen, is what the hell he was doing here? I didn't put in any call."

"Why not?"

"Why—I—there wasn't time . . . I—"

"Clippert, it's after four. When your doctor gets there, why don't you take a pill and go to bed. I'll be in my office by nine o'clock. Why don't you be there too?"

"What? I've had about enough of this insolence, Sergeant. I'll be down there, all right, with my attorney. You're going to wish you had never heard of me."

"Fine. I want to talk to you about a man named Wienoshek."

"What? Who?" Clippert paused. "I don't know what you're talking about. What is this?"

Mulheisen noticed that some of Clippert's rage had dissipated. "This guy Wienoshek is a burglar," Mulheisen said.

"Do you think he's the man who broke in?"

Mulheisen laughed. "Could be. See you in the morning. Nine o'clock. The Ninth Precinct, that's on Chalmers. You know where it is? Good. Now let me talk to Sergeant Maki."

To Maki he said, "Make it sound like I'm sending you off duty. Maybe he'll go for it and run. I'd like to see that. But I doubt it."

Maki managed a poor smile. "Well, thanks, Mul. Should I split, or just go back to the station?" His smile faded. "Well, at least it's warm there."

Mulheisen laughed. "That's too good. Keep an eye on him."

It was after five before Clippert was alone again. The doctor had left some sleeping pills, but Clippert didn't take them. He had another shot of brandy and trudged back up to the guest room. He lay there, thinking about Wienoshek. What could they make of Wienoshek? He finally decided they could make anything they wanted of Wienoshek, it would have nothing to do with himself.

After a bit he forgot about Wienoshek. He became more conscious of the present, of lying in bed. He rehearsed all the events of the past few hours, going over again how he had awakened, feeling the fear again . . .

And then he was really afraid. Pure, mindless terror seized him and he went stiff, shaking. After a few moments the feeling passed and he was limp, with cold sweat all over his body. It's just shock, he told himself, like trembling an hour after a near accident.

Then he remembered the .45. Where was it? He had left it down-stairs, on the mantel of the fireplace.

He got out of bed and went down to get it. It was still there. He had not turned on the light. Once again he stood in the dark room, seeing only by the faint light of the street, holding the .45. He looked down at it. Then he laid the cool muzzle against his cheek, smelling the cordite of the recent explosions mingling with the scent of the gun oil. He flicked his tongue at the barrel and tasted the metallic tang. He edged the muzzle up to his temple.

This is how you do it, he thought. It's easy. You just pull the trigger, like this . . . his finger tightened against the trigger. He lowered the gun.

It was still snowing. He looked out into the swirling cloud around the streetlight. There were no cars parked but he knew they were out there. Oh yes. They were out there, snow or not. But *who?* Mulheisen? Wienoshek? Who else? The FBI, the U.S. Attorney, the grand jury. People. That's all it was. People. They wanted you and fed on you and tore you to bits when you didn't give them what they wanted.

He couldn't worry about them, he decided. He had other things to worry about. He had things to do. You have to do it alone, he told himself.

He went upstairs, taking the .45 with him.

Nineteen

Precinct Inspector Buchanan was the commander of the Ninth Precinct. He was short, just meeting the Department's physical standards. He was slender and handsome, with silky black hair. He reminded Mulheisen of a seal. Mulheisen could not imagine Buchanan as a young patrolman, but like everyone else, Mulheisen included, Buchanan had come up through the ranks. He did not like Mulheisen.

Buchanan had a theory that Mulheisen was independently wealthy and had secret but loyal connections with the very highest figures in police and political hierarchy in Detroit and the state. It was true that Mulheisen had some old friends through his late father, the water commissioner. His father had been an absolute Democrat, a solid party worker for fifty years. But the wealth and influence was all in Buchanan's mind.

"Why is he still a goddamn sergeant?" Buchanan would demand of his lieutenant of detectives, Johnson. Johnson would shrug.

"He won't take the exams," he would say. "No ambition, I guess."

Buchanan could never figure that one out. "Why the hell isn't he downtown, at least, instead of out here in the Ninth? How come we're stuck with him?"

"He was here when I came," Johnson would say. "I guess he likes it."

"He's got pull," Buchanan would insist. "Anytime McClain wants him, off he goes. He practically works for Homicide. And if I say anything, the chief just looks at me. Oh, to hell with it. Just keep him out of my hair."

Thus Inspector Buchanan was surprised to see his most independent detective in the precinct by eight o'clock. Not only that, he was wearing a coat and tie. Despite having had only four hours of sleep, Mulheisen looked alert and purposeful. He bared his fangs at Buchanan in what passed for a Mulheisen smile and sailed on down the grimy corridor to his tiny office.

A little later, having received his reports from his lieutenants and shift commanders, Inspector Buchanan stopped in at Mulheisen's office.

"Say, Mulheisen," he smiled, "I'm off to my morning meeting with the bureau chiefs downtown, and so forth. I wonder if you have anything to report on that Indian Village affair?"

Mulheisen puffed on a cigar. "Getting close, Inspector," he said. "I'm sure McClain can fill you in. But I can ease your mind on one thing."

"What's that?"

"The culprit was not what some of the boys around here have taken to calling *Americanus Alabamus.*"

Buchanan knitted his smooth and handsome brow. "I don't follow."

"No race problem," Mulheisen said.

Buchanan brightened and smiled. He left for downtown with his driver, feeling quite cheerful.

Mulheisen was reading Clippert's file when the telephone rang. It was the dispatcher from Dixieland Cab.

"Is this Sergeant Mulleye—what's that name again? Mul—Mil—"

"Mulheisen."

"That's it. I called cause you said, if I heard anything. About that cab. Ol' John's cab."

"What about it?"

"We found it."

"Where?"

"Airport parking lot. Metropolitan. They called up. They been noticin' it. But no sign of ol' John." The dispatcher chuckled. Mulheisen could hear the man's pipe burbling like a stream. "I just betcha ol' John took a fare out there and the guy musta bought ol' John a drink and next thing you know ol' John wakes up in some gal's apartment and can't remember where he lef' the cab. Mister Shapiro pissed. He say ol' John fired, this time."

"They say how long it's been there?" Mulheisen asked.

"They didn't have the ticket on it," the dispatcher said. "But they figure it's been there three or four days."

"Where's the cab now?"

"Still there."

"Good," Mulheisen said. "We're going to have to borrow it for a day or so. I don't want anyone going near that cab. This is a homicide investigation. If Mr. Shapiro is upset, you tell him to check with Lieutenant McClain, at Homicide. I'll let you know when you can pick it up."

Mulheisen went down the hall and found Jensen and Field. He told them to get the lab onto the cab, then go out to the airport with their photographs of Wienoshek and Carver. They were to question the airline personnel again and check passenger lists for both names for every day since the Clippert murder.

At nine o'clock, Arthur Clippert appeared with his lawyer. The lawyer turned out to be none other than Homer Ferman, a nice fat man who was approximately the hottest criminal lawyer in the city. Mulheisen had seen him in action more than once and was impressed.

"So nice to see you, Mul," Ferman said, shaking his hand and exuding great warmth. "How have you been? I hope the holidays aren't killing you like they're killing me."

Mulheisen almost smiled. "How are you, Homer? Have you been representing Mr. Clippert here for long?" Mulheisen was thinking of the fee that Ferman would be getting in the Fidelity Funding case, if that was his as well.

"For many years, Mul," Ferman said. His voice was deep and

comforting. It always reminded Mulheisen of a wealthy and hospitable innkeeper, somehow. "Art is an old and valued friend," Ferman said, "as well as a valuable client." He laughed mischievously and this time Mulheisen did smile.

And then Homer Ferman went to business. "Mr. Clippert is appearing voluntarily, Sergeant," he said, "and is eager to cooperate with the authorities in any way in the investigation of the death of his wife. Nonetheless, he naturally reserves his right to counsel and reserves the right to remain silent."

"Naturally," Mulheisen said. "Sit down, gentlemen. Smoke if you like." He rummaged in the battered gray desk and produced an ashtray that said "Sinbad's" on it, which he had stolen from that restaurant-bar.

Homer Ferman produced a cardboard package of cigars and offered one to Mulheisen, but when Mulheisen saw what they were he got out his own and prevailed upon Ferman to take one. Clippert lit up a pipe.

"I have a few questions for Mr. Clippert," Mulheisen said, "and I have some information, which I hope will aid us in apprehending the men behind this homicide. But first, I want to talk about burglary."

"Burglary?" Ferman said.

"Yes. It's beginning to look to us like Mr. Clippert is burglary prone. Apparently, there was a break-in at his home last night, the second one in a week. During the first one, of course, Mrs. Clippert was attacked and killed. Was anything taken last night, Clippert?"

"Not that I could tell," Clippert said.

"And during the incident, you fired a handgun, presumably at the intruder. Is that right?"

"I didn't hit anyone," Clippert said. "There was some damage to my own personal property, and then one of your detectives came in, and he—"

"Yes," Ferman interrupted, "that's something we want to discuss with you, Sergeant." He sounded grave and concerned. "Just how did Sergeant Maki happen to be on the scene? Is Mr. Clippert under surveillance?"

Mulheisen exhaled cigar smoke. "Like I say, we think Clippert is burglary prone. Evidently, someone wants something that he has. Why else two burglaries? What is it they're after, Clippert?"

"I can't imagine," Clippert said blandly. "I have a few items of value in the house, but nothing exceptional."

"No moonstone or Maltese Falcon, then?" Mulheisen said. Neither Ferman nor Clippert smiled.

Mulheisen tapped a finger on the folder that contained Clippert's file. Clippert's name was written boldly on the cover. "And you had an earlier burglary, too," he said, "not three months ago, at your place up north. But that was never reported. Why is that?"

"I don't know what you're talking about," Clippert said.

Ferman had turned to look at his client with evident interest. Mulheisen was surprised. He had been certain that, despite his injunction, or even because of it, Carl Joyner would certainly have notified Clippert of Mulheisen's visit yesterday, and his discovery of the unreported Jasper Lake burglary. Mulheisen was curious. He could see that Ferman was too. He pressed a button under his desk that lit up a light at the front desk. Almost immediately, his telephone rang.

"Yes?" Mulheisen said.

"Awright, what do you want?" the desk man said.

"Oh?" Mulheisen said. "Ayeh? What does he want? Is it urgent?"

"Send not to know for whom the bell tolls," the desk man said. "Yeah, he's here. I'll get him. You coming out?"

Mulheisen sighed. "All right," he said. He hung up. "Excuse me a moment, gentlemen. The lieutenant wants to see me. I'll be right back."

He found Ayeh in the squad room. "Where did Clippert go yesterday?" he asked.

Ayeh opened his notebook. "Up about eight. Left the house at nine. Went to his office. Left the office at eleven and went to his club with a young fellow from the office. Fellow's name is Avery, according to the doorman. They played handball for a couple hours. Left the club at one-thirty and went to lunch together for an hour at the London Chop House. Left the London Chop House at two thirty-seven and Clippert dropped Avery off at the office. Clippert drove downtown to the office of Homer Ferman, his lawyer, and stayed there till four fifty-five. Walked from Ferman's office, alone, to the Ponchartrain, where he had several drinks and made two phone calls, apparently no answer.

"Walked downtown at five forty-five, to J. L. Hudson's, where he purchased several toys in the toy department and had them sent to a Miss Shirley Carpenter, 1296 Seaforth Tower, on Lafayette Boulevard. Made another phone call from the store at six-fifty, apparently connected. Got his car out of the garage and drove to Seaforth Tower. Arrived seven twenty-three, and went up on the elevator, apparently to visit Miss Carpenter. He came out at eleven-ten and drove home. Lights out before twelve, and I was relieved by Maki."

"Who's the girl?" Mulheisen said.

"She works in Clippert's office."

"Thanks, Ayeh. Keep on him. I'll try to get you relieved a little earlier tonight."

Mulheisen had a cup of bad coffee from the urn and then, thinking that Ferman and Clippert had had enough time to confer, he went back. They were standing and smoking.

"Sorry about that," Mulheisen said. "Sit down." He sat down himself behind the desk. "Now, what about this earlier burglary?"

Clippert looked at Ferman, then smiled sheepishly at Mulheisen. "I don't know how you found out about that," he said. "But it's true."

"When did this happen?" Mulheisen had a pad out, taking notes.

"Oh, let's see. I guess it was about September twenty-fifth, somewhere in there. I suppose I could pinpoint it for you."

"Do," Mulheisen said.

"Very well." Clippert got out a pocket secretary and consulted some dates. "It was September twenty-fifth, a Friday."

"What exactly happened?"

Clippert looked at his lawyer, then plunged into a narrative about how he had driven up to Jasper Lake to spend a weekend alone, working, and had discovered the burglars in the process of looting the house.

Homer Ferman listened to his client and looked unhappy. No criminal lawyer likes to hear the sound of his client's voice.

"As they hadn't had a chance to actually remove anything," Clippert said, "I just gave them a good scare and told them to get the hell out. Believe me, they ran."

"Just a couple of kids, I suppose," Mulheisen suggested. "Local boys?"

"Ye—uh, no," Clippert said. It was as if he had wanted to say yes, but reluctantly decided that the answer had to be no. "They weren't kids, really. I don't know where they were from."

"Well, we'll get back to that in a moment," Mulheisen said. "Now, you say you were alone. Nobody with you?" He looked pointedly at Clippert.

Clippert broke into a boyish grin. "Well, perhaps I wasn't quite alone," he said, grinning over his briar pipe. Mulheisen thought he looked like a model in an *Esquire* ad. "There's no point in denying it. I took along a girl, one of the secretaries from my office, to sort of . . . well, you know . . . to assist me, do some typing and take some dictation."

His grin had given away to a roguish look of amusement. Mulheisen could have sworn that he had winked. "What's her name?" Mulheisen asked.

"Uh, Shirley. Shirley Carpenter. I know what you're thinking, Sergeant." The roguish smile again. "If you're thinking what I think you're thinking, you're absolutely right. There's no romance, though, not really. Actually, my wife more or less knew about Shirley, though nothing direct was ever said. Jane certainly did not approve, but I don't think she really minded. She could never be jealous of Shirley. If you like, you can verify all this with Shirley."

"I'll do that," Mulheisen said. " Did she witness the burglary scene?"

"No," Clippert said. "She was in the car. I'd noticed some lights in the house when we drove up and told her to stay put. She may have seen the men as they left, but I doubt it. It was very dark."

"Then you are the only one who saw the men?"

Clippert nodded. Mulheisen picked up Carl Joyner's affidavit and glanced through it. He looked up at Clippert.

"I have here evidence that you were acquainted with the

burglars. That you recognized them, and that's why you let them go and did not report the crime. What about it?"

Clippert stared at Mulheisen, then he looked at Homer Ferman. "I think I'd like to confer with my attorney before I respond to that."

"Sure," Mulheisen said. "I'll get some coffee. You fellows care for some coffee? It's pretty vile."

They did not want coffee. Mulheisen left, saying he would be just down the corridor. He had a cup of coffee and looked through Sergeant Maki's report. Then he called Shirley Carpenter at Clippert's office and made an appointment to see her for lunch. Since the offices were downtown, he suggested that she meet him at Schweizer's restaurant. "Or I could pick you up," he said. She quickly said she would prefer to meet him.

Homer Ferman was looking for him, so Mulheisen went back to his office.

"As Mr. Clippert's attorney, Sergeant," Ferman purred, "I'm not particularly pleased with this line of questioning. Mr. Clippert came down here of his own free will, under the impression that you might have some helpful information about the death of his wife. What is the relevance of this interrogation about an earlier burglary?"

"I would think it would be obvious," Mulheisen said. "Mrs. Clippert was killed in the course of a burglary; Mr. Clippert had once seen and talked to the perpetrators of an earlier attempted burglary. It is conceivable that the earlier burglars could be the same ones who later broke into his house. Beyond that, we're assisting upstate officials in their investigation of a series of burglaries that occurred in the same area as Clippert's Jasper Lake house, at about the time he met these men. Since he is a lawyer, and an officer of the court, I'm sure he would be happy to cooperate in this investigation, despite the fact that earlier he helped to conceal a crime."

Ferman sighed. Nodding at Clippert, he said, "Very well, ask your questions."

"Who were the burglars?"

"I only recognized one of them," Clippert said, "and I don't remember his name, if I ever knew it. Actually I didn't even recognize him, at first. But he recognized me, he said, and mentioned an incident from a few years ago and then I recollected him. He didn't mention his name, however, and I didn't think to ask it."

"What was the earlier incident?" Mulheisen asked.

"Uh, an auto accident," Clippert said. "Just a minor thing, really. I had bumped into his car at an intersection, here in Detroit. I had been drinking a bit, I suppose. Rather than go to a lot of trouble with insurance companies and police reports and so on, I offered the fellow some money. Fifty dollars, I think it was. There was very little damage to his car, and it was clearly my fault. He was good enough to accept the money and go on his way. I figured I had avoided a ticket, and it could have cost me fifty anyway, to say nothing of bad publicity, so the man was doing me a favor. So, now I returned the favor, that's all."

Mulheisen shook his head. "You don't seem to like to report things to the police, do you? When was this accident? Where did it take place? Were there any witnesses?"

Ferman intervened at this point. "Mr. Clippert is being cooperative, Mulheisen. I don't see any need for this kind of bullying."

"Oh, that's all right, Homer," Clippert said. "I don't mind answering these questions. It happened three years ago, I think in March. Jane was with me at the time. We were coming from a party at a friend's house, quite late. I was driving a Buick at the time, and if you want to check with Al's Collision, I think you'll find that I had some front-end repairs done on the Buick."

Mulheisen puffed on his cigar. "Okay. I'm glad you're being cooperative, Clippert. But this story sounds pretty vague to me. What did this guy look like, for instance? It could help us in the upstate burglary investigation."

"Oh, he was young, in his twenties. A kind of short stocky guy, with short blond hair."

"What did the other burglar look like?"

"About the same as the other guy, in age, also short, only he was dark and, oh yes, he had a mustache."

"I'd like you to look at some mug shots, Clippert, to see if you can recognize these fellows. It could be very important. Also, I'd like to know if you are willing to sign a formal statement to the effect that what you've just told me about this incident—including the auto accident—is true, and that it was a voluntary statement made in the presence of your attorney."

"I'll be glad to cooperate," Clippert said.

For another hour, with the assistance of a stenographer and a typist, they labored over the statement which was then signed and witnessed. Mulheisen gave a copy to Ferman.

Clippert was ready then to look at the mug shots.

"One other thing," Mulheisen said. "Do you know a man named John Byron Wienoshek?"

Clippert stopped at the office door and looked puzzled. "You mentioned that name last night, on the telephone," he said. "I don't believe I know the fellow."

"Think carefully," Mulheisen said. "You were in the Air Force, for instance. Could you have known him there?"

"It's possible," Clippert said, "but I don't recall him."

"How about an Airman Wienoshek whom you were appointed to defend in a court-martial at Lockbourne Air Force Base in 1962, a charge of attempted burglary?"

Clippert clapped his hand to his head. "Oh, yes! Of course. How could I have forgotten? I won that case. My God, that's ages ago, just before I got out of the service. But what about him?"

"Attempted burglary," Mulheisen said. "I thought he might be the man involved in your burglaries, but he doesn't resemble the description you gave at all. Still, he could be the man involved in the burglary in which your wife was killed."

Mulheisen stood up then and said good-by to the two men. "Sergeant Maki will help you on the mug shots," he said. "As for me, I've got a luncheon appointment."

Twenty

In the morning the sun was shining. It had been that way every day
this week. He woke up and looked out the window and was surprised again. It wasn't that he didn't expect the sun to be shining.
Consciously, he knew it was right. But something in the back of
his mind told him it was wrong.

Well, this is Florida, he told himself. I've been living in Ontario too long.

So he got up and dressed in a short-sleeved shirt and thin
slacks and wore dark glasses when he went out. He drank the
freshly squeezed orange juice, ate a big breakfast, and read
the *Miami Herald*. He didn't like the *Herald*. The funnies were in
the wrong place and he didn't like the looks of the sports page.

In the afternoon he went to the race track and lost money. At
night he went to the dog track and lost money. It didn't bother him;
he still had a lot left.

He would go downtown and buy a Detroit newspaper and sit
on a park bench to read it. Then he would throw it away. He didn't
want anyone to see him reading a Detroit newspaper.

At other times he walked along the beach in sandals and
Bermuda shorts. He stopped to look at the dried-out Portuguese
man-of-war that had washed up on the beach. An old black man

was raking the sand, raking away the man-of-wars. He stopped to talk to the old man. They were almost the only people visible on the beach, although the weather was very fine and the sea was warm.

The old man said that he was from Jamaica, but that in order to get into the United States he had to move to Canada first. He had lived in Toronto, he said. He hadn't liked it. After a while they had let him come to the States and he came directly to Miami.

"Toronto no damn good, mon," the old man said. "No sun. Cloudy all day."

The big man said he understood, but all the same he liked it in Toronto, himself.

The old man smiled. "Maybe it's okay, mon. But too damn cold."

That afternoon the man bought himself a paperback copy of Byron's poetry. He put on swim trunks, covered himself with suntan lotion, and settled in a lounge chair by the big hotel pool. He drank gin and tonic and read the poetry, surrounded by elderly Jewish women. They wore swimsuits that were too youthful for them. They noticed him and thought he looked sexy. They were intrigued by the fact that he was big and rough looking, yet he was reading poetry. Some of them asked the waiters who he was.

"Mr. Gordon," they were told. "He is registered as George Gordon, of Chicago."

The name meant nothing to the ladies. But he must be rich, they thought. This is a rich hotel. He is a rich tough guy who reads poetry, they told each other. They supposed that a man who read poetry was sensitive, no matter how tough he looked.

Mr. Gordon *was* sensitive. He was sensitive to heat. He disliked the hot Miami sun. And he was sensitive to another kind of heat. The kind that is known as the Heat.

At about four in the afternoon, Mr. Gordon became very sensitive to the Heat. He felt restless. He looked around frequently. There was nobody there, just old ladies with blue hair and dark glasses. Very few men, except for the cabana boys and the waiters. He supposed the men were either dead or still working themselves to death in New York.

Mr. Gordon was restless and felt out of it. I should be working, he thought. Other men are working, but I have nothing to do.

And then he saw the Heat.

He was short and stocky with thick black hair and wore a tiny swim suit. He came out by the edge of the pool and removed his sunglasses. He took off his sandals and left them with his sunglasses and towel. He dove into the pool and swam back and forth the length of the pool with powerful strokes. He was the only person in the pool. The ladies watched.

He got out of the pool and swept his wet black hair back with both hands. Then he put on his glasses and looked around, hands on hips. Little droplets of water gleamed on his very muscular torso. He had at least the beginnings of a tan, unlike Mr. Gordon, who had put his shirt on to keep from getting sunburnt.

Mr. Gordon watched him over the edge of his book.

The man strolled along the pool and flopped into a lounge chair next to Mr. Gordon.

"Whew," the man said. "Out of shape." He slapped his stomach, which was so flat and muscular that it almost didn't seem to have skin on it.

He beckoned to the waiter and ordered a vodka and tonic. Then he leaned back in his chair and sighed. "Ah, that sun. That's great, isn't it?" There was nobody else near them, so Mr. Gordon had to assume that the man was talking to him.

Mr. Gordon grunted something that may or may not have been agreement.

"Just think of those poor saps up north, slogging through the snow," the man said. "That makes this even better."

Mr. Gordon grunted again.

"Now this is the way to spend Christmas," the man said. "Don't you agree?"

Mr. Gordon lowered his book and looked with his dark glasses at the dark glasses of the man. The man looked at him.

"It's all right," Mr. Gordon said.

"All right? It's better than all right. It's terrific!"

"Depends on what you like," Mr. Gordon said.

The boy came back with the man's drink and Mr. Gordon asked for another gin and tonic. "Make it a double," he said.

The man sat up and held out his hand. "Service," he said. "Joe Service, at yo' service." And he laughed.

Mr. Gordon took the man's hand, briefly. "Hello," he said. He looked intently at Service and thought, This is the Heat. He was certain of it. But he was a strange kind of Heat. Mr. Gordon couldn't quite put his finger on it. But there was something wrong. For one thing, the guy was too small to be a cop.

"What's your name?" Service asked.

"Gordon."

"Gordon what?"

"George Gordon," the big man said, reluctantly.

"Gordon," Service said, "that's funny."

"Funny?"

"Sure. Your name is George Gordon and you're reading Lord Byron."

"So what?"

"So, that was his real name."

Mr. Gordon felt cold. "What do you mean?" he said slowly, "his real name?"

"Byron's real name. His family name. George Gordon, Lord Byron. See, his real name was George Gordon and then when he inherited the title he became Lord Byron."

Mr. Gordon relaxed slightly. "I see. I guess I knew that but it slipped my mind."

Service sipped his drink. "Oh, that's all right," he said. "Most people don't know that. It's the same with movie stars. How many people know that Roy Rogers' real name is Leonard Slye?"

"Leonard Slye?" Mr. Gordon smiled, despite himself.

"That's right," Service said. "And you know who Cary Grant used to be?"

"No."

"Get this. Archibald Leach!"

"You're putting me on," Mr. Gordon said.

"No, I'm not," Service said. He spoke with sudden intentness.

Mr. Gordon just looked at him, waiting.

Service laughed. "Lots of people change their names, these days," he said. "All kinds of people. Show business people, people who are running away from another life. Why, I even knew a farmer, in Iowa, who changed his name."

"Is that right?"

"Yeah. He was a Bohemie. A Bohemian. Lots of Bohemians in the part of Iowa I come from. Anyway, this farmer's name was Someshit. Well actually, it was Zumcek, Z-U-M-C-E-K. Really, it should be pronounced 'Zumchick,' but everybody called him 'Someshit.' " Service laughed. "So, old Someshit goes to probate court and tells the judge he wants his name altered. Get it? All-turd. Ha ha ha hahahaha."

Mr. Gordon stared at Service. He did not smile.

Service flopped back in his wooden lounger, still laughing. "Oh, it's a pretty bad joke, I guess. Sorry about that."

Gordon was amazed. What the hell is this? The Heat makes jokes?

Service took a long drink of his vodka and tonic. "Ah, that's great," he said. Then, "Yeah, lots of people change their names. Especially writers. You know that guy David St. John, wrote a whole bunch of spy novels? He was really E. Howard Hunt, the Watergate guy."

"You know a lot about names," Mr. Gordon said. "How about your own? Service? Is that for real?"

"Yeah, but, there too, it's been changed. My grandfather was named Guido Surface, pronounced 'sir-fah-chee,' " he explained. "He came over on the boat and he wanted to go into the restaurant business. So he figured that 'Service' would be a good business name. Or else he just didn't like the way the immigration people pronounced his real name."

Mr. Gordon downed his gin and tonic and ordered another double.

"Names fascinate me," Service said. "Now, you take a name like, say, Wienoshek. The average person looks at that name and thinks, Wieno? Like wiener? Or maybe they think, Wino? Actually, I imagine that wiener is closer to the origins of the name. It probably comes from Wien, which is German for Vienna. That's the origin of wiener, you know. Vienna sausage—wiener sausage. Maybe this Wienoshek's ancestors came from Vienna, originally, before they moved to Czechoslovakia."

"Names are beginning to bore me," Mr. Gordon said. "What else are you interested in?"

"I'm much more interested in money," Mr. Service said.

Mr. Gordon shrugged. "So is everybody."

"Especially twenty million bucks," Service said.

"Twenty million? Like you say, it's interesting."

"Yes," Service said. "Twenty million. You know what I do for a living, Mr. Gordon? I'm a finder. Somebody wants to find something, or somebody, they come to me. I'm good at it. Usually, I get a flat fee. I don't mind telling you that my fee is higher than the fee paid to any other man in my profession. But sometimes I work on commission. Especially if I'm looking for lots of money. Then I have a sliding scale."

"Sounds like interesting work," Mr. Gordon said.

"Interesting? Hah! You're damn right it's interesting. It may not look like it, Mr. Gordon, but I'm on a case right this minute." He laughed. "That's right! Even as I sit here in this lovely Florida sun, drinking vodka."

Mr. Gordon was restless again. He was also baffled. Was this the Heat, or wasn't it? He drank deeply from his glass of gin.

"Am I boring you again, Mr. Gordon?"

Mr. Gordon did not look at him. He looked across the pool at two blue-haired ladies in bikinis. They didn't look too bad, for sixty-year-olds. Their flesh was still fairly smooth and firm. They didn't look young, but many women in their forties would like to look like that, Mr. Gordon thought. He tried to imagine his old mother in a swimsuit, then pushed the notion out of his mind, embarrassed.

"I wonder how they do it?" he said.

"What? Who?" Mr. Service looked where Mr. Gordon was looking. "Oh, them. Good living. Tennis, masseuses, cosmetic surgery ..."

"I'm sorry," Mr. Gordon said. "What were you saying?"

Service laughed and shook his head. "You're too much, Mr. Gordon. Here I am talking about twenty million and you're looking at a couple of old bats in bikinis."

Mr. Gordon turned and looked at Service. "All right, Service, let's drop the comedy routine. What's your story?"

"Twenty million. Actually, ten percent. That's my fee this time. So I'm really only talking about two million. Fifty-fifty. A million apiece."

Mr. Gordon frowned. "You're coming in about one-by," he said.

"One-by?"

"That's radio talk," Mr. Gordon said. "If you're not receiving a transmission very well, you say it's one-by. Or maybe two-by. If you're hearing it loud and clear, you say it's five-by."

"Fascinating," Service said. "I'll give it to you loud and clear, then. I'm talking about a man in Detroit, name is Clippert. Is that five-by?"

Mr. Gordon nodded slightly. "Name's familiar."

"Yes, the Flying Clipper," Service said. "Something like twenty million Mr. Clippert has, or had. In cash. Or maybe it's in negotiable bonds. We're not sure."

"We?" Mr. Gordon said.

"My clients and I."

"Who are your clients?" Mr. Gordon wanted to know.

"At last," Service smiled, "some interest. But who my clients are is no immediate concern of yours. Not yet. But I will say that Mr. Clippert is not one of them. Mr. Gordon, my clients are not nice people. Of course, Mr. Clippert isn't so nice himself. Anyway, we figure that the Flying Clipper doesn't really own that twenty million. That twenty million is up for grabs, Mr. Gordon. And that's where I come in. I may be short, but you ought to see me on a jump ball. And I figure you're probably good in the jump circle too."

Mr. Gordon sat back in his lounge chair. He signaled the waiter for another double gin. "I don't know anything about basketball," he said, "or any twenty million."

Joe Service sighed. "All right, here it is. Five-by. About a week ago, somebody—just a couple of snatch-and-grab artists—broke into Mr. Clippert's house. Now maybe they were just after a couple of color televisions. But they didn't take any color televisions. I don't know what they did take. But I do know that Clippert had twenty million. The boys who broke in left the TV's. They also left a dead woman. Or, to be more exact, they left a woman for dead, only she didn't die right away."

"Didn't die?" Mr. Gordon was intensely interested. He looked very thoughtful. Then he said, "So what?"

"She lived long enough to walk next door. There's a chance she might have said something before she died. The cops won't say."

"It doesn't matter," Mr. Gordon said firmly.

"Possibly not. What matters is twenty million. I want to know where it is. I mean to find out. Now if those boys took it . . . well, actually, only one of them is still alive. If he's got it, the money, we're willing to let him keep a whole million of it for himself. He'll be a millionaire. And he won't have to worry about what the woman said to the cops. We'll help this enterprising lad out of the country, if that's what he wants. We think he's an amateur, see? We think that, left to his own devices, the cops will get him. There's all kinds of cops on this case. Not just Detroit cops. So far, none of the federal agencies seem to have tumbled to the idea that the amateurs may have gotten the money. But they will.

"So, we make an offer. If our hero wants to play ball, he can have a carefree million. If he wants to take the ball and go home, he's dead. But we don't want to kill him, understand—we want to help. Hell, a guy this enterprising might even find employment with my clients. A million dollars could buy a man's way into a casino setup, say in Brazil. And then, he'd have more than a million."

At this point, Joe Service leaned forward, and with his face close to Mr. Gordon's said, "Is that five-by, Gordon?"

Mr. Gordon surprised Service. He screwed his face up in disgust and said, "Five-by-five. I've been shafted."

"What?"

"Look, Service, or whatever your name is, you're not a bottle, are you?"

"A what?"

"A cop."

"For Christ's sake," Service said.

"All right, all right," Mr. Gordon said. "I'm just telling you that I didn't know anything about any twenty million. What I know about is much less. Much, much less."

Joe Service looked at the pitted face, the big body, the blunt-fingered hands. Finally, he said, "I see."

"So I can't help you," Mr. Gordon said. "Sorry. I wish to hell I could. At the prices they charge here, I'm not going to be here for long."

Service was silent. "I'll have to think about that," he said at last. "You might be able to help, after all." He got up. "I'll let you know. See you around, Lord Byron."

Mr. Gordon watched him walk rapidly away. He picked up his double gin and tonic.

Twenty-one

On his way downtown to lunch with Shirley Carpenter, Mulheisen stopped by Headquarters. He gave McClain a complete briefing on events since the evening before.

"Despite the Clipper's denials," Mulheisen said, "we have definitely tied him to Wienoshek. This other story about the auto accident is pure bullshit. But that's all right. In fact, it's fine. Better than a confession, as far as I'm concerned."

"How so?" McClain asked.

"Confessions aren't worth a hell of a lot in court, these days," Mulheisen said. "You know that. But here I've got a signed and attested statement that will show him to be a liar."

"Not really," McClain said. "You can't prove that he didn't have an accident, can you? Or that he didn't give somebody fifty dollars to forget about it. I think a jury would believe that part at least."

"Yes, but I think we'll be able to prove that Wienoshek was the burglar at Jasper Lake, and that the real reason that Clippert recognized the burglar was because he had once defended him in a court-martial. Then that story about the accident will look like what it is—a clumsy lie. That will be hard for anyone, even Homer Ferman, to overcome. Especially if we can then turn around and show that Wienoshek was involved in the second so-called burglary and the murder of Mrs. Clippert."

McClain agreed. "Maybe we should pick up Clippert," he said. "Do we have enough to hold him on?"

"I like him dangling, better," Mulheisen said. "He knows now that we definitely suspect him, but he doesn't know how close to the truth we are. If we pick him up and arraign him, then discovery rules are in effect and he learns what we know. And what could the prosecutor bring? A conspiracy charge? The prosecutor won't like that. No, I like him free, and nervous, and ignorant. He could lead us to Wienoshek, even, or to the money."

"You know," McClain said, "that's another funny thing—"

"I know," Mulheisen interrupted. "You're wondering why we haven't heard anything from the Feds lately. I'm wondering too. But I think that after last night's break-in that we will hear from them."

"Well, is there anything you need?" McClain asked.

"If you're going to be seeing the prosecutor, ask him if we can't have a couple of warrants ready on Clippert and Wienoshek. We won't use them until we have to."

Mulheisen got to Schweizer's before Shirley Carpenter. She was only a couple minutes late. She was not at all what Mulheisen had expected. He had expected a young sexpot.

Mulheisen figured this woman to be thirty-five. She had divorcee written all over her. It's an air of diffidence and confidence, undercut by an edge of anxiety.

She was not pretty. Five foot six and too thin. She did not have an attractive figure, except for long and handsome legs. She was a bit high-waisted. That was the point. Physically, she just missed in almost every category that convention has decreed as attractive. Her face was a bit too round for a thin girl, her nose a bit too large and blunt, her eyes just a mite small. Her hair was just too blond and too overdone at the hairdresser's. Her breasts were just too small and her hips not quite wide enough, nor slender enough to provide the willowy look of a fashion model.

Nonetheless, she was very appealing. It was something to do with a candid manner and a good, quick smile.

Over her Dieter's Special (something that Mulheisen couldn't fathom) she explained that her maiden name was Walton. "Well, not actually," she amended. "It should be Gombrowicz, but my father is a used-car dealer and he claimed that he had so much trouble getting the name spelled right on title transfers that he had to have it changed."

"But Walton?" Mulheisen said.

"He used to have a sales lot across the street from the Walton Hotel on Dequindre. He always liked the name. Anyway, my first husband's name was Carpenter, so I kept that, so as not to confuse our son."

"Your first husband?" Mulheisen said.

She smiled. "I expect to marry again, Sergeant."

"To Arthur Clippert?"

"Why not? It may sound like the old familiar secretary's folly to you—sometimes it seemed that way to me—but now that Arthur is . . . no longer married . . ."

Mulheisen had a sinking feeling. He was sympathetic toward the woman, but it still seemed to him like the old familiar secretary's folly. He couldn't see Clippert marrying this woman. Not when he could have his pick of the likes of Lou Spencer. Or did he have his pick? Lou had seen through Clippert readily enough.

Shirley Carpenter went on to talk of her twelve-year-old son, Scott. Yes, they had named him after the astronaut.

Lunch was over before Mulheisen could do little more than get a fair impression of the woman's character. "Would you like to go somewhere else, have a drink?" he suggested.

"I've got to get back to the office," she said.

"No, you don't," he said. "It is within my power to arrest you. Besides, Clippert knows where you are."

"Perhaps my apartment would be more comfortable than the precinct house," she said. "It isn't far."

She had a twelfth-floor apartment in the Seaforth Tower. It was a modern, high-rise building that stood where once there had been thousands of hovels and tenements, the old "Happy Valley" of Hastings Avenue. The urban planners had relocated the slum to less valuable real estate around the city, and erected themselves some lucrative and luxurious housing with a view of the river and Canada, and called it Lafayette Plaisance.

Shirley Carpenter drew back the draperies, and through the full-length glass wall Mulheisen could see the snow falling on Detroit, on the river and on Canada.

"I know what you're thinking," she said. "This, on a secretary's salary. But I'm paid quite well, my ex-husband is a foreman at the Rouge plant and pays his alimony and child support promptly—and Art takes care of the rest."

"It's nothing to me," Mulheisen said. "Do you mind if I smoke?"

"Not at all. Art always smokes his pipe. I like it. What would you like to drink? I think I'll have Scotch, myself."

Mulheisen accepted a generous glass of bourbon and water. He lit a cigar and got down to the basic questions. About Jasper Lake: did she go there often? Answer: more than once. What about on the night of the burglary? Yes. Did she see the burglars? Yes. One was tall and one was short, that's all she could say for sure. They had passed by the car where she sat, but it was dark. She didn't think they saw her, nor did she think she could identify them.

Did Mr. Clippert say anything to her about what had happened? Yes, but only, it seemed, what Clippert had told Mulheisen.

Did Mr. Clippert coach her on what to say if she were asked? No. He trusted her to keep her own counsel; it was in her interests.

She told Mulheisen that she was convinced that Arthur Clippert was innocent in the Fidelity Funding affair. As for the murder, there was simply no question of his innocence.

"Surely you must have known something about the Fidelity Funding business," Mulheisen said.

"I've been all through that with the Michigan State Insurance Commission, with the U.S. Attorney, with the FBI, with the Securities Exchange Commission, the grand jury . . . Art had nothing to do with it. I'm sure he knew nothing about it until it appeared in the newspapers."

She sat across the living room from Mulheisen in a large furry yellow chair. She had taken her shoes off and had her feet tucked up under her. She wore a short skirt and Mulheisen once again admired her nice legs.

The phone rang.

"Yes," she said. "He's here now. We're just talking. Of course . . . it's all right, I don't mind . . . yes . . . mmmhmmm . . . yes. Sure. Later." She hung up. She didn't have to tell Mulheisen who it was. He didn't ask.

By this time they were both on their third drink and Mulheisen felt mellow. He gazed out the big windows as she talked quietly. The snow fell and fell. The room was darkened by the heavy overcast. There were no lights on in the room. Mulheisen liked it that way. It suited his mood. He sat silently, watching the traffic crawl along Jefferson Avenue. He drew on his cigar and sipped at the whiskey. After she hung up they sat in silence for a long time, watching the snow.

She got up and plugged in the lights of the Christmas tree in the corner. All the lights were blue and winked on and off on some thermal principle. She poured more whiskey in both their drinks and sat down again in the yellow chair.

After a while, Mulheisen said, "I've heard everything I want to hear from you, Shirley, for now at least. And I believe you. That is, I think you believe what you are saying. I can't tell you what I think about these things, but I'd like to know what you think. I want to ask you some personal questions. You don't have to answer."

"I don't mind," she said.

"What do you think of Arthur Clippert?"

"Arthur Clippert is a fine man," she said, "a brilliant man. I believe in him. I trust him."

"But . . . I don't get it," Mulheisen said. "You said yourself, something about a secretary's dream. Even if he's not a criminal, if he has done nothing against the law . . . look at all this. He set you up here long before his wife died. I suppose he said all kinds of things to you, talked of getting a divorce . . ."

"Yes, we talked about that. Not as much as I would have liked. He meant it though, I'm sure. We didn't set a specific date. We knew it would happen, in its own time."

"All right. That's it," Mulheisen said. "You chose to believe him. That's okay, but finally, let's face it, you're no dumb kid . . . ah hell, maybe I'm out of line." He took a drink.

She was calm. "Yes, you are out of line, but I don't mind.

What you think doesn't matter. It won't change things. It is a dream. It is folly. I know that. But I *am* thirty-five. I have a son who is almost a teen-ager. I know I'm not beautiful."

"You have nice legs," Mulheisen smiled.

"They are my best feature," she said. She smiled. "But what I'm saying is that I have to go with this dream. It's not my last chance, but it's my last best chance. And when it comes down to it, I feel I can make it happen."

"You have a lot of confidence," Mulheisen said.

"I know I'm not beautiful and I didn't go to finishing school in Switzerland. I don't have Jane's looks, her money, her style, her leisure. But I'm a woman. A damn good woman, too. Of that I'm confident. Enough men have told me so."

Mulheisen didn't quite understand. "Told you what?" he asked stupidly. It was the whiskey.

Shirley Carpenter stood up. She faced him with the window behind her, hands on hips. "I'm a hell of a lay," she said, "I might be the best lay in this town."

Mulheisen stood up. He set his glass on the coffee table. He looked at her across the darkened room. Her expression, the way she held herself, told him that she meant what she said. She had pride and he thought she was brave. He was moved.

"I don't mind showing you," she said.

He knew she was serious and that it wasn't an idle proposition, nor a cynical one. She wasn't doing this for Arthur or for him. She meant to show him how good she was. He thought she might be very good indeed.

His tongue probed at a favorite molar. He looked away from her out the window, at the snow falling on Detroit and Canada. He put the cigar in his mouth and noticed that it was out.

"I have to go," he said. "No offense."

He picked up his overcoat and hat and walked out. She was still standing by the window, hands on hips. In the corner, the blue lights of the Christmas tree blinked on and off.

Twenty-two

Mulheisen came down the elevator nervous and dissatisfied. He had just turned down a proposition and he didn't know why. That was the trouble, he thought, I don't know why I do anything. He had been aroused. It wasn't as if he was getting a lot lately. And it wasn't because he was so ethical. Shirley Carpenter was just about his speed, too.

It was the room, he thought. Too many vibes, too many changes, as Ayeh would put it. He had started out doing a normal, if informal interrogation. Somehow, the light in the room, the whiskey, the woman herself, had changed all that. He had become almost drowsily comfortable. And then she had turned on the electricity with that straightforward offer. It was too much.

But more than that, she had aroused him and, in doing so, had reminded him that there was another woman around. Lou Spencer.

He suddenly realized that for a couple of days now, he had wanted to see Lou, to talk to her. What he wanted to tell her was what everyone wants to tell those who are important to them: Who I am. The trouble was, Mulheisen didn't know.

He dialed her number from the pay phone in the lobby. "Busy?" he said.

"Yes. I've been out in the mobs, shopping, and now I'm wrapping presents."

"Damn. I forgot. Today's the twenty-third, almost the last day. And I didn't get anything for Mother."

"Dear old Mom," she said. "Breaking her heart again, eh? Is that what you called to tell me?"

"No," he said, "I just called to tell you that I just got a terrific proposition and I turned it down."

"Proud of yourself, are you?" she said. "And what do you want me to do about it?"

"I thought you might come to dinner tonight."

"Where?"

"At my house," Mulheisen said.

"To meet your mother, you mean?"

"No. Mother's gone to Miami."

There was silence on the other end and Mulheisen cursed his rashness. He was a fool, he decided—at least he knew that much about himself.

"I'm not sure I know you that well," Lou said, finally.

"As a matter of fact, I meant to tell you that, also. I mean, that I don't know myself that well, either. That's one of my problems."

"And you thought I might tell you who you are?" she said.

"Mmmm . . . yeah, well . . . what do you think?"

"You're Sergeant Fang," she said.

"How did you find that out?"

"I called the precinct to see why I hadn't heard from you," she admitted. "The desk sergeant referred to you as Fang."

Mulheisen suddenly felt elated. It was the holiday season after all. " 'Tis the season to be jolly," he said. "I can cook a steak. I have wine and booze. I won't bite."

There was another long silence and Mulheisen's spirits drooped. Then, "All right. Pick me up at eight."

With a light heart, Mulheisen called the precinct and chewed Sergeant Dill's ass for referring to him as Fang.

"I thought it was your girl friend," Dill said. "She sounded like she knew you real well."

"I don't have a girl friend," Mulheisen said.

"You don't? Sorry. Sorry on both counts," Dill said. "Anyway, you're supposed to get your ass over to the U.S. Attorney's office, pronto."

Mulheisen went nowhere "pronto." He drove slowly, mulling over what he would tell Lou. He would tell her that he was contrary, that he sometimes appalled himself with his compliant nature, that he often thought he was full of crap and then the next day knew he was dead right about everything. It was a burden to be so indeterminate, so changeable, inconstant even.

Now, a man like Clippert, he would always know who he was. He would have no doubts. He might be dead wrong, but he would never know it about himself. So, he thought, it ends up that Clippert knows less about himself than I do. Only, in terms of conscious behavior, Clippert seemed to know himself better. He was in for a big shock, Mulheisen thought.

Downtown was so crowded that Mulheisen couldn't park anywhere. All the parking ramps had "Full" signs at their entrances. Mulheisen cruised round and round the Federal Building for at least fifteen minutes. The streets were slushy and traffic jerked and slid. A number of the giants from the traffic division were lording it about, so Mulheisen finally pulled into an alley and parked behind a horse from the mounted division that was tethered to a drainpipe and had an oat bag on its nose. An officer in riding boots and fur-collared jacked spotted him and came toward him. Mulheisen flashed his badge and the officer waved him on.

U.S. Attorney James Dunn was a man of thirty or so, sitting in his office and wearing an austere blue suit with faint pinstripes. "We've been waiting over an hour, Sergeant," he said.

Mulheisen shrugged. "I didn't know anything about it until a half-hour ago. I thought McClain would be here."

"Lieutenant McClain informed us that you would be able to answer all of our questions," Dunn said. He gestured to a middle-aged man who sat in the corner. "This is the Assistant U.S. Attorney, Brandon Piquette."

Mulheisen nodded at Piquette. He knew him slightly. Piquette was reputed to be the brains and guts of the federal attorney's office. He came from one of the very oldest Detroit families, dating back to the days when the town was called ville d'Etroit, and was merely a tiny civilian community attached to Fort Ponchartrain. Over a period of twenty years, Piquette had educated and molded a series of federal attorneys who were nominally his superiors. Many of them had gone on to be judges or to take higher positions in the Justice Department.

Mulheisen supposed that Dunn was probably the usual sort of bright and ambitious young man that Piquette had been dealing with for years. He decided to take his cue from Piquette and see what developed here.

What developed was that Dunn scolded Mulheisen for the failure of the city police to cooperate with the federal agencies. Mulheisen accepted this without complaint. Dunn went on to demand the complete files of the police investigation of Arthur Clippert's affairs.

"I'll be happy to tell you anything I know," Mulheisen said, "and if you want the files themselves, I'm sure that a formal request through the Commissioner will be favorably acted upon. Or you could go to Lieutenant McClain's office and view what he has."

Dunn looked angry. Piquette intervened. "That probably won't be necessary, Sergeant. We are mainly interested in Clippert's alleged involvement with the Fidelity Funding case, and we thought that your own investigation might have turned up some information that may be relevant. For instance, we see that there have been two break-ins at the Clippert residence, apparently with burglary in mind. Now, it occurs to us that these break-ins may be related to Mr. Clippert's involvement with Fidelity Funding. What do you think?"

"I've been thinking along those lines too," Mulheisen said, "and in fact, I questioned Clippert this morning with that in mind. But nothing came of it. And we have no other evidence, as far as I know, that points specifically in that direction. All we have is suspicion. I do have some ideas on the subject, if Mr. Dunn would care to hear them?"

Dunn scowled. He tapped a pencil on a yellow legal pad. "All right, Sergeant," he said, "let's hear your, uh, ideas. As Mr. Piquette suggests, we are interested in anything that will further the interests of justice."

Mulheisen smiled his long-toothed smile. "For the last few

days there has been someone else interested in our murder investigation. I assume that it is not a federal agent, since this man has represented himself variously as a Detroit policeman and as a friend of the number one murder suspect, in order to obtain information."

Mulheisen went on to tell them about John Byron Wienoshek and the "small, dark, Eyetalian" character. Dunn and Piquette assured him that the latter was none of their men.

"What do you conclude from this?" Piquette asked.

"It suggests to me that the Mob is interested in Clippert," Mulheisen said, "perhaps because rumor has it that Clippert is holding twenty million dollars. That, if true, is a mighty tempting target for the organization. The fact that one of their people is investigating John Wienoshek further suggests to me that the Mob believes that Wienoshek may have stolen the big pot from Clippert. It seems unlikely to me, personally, since Wienoshek doesn't have any kind of reputation for making a score like this. But then, Wienoshek is a peculiar guy. He may have stumbled onto the money by accident, even, during the course of the burglary in which the woman was murdered. Or he may be working with Arthur Clippert himself."

"I don't follow," Dunn said.

"Well, we know that Wienoshek, or a partner of his named Elroy Carver, killed Mrs. Clippert. Most likely, it was Carver. We know that he, at least, was at the scene of the murder. And we know that Carver is now dead, apparently killed by Wienoshek."

"Why?" Piquette asked.

"It's impossible to say," Mulheisen said. "Perhaps because Carver had badly botched the killing of Jane Clippert. Perhaps because Carver had something that Wienoshek wanted, like twenty million. More likely, it was simply to get rid of a liability: Carver doesn't seem to have been very competent. He might have seemed a danger to a man like Wienoshek, or Clippert."

"Are you suggesting that Clippert had his wife killed?" Dunn said. "That's ridiculous." He threw his pencil down.

"Why would Clippert want to kill his wife?" Piquette asked.

"I don't know. In cases like these, no matter how much we may want to know, we rarely find out why. Our simplest motive here is that Clippert stood to collect as much as two million dollars in insurance, if his wife's death could be made to look like an accident. She was taking a bath at the time she was attacked. A simple blow to the head could have made it difficult for the insurance company to prove homicide."

"But why would a man who has twenty million kill his wife for a measly two million?" Piquette asked.

"Measly?" Mulheisen said. "Anyhow, does Clippert have twenty million? And if he has it, how much of it is his? All of it? A part? How much? I understand that there are as many as twenty other people involved in the Fidelity Funding scandal."

"But embezzling is one thing," Dunn protested. "What makes you think that Clippert would turn to murder, as well?"

"Because I've talked to him," Mulheisen said. "I'm not a psychiatrist, but I'll say that this man does not know what murder means. Not yet, anyway. All he knows is what he wants, or what is to his advantage. I'm not saying he's crazy, now, but that he's cold-blooded. Maybe it's as simple as that his wife was in his way, she was blocking him from something he wanted.

"Do you remember him as a football player? He was terrific. All he needed was a block and he was gone. He ran away from tacklers. But when there was no block, he ran right over them. They called him the Flying Clipper, but they also called him the Gingerbread Man, because he was so sure of himself. He had no respect for his opponents; he was contemptuous of them."

"This is getting us nowhere," Dunn said exasperatedly. "Just a lot of speculative psychoanalyzing."

"I'm afraid Mr. Dunn is right," Piquette said. "Don't you have something more solid, Sergeant? Is there any reason to believe, for instance, that Mrs. Clippert was involved, or had knowledge of the Fidelity Funding business, and therefore had to be eliminated? Perhaps she had come across some evidence, for instance."

"You mean like tapes?" Mulheisen said, smiling. "Now you're being speculative, Mr. Piquette. No, I'm sorry, but we have no such evidence. In fact, Jane Clippert is the deepest mystery of them all. I can't figure out much about her at all. Evidently she had become rather reclusive in the last few years, despite the fact that she used to be something of a heller. I've been talking to old friends of hers, well, one of them, anyway, and this friend can't shed much light on Jane Clippert, either."

Mulheisen shook his head. "It's a sad thing about a case like this. The real victim gets forgotten. Nobody seems much interested in Jane Clippert. Everybody is keyed on the money."

"I have it," Dunn said brightly. "She found the money! She wanted to turn it in, but Clippert didn't. He probably couldn't talk her out of it. There was no way out for him. Prison, or get her out of the way."

Mulheisen looked at Piquette. Piquette's eyebrows barely quivered. Mulheisen looked thoughtful. "That's an interesting theory, Mr. Dunn," he said, "but it's unlikely that we'd ever be able to prove it. Jane Clippert is dead. That's what is significant, finally."

Dunn was sobered. He hunched his shoulders resignedly, then let them slump. He turned his chair to look out the window at the falling snow. The Ambassador Bridge, which ought to have been visible from this floor of the building, was a bare trace of an arc.

"Mulheisen," he said, without turning around, "you're right. Theories don't matter. In the long run, motives don't matter. All that counts is what happened. Jane Clippert is dead. The money is missing from the till at Fidelity Funding. What are we going to do about it?"

"You asked for information and assistance," Mulheisen said, talking to Dunn's back. "How about a little reciprocity?"

Dunn turned around. "What?"

"I think there's a connection between Wienoshek and Clippert. I think Wienoshek and Carver were paid to kill. Somehow, I don't believe that Clippert could lose twenty million to Wienoshek. But Wienoshek, wherever he is, must know by now that Clippert is onto some big money, whether from the insurance or from the Fidelity Funding ripoff. These two men, Clippert and Wienoshek, are tied together for life. Each is dangerous and/or valuable to the other. I can't believe that they won't get in touch with each other."

"So?" It was Piquette, speaking from his chair in the corner.

"So, I can't get a phone tap. But I know that the FBI can, and does." Mulheisen waved his hand to indicate that he didn't want to hear Dunn's disclaimers. "Okay, say you don't have a tap on Clippert's phone. But if you did . . . I mean, supposing that the FBI did have a tap, and supposing that they happened to overhear a conversation between Wienoshek and Clippert . . . I'd like to hear about it."

"No way," Dunn said, putting his hands flat on the desk.

"I'm not asking for a transcript, or for evidence that would be introduced in court. I won't even say anything about it to the prosecutor, if you don't want me to. I just want to get a line on Wienoshek. I can always say it came from a confidential informer. We've got a warrant on Wienoshek for the murder of John Doe— that's because we still don't have a definite identification of the body that we think is Elroy Carver. Just a little help, if it's available. And anything else you want from us, name it."

Piquette spoke up. "That's an interesting suggestion. Of course, under the circumstances, it's irrelevant because we have no such information. Nor could we promise to provide it if we had it. But it might be possible to make enquiries along these lines, just to see what develops."

Mulheisen privately marveled at the ambiguity of the statement.

"And what's to be done about this so-called private investigator?" Dunn asked.

"What can be done?" Mulheisen replied. "As far as I know he's done nothing illegal. The Mob has the right to hire a private eye, if they want. The way I look at it, he's probably trying to trace the shadowy twenty million dollars. The odds are with him, at that."

"Really?" Piquette said. "Why do you think so?"

"He has special sources of underground information," Mulheisen said. "He probably has unlimited funds for his search. In a way, I have to admire his position, as a detective. But most importantly, he is more interested in the money than I am. I want Wienoshek, and then, if it works out that way, I want Clippert. The money is least important to me."

"I see," Piquette said. "Also, this private investigator doesn't have to worry about jurisdiction, for instance, and he needn't be

150

bothered by Supreme Court decisions on methods of interrogation."

Mulheisen agreed.

Dunn stared at Mulheisen for a moment, then turned back to the window. Over his shoulder he said, "We'll let you know if anything develops, Sergeant. Thank you for coming down." Then, more to himself than anyone else, he said, "God, this snow! It just keeps coming down."

Mulheisen wished everyone a Merry Christmas and left. He came out of the Federal Building and saw how much snow had fallen in just the hour or so he had spent upstairs. Traffic was a hopeless snarl. He walked down Fort Street to Marvin's Pipe and Tobacco Shop.

He was pleased to find the proprietor, Marvin Berg, behind the counter. Marvin Berg was an enormous man. He weighed over three hundred pounds. He had a great, amorphous, sad face with sagging eyelids and sagging lower lip.

"Fang," he said slowly, coughing with a gentle liquid sound, "how nice to see you on this joyous occasion. I have your cigars."

The aisle behind the counter was barely wide enough to permit Berg to squeeze along it, his body brushing both sides. He forced himself down the aisle and into the back room.

Mulheisen saw that Marvin had a new girl working there. This one was small and had dark hair cut as short as boys' used to be. She had a wicked look. Mulheisen supposed that she would last no longer than most of Berg's girls did. That was due, as Berg himself confessed, to his gross suggestions and lewd behavior. "Hardly any girl is sufficiently depraved these days," he would complain, "to accept as a lover such a burden as myself. Not that I would dream of mounting the creature. Oh, no indeed, Fang. I have developed a peculiar variety of activities, some of which might even astonish such a one as yourself."

The new girl looked at Mulheisen with a malicious grin. "Are you a friend of his?"

"More or less," Mulheisen said.

"Another pervert, hunh? You look it. What'd he call you, Fang? What kind of name is that?"

"The better to eat you with, my dear," Mulheisen said.

"I knew it," she said triumphantly. "Oh well, what's a little scum between friends?"

Marvin came squeezing back, carrying two boxes of cigars. "This is Becky," he coughed. "She is easily the nastiest bitch I have ever come across, Fang. But she is complaisant. Now, these are fifty dollars apiece, dear boy, but I shall let you have them for only thirty-seven fifty. They are genuine Havana."

"Put them on the bill," Mulheisen said.

"Of course." Marvin shifted toward the girl. "Becky, this is Sergeant Mulheisen. He is not precisely a nice man, but I maintain a modest account for him. Please add seventy-five dollars to it. And bring us two of the Dunhill Corona Coronas."

The girl brought the Dunhills, saying, "Jesus, you really are a couple of faggots, sucking on these dildos."

"Thank you, my dear," Marvin said. He carefully clipped the ends from the cigars and the two men lit up. "Merry Christmas, Mul," Marvin said.

"What do you hear about a short, dark type who does a little investigating for the Mob?" Mulheisen asked.

Marvin sighed. "I thought you would never ask, dear boy. Round about, the conversation is all about this mighty mite. My friend Morrie the Shoe tells me that the little fellow is a Star." Marvin shook his great head solemnly. "It appears that he is an important person. He appears to be named Joe Service. He is no longer in town. They say he has taken the sun."

"You mean he found what he was looking for?"

"Perhaps," Marvin said. "Or maybe he simply tired of this wretched weather. At any rate, he is supposed to have left for sunnier climes. He is very good, they tell me."

"Don't they always say that?"

"Yes, they always do."

"What is he looking for?" Mulheisen asked.

"Money," Marvin said. "And that is the extent of my knowledge. Of course, if I hear anything . . . but now I believe I shall close my tiny shop. I am contemplating taking this scabrous slut to dinner. Perhaps you would like to join us?"

"No. I've got a date," Mulheisen said. "Nice meeting you, Becky." He waved. She gestured with an upthrust middle finger.

The streets were dark and snowy. Despite the mounted cop's recognition of him, Mulheisen had gotten a parking ticket. It took him most of an hour to get to Lou's house in Grosse Pointe. The snow swirled across Lake St. Clair, drifting already in the long driveway. Lou did not keep him waiting long.

She brought a large leather handbag. In Mulheisen's car she surprised him by saying, "I brought along some clean underwear. It occurred to me that we might get stuck in this storm. Today's smart young woman is always prepared."

"Sounds like the Boy Scouts," Mulheisen said.

"Oh, I'm better than a Boy Scout," she said. "Anyway, tell me about your proposition."

"Which proposition? The one I got, or the one I made?"

"Both," she said, "but start with the first one."

As they drove out on the long curve around the dark lake, Mulheisen told her first about Shirley Carpenter, and then Marvin Berg's new girl.

"I can certainly understand Shirley," Lou said, "though it seems a rather masculine thing for her to do, in a way."

"Well, then, what about Marvin's Becky?" he asked.

"Oh, she sounds merely venal."

When they got to the house, Lou walked around looking at everything while Mulheisen got some steaks out and mixed a couple of drinks.

"Where's your Christmas tree?" she asked, when they sat in the living room.

"Don't have one. Mother usually puts one up, but it's too much bother for me. When I got out of the service I had an apartment for a few years, on the near East Side. Every Christmas, Mother would come over and put up a Christmas tree for me. She loved to do it. But she quit, finally, when she discovered that I had left the tree standing until April, at which time it fell over of its own accord. By then all the needles had fallen off and the decorations hung on the bare branches, sort of like baubles on a naked chicken."

They laughed. Mulheisen told her to make herself at home. He was going to take a shower. After that, he would prepare the feast.

"Which is?" she asked.

"Steak and hot potato salad from a can."

"Ugh."

"I could cook some frozen asparagus," he suggested.

When he came down from the shower, dressed comfortably now in slacks and a sweater, he was glad to see that she had not attempted to do anything in the kitchen.

Over dinner, she said, "The steak is good. And the asparagus isn't too limp. Do I have to eat the beans?"

"I'll let you off on the beans if you cook breakfast," he said.

Lou raised an eyebrow at him. "And how do we fill the hours between now and then?" she asked.

"I had something in mind."

"I have a feeling that it's something carnal," she said.

"Well, that too, of course." He got up and peered out the dark kitchen windows at the snow that was blowing thickly against the house. "Looks like a sure-enough blizzard," he said. "If it keeps up we may not get out tomorrow. Which will give us time."

"For what?" she asked.

"To put together my puzzle. It's a thousand-piece picture puzzle of the Grand Canal, in Venice. From the Turner painting. I always used to do one at Christmas, when I was a boy."

Lou came to stand by him at the window, looking out into the snow that tumbled into the light from the window. She smiled into the darkness.

Twenty-three

Early one morning in June, 1805, in ville d'Etroit, the "village by the strait," a hostler rose early to hitch up a team of horses. He was to take a wagon out to the prosperous farm of the Campau family. While he worked in the stable he smoked his clay pipe. Absent-mindedly he knocked the ashes out of his pipe and went on his way. Every single building in the village burned to the ground, except for St. Anne's church. Miraculously, only two persons were injured.

The disconsolate former Detroiters camped on the plain just south of the gutted village. They were found there a couple of days later by the newly appointed governor of the Michigan Territory. The territory included Michigan, Wisconsin, and parts of Minnesota, and had just been created. With the new governor was Augustus Woodward, who had just been appointed a judge of the territory by his friend President Thomas Jefferson.

Judge Woodward was not at all dismayed to discover that the capital of the new territory no longer existed. "I just happen to have in my saddle bags here a complete plan for a new town." It was actually the plan for Washington, D.C., as designed by the French-American engineer and architect Major Pierre Charles l'Enfant. It was basically a radial plan, with broad thoroughfares emanating outward from a central hub. Judge Woodward adapted the plan to the new Detroit. The fledgling town had amazingly wide boulevards and avenues, named after Jefferson, after the early founder of Detroit, Antoine de la Mothe Cadillac, or for Grand River. Other streets were named for early settlers like Joseph Campau. But the main avenue, which remains the main street of Detroit, was called by its designer Woodward Avenue.

Apparently some of the citizens objected. But the judge responded with the interesting explanation that the avenue was not, after all, named for himself. "The street goes north, toward the forest, to the woods. Hence, Wood-ward."

On this morning of Christmas Eve, a semitrailer truck was jackknifed across Woodward Avenue, just north of Grand Boulevard. The truck blocked five of the six traffic lanes. But there was no traffic on Woodward Avenue this morning. The truck was abandoned and snow had drifted well over the tops of the wheels. All night long the snow had fallen heavily and continued to fall. It was driven by gale-force winds between the dark and quiet office buildings.

Like the fire of 1805, the Christmas Blizzard had a purifying effect on the city. The raw rubble of urban renewal was blanketed in white, the deep scars of the expressway system that lay over Judge Woodward's radial plan like a plastic overlay on a field map were softened and filled, the sky was not yellow and red with industrial pollution, the atmosphere above Woodward Avenue itself did not shimmer with automobile exhaust. Most importantly, crime had nearly vanished in Detroit. The city had changed its infamous ways overnight.

Detroit is Murder City. After the riots of 1967, the sale of handguns greatly increased, and with that came an increase in monthly killings, so that as many as eighty-nine have died in a single month. In a single precinct there have been as many as thirteen killings in a weekend. In the Orient, we like to say, life is cheap. But not cheaper than in Detroit.

But on this Christmas Eve, when the city should have been thronged with shoppers and shoplifters, office-party drunks and drunk-rollers, with thieves and bonus-flush victims, Santa Clauses and maniacs . . . the city was practically empty. There was no one to rob or be robbed, no one to kill or be killed.

Not a single murder was recorded for eighteen hours. Then an auto worker named Wiley Hatton shot his wife in their East-side home because she had failed to lay in a sufficient supply of whiskey against the coming of the Christmas Blizzard. Mr. Hatton called the police himself and then had to wait more than an hour and a half for them to get to his house.

The great office buildings downtown were virtually empty. The hotels were full and likely to remain so. The only cars on the streets were stuck there. No one came to relieve the caretaker staff at the General Motors Building. The Henry Ford Hospital was accepting patients, but discharging none. There were fires and the fire department battled their way to them, not always in time. Policemen delivered babies, used helicopters to rush heart-attack cases to the hospital, and not always successfully in either case.

The whorehouse/motels had an unprecedented number of all-nighters. Robbers stayed home. The stores stayed closed. Concerts were canceled. Many people were hungry and cold. Some died. Linemen froze their fingers and feet repairing power and telephone lines.

The temperature dropped to zero, the wind grew to thirty knots, then thirty-five.

A city the size of Detroit can take only so much shutting down before it collapses. The collapse began immediately, but was still not significant. If the snow and wind would let up by Christmas Day, everything would be all right. Even two more days would not be cataclysmic, although food supplies would dwindle, especially the milk supply. People would then have to get out, into the blizzard. Supplies would have to be brought in, somehow. But for now, the population could sit quietly inside.

The weather prognosis was promising. A strong high-pressure system was moving inexorably from the west. Already it was clearing in Minneapolis, where the sky was a brilliant blue and the temperature was a brittle $-15°$ F.

At the U.S. Weather Bureau at Metropolitan Airport, the main concern was that the blizzard—which they referred to as a low-pressure system—would not be able to continue its normal eastward course. It was now centered just northwest of Detroit. But there was a ridge of high pressure lying along a line from Quebec to Kentucky. If the ridge did not move, the blizzard would not move. The low-pressure system would stick, it would probably deepen, winds would increase, there would be warmer, moister air coming up from the Mississippi Valley to feed the system . . . oh, what a blizzard they would have then!

The problem was, the weather bureau was not getting sufficient information about the upper air movements. Most air traffic in the Midwest—the main source of upper air information—had stopped. Only the transcontinental flights were operating, cruising at sunny altitudes high above the storm-stricken Midwest. Businessmen en route to New York from Los Angeles sipped their whiskies and gazed down on the beautiful golden billows below. Bored SAC bomber crews calculated the precise but invisible spot in the sky where they would rendezvous with bored refueling tanker crews; they ate stale sandwiches and wrote letters to girls in Falfurrias, Texas.

Mulheisen woke up to the storm with a tousled blond head on his arm. A little later, he made a token effort to get his car out of the driveway, but it was futile. Even if he got to the lane that was as full of snow as the drive. And if he got to the highway, would that be plowed? He abandoned his snow shovel just as Lou called to him from the kitchen door. It was Lieutenant Johnson.

"Might as well stay home, Mul," Johnson said. "I had to hitch a ride with a plow, myself, to get in. Thank God there's nothing much going on, just emergency calls."

"Who's there?" Mulheisen asked.

"Well, Jensen and Field," Johnson said. "Which reminds me, Jensen wants to talk to you. Oh yeah, I called Ahab off on that Clippert stakeout last night. I didn't have anyone to relieve him. He barely got home as it was."

"What?"

"Don't get excited, Mul. Believe me, Clippert isn't going anywhere in this weather."

"All right, all right," Mulheisen said, "but if it starts to break, get someone over there right away."

"If I can spare anyone," Johnson said. "Here's Jensen."

Peter Jensen came on the line. "Mulheisen? Me and Field checked out the airports and ticket offices on those two guys, yesterday."

The line was silent. Mulheisen waited, then sighed. Why was it so difficult to get information out of Jensen? Finally, Mulheisen said, "That's good, Jensen. What did you find out?"

"Wienoshek flew out of Metro Airport on the eighteenth, the noon flight on Delta. Nonstop to Miami. The seat was originally reserved for an earlier flight in the name of Elroy Carver."

Silence.

"That's very good work," Mulheisen said. "Is there anything else?"

"Yeah." There was another brief silence, then Jensen cleared his throat and went on. "The girl from Delta's ticket office downtown identified Carver's picture as the man who bought the ticket."

There was a voice in the background, then Jensen said, "Uh, Bud wants to talk to you, Mulheisen. Here."

The calm precise voice of Bud Field came on the line. "Hello, Mul? I did the downtown work. The Delta girl was very cooperative, very helpful. She said Carver seemed nervous and in a hurry. She sold him a ten o'clock ticket even though it seemed unlikely that he would make the flight in time. He flashed a big roll of bills. He was wearing an overcoat that was too large for him, she says, and he was carrying an airline bag. She said he took a cab just outside the office, but she didn't see what company it was."

"I guess Carver didn't make his flight," Mulheisen said.

"No, he didn't," Field said. "Airport personnel definitely identified Wienoshek as the man who used the ticket. Not only that, the desk man out there tore off the top part of the ticket and kept it, as usual. Jensen picked it up. I was thinking there's a good chance we might get prints of both Wienoshek and Carver from the ticket. Also, it is definitely the same ticket the girl sold to Carver, the same number, her handwriting."

"Very good, Field," Mulheisen said. "So, he went to Miami. Did you get out a bulletin to Miami?"

"Right. And also to the FBI."

"Wonderful. What about the cab? Did the lab do a job on it?"

"They did. Frank told me that he is pretty sure that he can

prove that Carver was in the cab. He said he would send a full report on fingerprints, hair, a saliva test on some cigarette butts, and also some dirt samples that he hopes to match with the dirt found in Mrs. Clippert's bathtub. Of course, Frank isn't working today, and probably won't be in for a couple days."

"No hurry," Mulheisen said. He was delighted.

"Oh yeah," Field said, "there's a pathology report here, too. Some bright boy over there compared x-rays from Carver's military record with x-rays of the corpse, and he says they can prove through old bone fractures that the body is Carver."

"Well, that's it, then. All we have to do is find Wienoshek," Mulheisen said.

"That may not be so easy," Field said. "The trail is kind of cold."

"Don't worry," Mulheisen said, "that boy is down the tubes. I'm going to have him." He told Field that he would be at home, naturally, if he was needed, and hung up.

"You look very pleased with yourself," Lou said, "like an owl with a mouse's tail in its mouth."

"And you look great, even if that bathrobe is too big for you," he said. He came up behind her at the stove, where she was frying bacon, and slid his arms around her. She turned her head and kissed him lightly. He ran his hand into a fold of the robe and found her breast.

"Oh, your hand is cold!" But she arched her back against his chest. "Stop it, now. I'm cooking."

"I'm starving," Mulheisen said. "You look great, the bacon smells great. I feel like an old married man."

"Don't presume on such a short acquaintance," she said. "You move too fast."

"That's what Laddy McClain tells me," he said, "but I'm also quite patient."

He sat down at the kitchen table with a cup of coffee and talked to her while she fried the eggs. He told her about Jensen and Field. "Together they make one very good detective," he said. "Jensen is methodical, tireless and tough. Field is intelligent and imaginative. Apart, they're just average. They work for each other, I think, to help each other."

Lou brought the eggs and bacon to the table. "That's sweet," she said. "Are they married?"

"I don't know," Mulheisen said. "I've never heard them mention wives."

"Didn't you ever ask? Aren't you curious?"

Mulheisen laughed. "They're married to each other. Anyway, that's the sort of question a woman asks."

"Ugh, what a sexist pig you are. Don't you think a woman would be a good detective?"

"I don't know," he said. "I never thought about it. I mean, we have women detectives, but they aren't really detectives, somehow. They work on muggers and rapists, that sort of thing, and they help question female suspects, do personal searches and so forth."

"You mean they do specialized kinds of work," Lou said. "They're categorized. You don't see them pulling a routine shift like any other detective. A social worker might be a man or a woman, it doesn't make any difference. But a detective is a man, and then there are *women* detectives who do special things."

"Something like that," he said, forking bacon and eggs into his mouth.

"I think a woman would make a very good detective," Lou said.

"Maybe."

"I imagine that we women are very interested in personal things, in the nature of relationships. It seems to me that apart from economic pressures and social conditions, it is human relationships that are at the source of problems that develop into crimes."

"Sounds like a theory," Mulheisen said. He sipped his coffee. "But I agree with you. I believe that."

"And then, of course," she went on, "there's all that stuff about women's intuition. I imagine that good detectives are intuitive as well."

"Intuitive or imaginative," Mulheisen said, "I'm not sure how you would define it, if you had to. But now that we're talking about intuition and human relationships, what do you think it may have been in Arthur Clippert's relationship with his wife that led him to kill her?"

"I'm not sure that he did," Lou said.

"But if he did? If he arranged to have her killed?"

Lou ate for a moment and chewed, then drank some coffee. "Jane had one quality," she said, "that could have gotten to Arthur. She was proud. If she was in danger of losing Arthur, I don't think her pride would permit it. I think she would do almost anything to hold on to him."

"That's not what Clippert suggested. He said that she didn't mind his having a mistress."

"That's possible, I guess, but I doubt it. I remember with the ski instructor, Dieter, even after she got over the romance and wasn't seeing him anymore it still irritated her to see him flirting with some new young thing. She even ran one of Dieter's girl friends down on the slopes. Jane swore it was an accident, but I'm not sure it was. Of course, that was ages ago, when she was only seventeen. Maybe by now she wouldn't take someone like Shirley Carpenter seriously, but I still think it would bother her if Arthur was getting too independent."

"Independent of her, or her money?" Mulheisen asked.

"Her, her influence. If he was involved in the Fidelity Funding fraud it was quite a coup for him," Lou said. "I mean, aside from its criminal aspects it was a spectacular bit of wheeling and dealing, and so far Arthur seems to have come out of it smelling like a rose. On top of that, it looks like he got more money than even her father did . . . that's assuming that Arthur was involved at all."

"Poor little rich girl," Mulheisen said.

"Yes. She had pride, but I don't think she ever felt secure. Maybe that's why she liked older men."

"Ah yes," Mulheisen smiled, "The older-man syndrome. I remember I asked you what your feelings were toward the aged."

Lou sat back in her chair and smiled. "I haven't made up my mind. I've heard so much about their lack of stamina. You know, all that stuff about once a night, once a week . . ."

"It's still only nine o'clock," Mulheisen said, looking at the kitchen clock. "We've got a long day ahead of us, marooned in the storm. And I'm a little tired from all that fruitless shoveling. I was thinking I might retire for a bit."

"Now that's what I mean about old men," Lou said. "Just when you think they want to get it on, they talk about taking a nap."

Later they worked on the picture puzzle. The outside pieces were all done, and part of the Grand Canal itself. Neither had gotten very far on the sky.

Snow fell and the wind drove it in level sheets. One or the other of them would remark, looking up at the windows from time to time, "Look at that snow!" They snacked on cheese and wine, they drank some calvados and Mulheisen smoked his Havanas. Sometimes one of them would wander off to read, or to make a phone call—Lou to assure her family that she was all right, Mulheisen to see what was doing at the precinct. It was an excellent day.

For dinner, Mulheisen outdid himself with baked pork chops and boiled potatoes, while Lou made a green salad. After that they watched television for a bit, worked on the puzzle, and talked a great deal about who they were, and what they liked, and what they didn't like.

In the evening the snow seemed to diminish, but the wind was still very strong. Snow covered the driveway completely. It was a rural house, with trees that hid the nearest neighbors' houses even in good weather. Now they seemed in the midst of a northern forest, alone and safe and snug.

"The only thing we lack is a fireplace," Mulheisen said. They were on the couch, listening to some old Stan Getz records.

"That would be a bit too much, maybe," Lou said.

Mulheisen knew what she meant. He kissed her. And then he realized that she was crying.

"What's wrong?" he said.

"Nothing," she said. "It's been a nice day, that's all."

Mulheisen grimaced. He felt nervous. "Would you like to talk?" he asked.

"About what?"

"Sociology and crime and sex and love and history?"

She laughed and said, "Let's go to bed."

While she was in the bathroom, Mulheisen undressed and sat on the edge of the bed, distracted. He was thinking about Clippert. He suddenly had a powerful urge to telephone Clippert, to make contact with him, to be sure that he was there. He could think of no pretext. He couldn't just call him up, he felt, and say, "Hi, Clip, just thought I'd check and make sure you were safe and sound."

Lou came back into the bedroom, wearing Mulheisen's robe again.

"How would you like to call up Arthur Clippert?" he asked her.

She looked at him in surprise, then a touch of fear. "Call him up?" she said. "You mean, right now?"

Mulheisen was embarrassed. But he persisted. "Why not?" He tried to sound nonchalant, but knew he didn't sound that way at all. "You could wish him a Merry Christmas."

"Why do you want me to do this?" she asked.

"I just want to know if he's home," he said. He knew that it was more than that. It was more than a callous willingness to use her. There was something perverse in it, as well. Perhaps something perverted, even. He wanted to hear her talk to her former lover.

"You're a calculating bastard, aren't you?" Lou said.

"Don't do it, then," he said, an edge of anger in his voice.

"I'll do it."

He looked at her carefully. "I've got the number here, someplace," he said.

"I know the number," Lou said. She went to the telephone by the bed and sat down, crossing her bare legs. It was a movement so casual, so intimate somehow, that he cursed himself for having asked her in the first place.

He watched as she dialed the number swiftly and surely. She waited. After several seconds she looked up at him, frowning. After several more seconds she held out the phone to him. He listened to ten unanswered rings, counting them silently. Then he set the phone back in its cradle.

"He's not there," he said.

Mulheisen walked away from the bed. He stood by the window and looked out into the storm. He wore only patterned shorts and his hands were on his hips. His pistol lay on a small table next to the window, along with binoculars and the book on Christopher Columbus. Absentmindedly, he picked up the .38 and hefted it. He pursed his lips and whistled very softly.

"What's that?" Lou asked. She sat on the bed still, by the telephone.

"What?" he said, startled.

"That tune. What is it?"

"I don't know . . . an old nursery tune."

"How does it go?" Lou asked.

Mulheisen set the gun down on the table and came back to where she sat. He took her by the shoulders and brought her to her feet. She came into his embrace and he sang softly into her hair, tunelessly:

"The north wind shall blow,
And we shall have snow.
What will the robin do then, poor thing?"

He released her. She turned back the covers and then undid the belt of the robe. She let the robe fall. She was very beautiful, he thought.

In bed, she crooned the rest of the rhyme for him:

"He'll sit in the barn,
To keep himself warm,
And tuck his head under his wing, poor thing."

Her hair spread softly across his chest. It was dark, and they listened to the snow ticking against the windows.

Twenty-four

Mulheisen sat up in bed. "This won't do," he said. "I've got to call in. I've got to know what's going on."

Lou did not say anything.

The telephone rang. Mulheisen snatched it up.

A voice said, "Sergeant Mulheisen?"

"Yes?"

"Listen."

Mulheisen listened. There were clicks, then a series of low buzzes.

"What the hell?" Mulheisen said.

The buzzes were interrupted by another click, then a sleepy voice said, "Hello?"

"Hello," Mulheisen said.

"Hello," a third voice said.

"Hello," Mulheisen said.

The third voice seemingly ignored Mulheisen, and went on to say, "Mr. Clippert?"

"Who is this?" Clippert said.

"You know who this is."

"What do you want?" Clippert said guardedly.

"I want to talk to you. About some business."

"Business?"

"It's about money."

"I see," Clippert said. "Where are you calling from?"

"Florida," the voice said.

"Well, I'll have to get back to you. There's a blizzard going on up here. Everything is shut down. I can't get out."

"I heard about the blizzard. You'll be able to get out tomorrow. Call me tomorrow. It's important, Mr. Clippert."

"I don't want to call you," Clippert said. "I don't think that is a good idea. We'll have to think of something else."

"So? Think of something."

"Hmmmm." That was Clippert. There was silence on the line. "How about if you call me again?"

"This number?"

"No. I don't think that's a good idea. Let's see . . . you could call me at my office, in a day or two . . . no, that won't do, either."

"I've got to go now. You think of something. I'll call again."

"When?"

"I don't know."

There was the sound of two telephones hanging up, then another couple of clicks. A dry voice said, "This conversation originated in Miami, Florida, at 9:47 P.M., Eastern Standard Time, December twenty-fourth." The line went dead.

"Thanks," Mulheisen said into the darkness.

"Who was it?" Lou asked. "The precinct?"

"No." He got up to dress in the dark.

"Is anything wrong?" she said. "Where are you going?"

"We might be on to something," Mulheisen said. "I'm going downstairs to wait."

"I'll come, too," Lou said. She turned on the light and they both stood foolishly in its brightness, squinting. She put on his robe again and followed him downstairs.

He went into the living room and found the bottle of calvados and poured himself a couple of fingers. "Want some?" he asked her.

"No, thanks. I'll make some coffee."

He lit a cigar. The unfinished picture puzzle was on the floor.

Mulheisen sat down cross-legged in front of it and studied the puzzle.

Lou came back into the room from putting water on. She sat down next to him and leaned against him.

"I have to wait now," he said.

She picked up a piece of pale-blue sky that had a tiny gold part. The gold part was the edge of a cornice on a palazzo that stood on the Grand Canal.

"You don't mind if I wait, too?" she asked.

He smiled. "No."

Together they fitted another ten pieces before the telephone rang again. Mulheisen took it on the wall phone in the kitchen.

"Sergeant Mulheisen?" asked the dry voice.

"Yes."

"Conversation number two."

Clickclick, buzzzzzz, buzzzzzzz, click. "Hello?" It was Clippert.

"Clippert? I got a plan. I want you to talk to a friend of mine."

"Hello," said a new voice. "Mr. Clippert? Pleased to make your acquaintance. I'm a friend of your friend. He says you are having some difficulty making connections. I understand the problem."

"Put Byron back on," snapped Clippert.

"Uh-oh," the third man said, "you made a boo-boo, there. Shouldn't mention names on this phone. It probably won't make any difference, but maybe you'll be more careful from now on. I'm not the law, Mr. Clippert, if that's what is bothering you. If I were, you wouldn't be talking to my friend right now. But here, let our mutual friend reassure you."

"Clippert? This guy's all right."

"How do I know that?" Clippert said angrily. "For all I know he's some cheap hood and you're cooking up dangerous plans. Dangerous, Byron. Get that?"

"I get it," Byron said. "But you better get wise. You don't have any choice in this. You better listen to my friend."

The third man came back on the line. "He's right, Mr. Clippert. You don't have any choice. But let's not discuss this on this phone. The problem is communications, right, Mr. Clippert?"

"What do you suggest?" Clippert asked.

"Communications are always problematical in a complex society," the third man said. "The usual solution is simplification. That is what everybody tells me. But I believe in complication."

"Get to the point," Clippert said.

"I understand the weather is terrible up there."

Mulheisen could practically hear Clippert's teeth grinding.

"So what?" Clippert said.

"I hate to tell you this," the man said, "but you have to go out into the cold night."

"What for?"

"To find a safe phone. A phone booth. When you find one, call this number: 885-5101. It's a Detroit number. When they answer, say, 'I want to talk about the South.' Use those words. They'll give you a number where you can reach us again. I'd go right now, if I were you. They know you'll be calling."

"What kind of crap is this?" Clippert said. "Code words?"

The other man laughed. "Well, forget the code words," he said, "just tell them who you are."

"And who are you?" Clippert asked. "How do you fit into all this?"

"We'll discuss that later. Good-by now, and Merry Christmas."

Click. There was a moment's silence, then another phone, presumably Clippert's, was hung up.

Several more clicks, and the dry voice came on. "The preceding originated in Miami, Florida, at 11:03 P.M., Eastern Standard Time." Click.

Mulheisen looked at the kitchen clock. It was almost 1 A.M., Christmas Day. What had taken so long, he wondered? Probably the messages had to go through channels, had to be listened to by various decision-makers. He hoped that they had awakened U.S. Attorney James Clarke Dunn for final approval. Whatever the case, it was clear that Clippert had flown. Of course, he might return home after making his phone call.

Mulheisen called the precinct. "This is Mulheisen. Who's got the duty tonight?"

It was Jensen. "Somebody's got to stay," he said. "I was lying down in the back room. You woke me up."

"Sorry," Mulheisen said. "Look in the telephone directory, the one that has the numerical listings, and tell me who belongs to this number: 885-5101."

A minute later, Jensen said, "It's Poppie's Bar, on the east side. You know the joint."

"Yes. Carmine Kusane, right?"

Jensen did not deign to answer. He assumed it was not a real question, since every cop in Detroit knew who and what Carmine Kusane was.

"Jensen?"

"Yeah."

"Can a vehicle move anywhere at all tonight?"

"The plows are out. They aren't making much progress, though."

"Can they get around?"

"Yeah," Jensen said.

"How about a four-wheel drive?"

"Maybe," Jensen said.

Mulheisen sighed. "Okay, thanks, Jensen. Good night." Jensen hung up before he could get the final words out.

Mulheisen stood by the kitchen phone for several minutes, not looking at anything. He dialed Clippert's number again. No answer. He hung up, wondering what he would have said if Clippert had answered. It occurred to him that he would have had his conversation recorded by the FBI.

He walked back into the living room and stood there, staring at nothing. After a while he said, "Who's going where?"

"What?" Lou asked.

"In this weather Clippert can't be going anywhere, or at least not far," Mulheisen said. "So where is he?"

"I don't understand," Lou said. Mulheisen told her about the taped phone calls.

"I think they're trying to arrange a meeting," he said.

"It sounds like it," Lou said. She shook her head sadly. "It's beginning to look like you were right. Arthur is involved with these people." She stared down at the unfinished picture puzzle. Unthinkingly, she picked up a piece and fitted it into the Turner sky.

Mulheisen walked about the room, thinking. Occasionally he wandered into the kitchen. Then he would return to the living room, throw himself into a chair and light up a cigar or sip calvados. He didn't seem very aware of Lou. He asked questions out loud, but they didn't seem to be addressed to her. "What's their big hurry?" he wondered. And, "Would they really try to set it up tonight?"

"The sooner the better, I imagine," Lou said. Mulheisen looked at her uncomprehendingly. "I mean, it's a perfect opportunity for Arthur to give the police the slip," she said.

"You're right," he said. He went to the telephone and called McClain. "I think they're trying to set up a meet," he told him, "but there's no way that Clippert could get a flight to Miami, so maybe they'll come to him."

"If these are Kusane's people," McClain said, "they don't have to come here. Kusane's here, he can deal direct with Clippert."

"What kind of a deal?" Mulheisen asked.

"Maybe Clippert thinks the game plan is blown. Maybe he wants their help in getting out, in exchange for a big payoff."

"I doubt it," Mulheisen said. "I think Clippert's too shrewd for that. He won't want to deal with Kusane. It's too risky for him. He'll want to see what Wienoshek and this other guy are up to, and make a deal from that point."

"Well, I'll get onto the Miami police and ask them to increase their surveillance. If you're right, somebody'll be going in or out of Miami, and it'll probably be the airport."

"Thanks," Mulheisen said. "I'll be here, waiting." He hung up and came into the living room again. He slumped into the big chair and looked out the window.

"The snow has stopped," he said. "Wind's still up, though."

A moment later he jumped up again and made another phone call. "Hello, Oz? Did I wake you? . . . I didn't? Oz, it's two in the morning, what are you doing up? . . . Oh. Santa Claus. I forgot . . . Yeah. Listen, I've got an emergency, Oz. I've got to get out. Do you think that four-wheel drive rig of yours would get through this snow? Can I borrow it? . . . No, I'll walk there, Oz. It's only a mile, I'll walk. You stay there and fill the stockings. I'll be by for the keys. I'm leaving now."

"Where are you going?" Lou asked. She seemed alarmed.

"Ozzie's marina," he said. "He's got a rig that I think will make it through this snow. A Dodge Powerwagon."

"I'll go with you," Lou said.

He looked at her as if she were crazy. "No, no," he said. "You stay here. I can't take you with me. It's cold out. You don't have the gear for it."

"I'll wear something of your mother's."

"Don't be silly," he said. "I'm just going down to the precinct, and maybe see if I can't locate Clippert."

"For what? To arrest him?"

"I don't know. He could be in bad trouble, if he's playing games with a guy like Kusane."

She stood there in his too-large robe, looking upset. "You could get in trouble too," she said.

"Well," he said, "so what?"

"So what?" She was angry.

"It's my job," he said. He walked over to her and took her by the shoulders. "Come on," he said, "don't be this way. I have to go out. I don't want to leave you, but I have to. Clippert doesn't want to go out either, but he has to."

She moved into his arms and he held her, smelling her hair. "Aren't you the one who wanted to know what it was like to be a cop?" he asked.

"A detective," she said, her voice muffled against his chest. She clung to him tightly.

"Yeah. Well, this is what it's like," Mulheisen said. He kissed her. The kiss was longer than he wanted it to be. Her arms were tight about his neck. At last, he gently pulled away from her.

"I've got to go," he said. "But I want you to stay here. Wait for me. I don't know how long I'll be. Maybe just a few hours. But if it's longer, if the plows get through in the morning, you can take the car and go home."

"No," she said. "I'll wait here. I'll do the puzzle for you."

"You go to bed," he said.

"Call me."

He promised that he would, as he got on his old Air Force parka. It was a big, bulky nylon thing with a fur-lined hood and reflective markings sewn onto it. He wore heavy wool pants, his old uniform pants, and boots that had felt liners. He kissed her again and left.

It was cold. The snow was waist-deep in places, but generally he found that he could avoid these drifts and walk where it was only knee-deep or less. After a hundred yards he wanted to go back, but then he hit a barren stretch where the snow was only six inches deep. What the hell, he told himself, my boots are warm. He stumbled on through the high wind, turning his face away from the icy buffeting. It took him forty minutes to get to the front door of Gary Oswald's house.

Oswald was a burly man in robe and slippers. He was balding and had a huge, drooping mustache. The tree was decorated and shining with lights and tinsel. There were children's presents everywhere.

"Damn, Mul, come in. Take your coat off and warm up. I'll get you some coffee."

"Oz, I'm in a hurry," Mulheisen said. But Oswald insisted, bringing a cup of coffee with a generous dollop of whiskey in it.

Mulheisen stood by the door and drank the coffee. "Where's the Powerwagon?" he asked.

"In the big shed," Oswald said. "Here's the key to the shed, and here's the key to the truck. Unplug the engine heater, and pull out the choke to start it."

"Do you think it'll get through this?"

"Mul, it's got snow tires, chains if you need them, and a high clearance. There's a winch, too. If you get stuck, just throw the cable around a tree and you can winch yourself out."

"How's the gas?"

"Gassed up yesterday. It should be full, and there's a couple of full five-gallon cans in the back."

Mulheisen took the keys and went out. Oswald closed the door, shaking his head. A wisp of snow had blown in while the door was open. Snow had melted from Mulheisen's boots onto the carpet by the door. Oswald thought about cleaning it up, thinking of his wife upstairs in bed. She would be annoyed by the mess. "Ah, to hell with it," he said, and turned out the lights.

Twenty-five

"What the hell?" said Sergeant Dill, the desk man at the Ninth Precinct. "Mul, I didn't recognize you. How the hell did you get here?" The sergeant peered out the back door at the Powerwagon. "Jesus, it looks like a weapons carrier."

"Where's Jensen?" Mulheisen asked.

"He got restless. He went to Clippert's house. He got a city plow to take him. Hey, are those uniform pants?" He gestured at Mulheisen's heavy blue pants.

"Yeah, I'm back in the blue," Mulheisen said. He went to his tiny office and dialed Clippert's home.

"Hello," a voice said. "Who is this?"

"Jensen, it's me."

"Oh. Mulheisen."

"I'm down at the precinct. Is Clippert there?"

"No. His car is, though."

"Both cars? His wife had an Audi, I think."

"Both cars. But I'll tell you one thing—"

Jensen volunteering information? This is new, Mulheisen thought.

"—this house is a mess."

Silence. "What do you mean, a mess?"

"There's mattresses ripped open, kitchen shelves emptied, closets dumped out, and he never picked up that Christmas tree that he blasted. Looks like he cleared out."

Mulheisen thought about that for a moment. "Anything else, Jensen? Did you notice anything else?"

"Not really. You want me to stay here?"

"No. Have you been to Kusane's?"

"Should I go to Kusane's? I still got the plow waiting."

"Go see Carmine," Mulheisen said. "Call me from there."

Mulheisen went out to the desk. "Any messages for me, Dill?"

"You're practically our only customer tonight, Mul. I was just gonna call you when you came in. A Lieutenant Mendoza from Miami called. He left a message."

Miami police had Miami International locked up tight, with the aid of the FBI, and they were canvassing the hotels, armed with a photograph and a description of Wienoshek. Apparently they had found where Wienoshek was staying, under the name of George Gordon, but he had checked out earlier in the evening.

McClain had called to say that arrest warrants were waiting downtown on both Wienoshek and Clippert, but that it would be impossible to have them delivered to the Ninth Precinct. Any other assistance Mulheisen required would be forthcoming by calling the shift commander at Homicide. Or call me, McClain's note said. Mulheisen read that to mean, call Homicide first.

Mulheisen told the desk man to get Miami police and put the call on his office line.

Lieutenant Mendoza came on the line. "Did you get our message?" he asked, after the introductions. "Looks like your boy has skipped. We've got checks on the bus stations, train station, and so forth."

"How about roadblocks?"

"Of course," Mendoza said. "But if you think he'll try to get back north, I imagine he'll want to fly, don't you?"

"Most likely," Mulheisen agreed.

"We've got Miami International covered," Mendoza said. "Of course, starting around six there'll be a hell of a lot more people in the terminal and then it'll be tougher to spot him. But the FBI is helping out, so we shouldn't have too much trouble."

"What kind of an operation do you have?" Mulheisen asked.

"At the airport? We've got men all over the place, watching from observation points, outside, inside, in the johns . . . the FBI has men behind the counters of the major airlines."

"Just at the one airport? Are there other airports?"

"Miami International is the only one with the big scheduled airlines. It's where he'd have to go if he wanted a flight north."

"Look," Mulheisen said, "check with Miami Flight Service. It's probably right there at the terminal. They'll have clearances on all air traffic in the area. See if there has been any kind of flight plan filed for private aircraft into the upper Midwest, especially to Michigan. And if they don't have anything, ask them to call you if they get anything."

Twenty minutes later Jensen called again. "I'm at Kusane's. They never heard of Clippert, of course, never saw anybody of that description. But I'll tell you one thing, there's been cars in and out of their parking lot tonight."

"Did you ask Carmine about Wienoshek?"

"My old buddy Carmine is kind of irritated with me," Jensen said, "for waking him up on Christmas morning."

"Did you lay it on him heavy?"

"Like a goddamn hammer," Jensen said. "Nothing."

"See if you can find out what kind of car he's got that could get around in this weather, then come on back."

As soon as Mulheisen hung up, the phone rang. It was Mendoza.

"Not much traffic on Christmas Eve," Mendoza said. "I checked as far back as 10 P.M. That good enough?"

"Fine," Mulheisen said. "What have you got?"

"Let's see here." Mulheisen could hear paper rattling, then Mendoza said, "They got a Twin Beech out of Miami International at ten-eighteen Eastern, for Atlanta—"

"No," Mulheisen interrupted, "just give me the destinations, for now. Anything into the Midwest."

"There's not much," Mendoza said. "The guy at Flight Service said most of these are small aircraft that don't have the instruments to fly into bad weather areas. The farthest north we have is a flight to Chicago."

"What's that?"

"A Convair 240 off at 0131 Eastern, for O'Hare International. A company plane, belongs to Northwest Properties. Sounds like one of those real-estate operations, where they fly prospective customers down for a day or two."

"That doesn't sound like Wienoshek," Mulheisen said. "What else?"

"Okay, here's one to Nashville."

"Nashville? What's that one?" Mulheisen asked.

"That's, ah . . . oh, here's one to Pittsburgh," Mendoza said.

"What's he sound like?"

"Lear jet, out of Miami at 0112 Eastern, for Greater Pittsburgh Airport."

Mulheisen copied the information, then asked about the Nashville aircraft. That turned out to be an Apache that had changed its flight plan shortly after take off and headed for Memphis.

"That's about it," Mendoza said.

"Thanks, Mendoza. Let me know if you hear anything interesting."

Mulheisen sat and smoked a cigar. He studied the note pad scribbled up with flight plans and was reminded of his own days as a control-tower operator. Almost twenty years ago. It didn't seem that long ago. In a way, he thought he should have stayed at it. He had enjoyed tower work. All the tower operators did, although they bitched constantly about the pressure and/or the occasional moments of boredom when there was no traffic. That was the way it seemed to go: one moment you had five guys on final and the next hour you had nothing. It was different in the big commercial airports, of course, where the traffic was heavy and steady.

Mulheisen had never tired of it. Standing in the tower before a bank of radios, clearing a flight of F-101 Interceptors for a hot scramble, telling a KC-135 refueling tanker to begin his jet penetration from thirty miles out, watching a loaded C-5A use every bit of runway on takeoff. When civilian aircraft entered his control zone he would advise them of what local traffic there was.

He used to sit in the darkened tower on nights of little traffic and listen to the big control centers passing on flight plans. Like this Apache out of Miami: someone would be calling Nashville tower to cancel that inbound; the same person would call Memphis tower with the change in flight plans.

On impulse, Mulheisen got on the telephone, and through a series of information operators was able to call the FAA Flight Service in Memphis. Memphis told him they had the Apache inbound.

"Is there any further amendment on the flight plan?" Mulheisen asked.

"No, sir. They're terminating here and requesting parking space for overnight."

Mulheisen thanked him and hung up. It was interesting talking to Flight Service again. Just like old times. He decided to call Pittsburgh.

Pittsburgh Flight Service said, "A Lear? Flight out of Miami? That's Juliet Tango One-Oh-Two-Oh-Seven Sierra Tango. Amended flight plan, en route to Chicago, O'Hare. Estimated time of arrival, 0217 Central. He ought to be there by now, sir."

Mulheisen went out into the hall and looked at the clock. Four-thirty Eastern, in Detroit, on Christmas Day. That made it three-thirty in Chicago. He called O'Hare.

O'Hare verified that they had a Lear, JT 10207 ST, out of Miami. "She was a little late," the man said, "but she got off okay, after refueling."

"Refueling? Where was she headed?"

"Milwaukee, with an open destination for Pellston, Michigan, if the weather cleared there."

"How does Pellston look?" Mulheisen asked.

"Last report had a fifteen-hundred-foot overcast, but breaks in the overcast all quadrants. I see that Traverse City is almost clear with fifteen miles visibility. That's just southwest of Pellston, so they could be all right by the time they get there."

"When will that be?" Mulheisen asked.

"About twenty minutes."

Mulheisen immediately called the Michigan State Police. "Where the hell is Pellston?" he asked.

"About three hundred miles due north of Detroit," said a Lieutenant Ackerman.

"I have information that an interstate fugitive, wanted here for murder, is aboard a Lear jet inbound to Pellston in about twenty minutes. Can you get a man there to make an arrest?"

"I understand that it's been storming up there," Ackerman said, "but not as bad as here. We should be able to get a car over there, and if we can't then I don't imagine they'll be able to get out either. We'll try."

Mulheisen gave the information to Ackerman and hung up. He stared at Jensen, who had just come in. Jensen was wearing an overcoat and galoshes, but no hat. He never wore a hat, even though his blond hair was only a half-inch long. Jensen believed that wearing a hat was an instant tipoff that one was a cop. "Anymore," he would say, "only cops wear hats." It didn't take a hat for anyone to know that Jensen was a cop.

"Kusane has a Lincoln Continental," he said. "It wouldn't get through that mess. Someone was there in his parking lot in a four-wheel drive, but of course, Kusane doesn't know who it could have been. I'm gonna sack out," he said. He looked beat.

Mulheisen nodded. He sat there, looking at his flight plans. After a while he began to look through the desk. Then he went out front. Snow was still whirling around the glass doors of the precinct. "Dill," he said, "have you got any whiskey?"

"Whiskey? Mul, are you kidding?"

"Dill, it's Christmas."

Dill looked around the deserted lobby. "Watch the desk, will you, Mul? I gotta go to my locker for a minute."

He came back shortly with two plastic cups from the coffee room. They were filled with an amber fluid.

"Merry Christmas, Mul," Dill said.

"Cheers," Mulheisen said. He sipped. "What is this stuff, anyway?"

"Kessler's. Took it off a drunk yesterday."

Mulheisen took the cup back to his office and sat there, sipping. He had another cup before the state police called back, forty minutes later.

"We got your man," Lieutenant Ackerman said gleefully.

Mulheisen let out a great sigh. So that's it, he thought. It was curiously anticlimactic. He had Wienoshek. That left only Clippert, and Clippert was out in the cold.

"That's great," Mulheisen said. "Good work. Did you get both of them?"

"No, only the one," Ackerman said.

"Only one? Which one?"

"He says his name is Oliver Lewis. We're checking on him now."

"What's the description?" Mulheisen demanded.

"Um, according to the officer there, he's five-ten, a hundred sixty pounds, Negro male—"

"What? I didn't give you anything on a Negro!"

"You said one of the guys might be short and dark," Ackerman said.

"I meant he might be an Italian. Besides, where's the other guy, the main one? Wienoshek?"

"I don't know anything about Wienoshek," Ackerman said. "All we've got is this Oliver Lewis. The pilot."

"The pilot! I'm not interested in the pilot! Oh, well, you might as well hold him, if you can. But find out about his passengers. Why was he late, anyway? He should have been into Pellston a half-hour ago."

Lieutenant Ackerman sighed. "I'll find out," he said. He called back ten minutes later. "Well, here it is. They stopped in Traverse City, according to the pilot, because the weather hadn't cleared yet in Pellston. But then it cleared up right away and he came on. He had two passengers who got off in Traverse City."

"Good Lord!" Mulheisen groaned. "Who were the passengers? Find out about the passengers. Get a description, and find out who employed this pilot."

Ten minutes later, the answer came back. The pilot was very cooperative. He said the passengers were named Mr. Gordon and Mr. Arthur. Mr. Gordon was tall and had a pitted face. Mr. Arthur was short and dark. The airplane belonged to a private corporation in New Jersey, the Seaboard Corporation, but was usually kept in Miami. Late Christmas Eve, the pilot was informed by his employers that the plane had been chartered by a Mr. Arthur, who would be leaving shortly with another gentleman. He was to take Mr. Arthur and Mr. Gordon wherever they wished to go, so long as it wasn't outside the country. Beyond that, Oliver Lewis was saying nothing until he had a lawyer.

Twenty-six

They were setting up a meeting. Mulheisen was sure of it, and he could guess what the meeting was about. The question was, how could Clippert get to the meeting? It didn't seem probable that he could, but Mulheisen knew that if he could get into town, other people could. It just wouldn't be easy, that's all.

Mulheisen went outside. The snow had stopped completely and the wind was dying. What the forecasters had hoped for had happened. The ridge of high pressure over eastern Canada and the Midwest had shifted, permitting the storm to continue its normal eastward course. Now a high-pressure system of cold, arctic air was moving in. Christmas Day would dawn brilliantly clear and the temperature would be well below zero. A great day for the kids to go down to the canals that lined the Detroit River and try out their new hockey skates.

Mulheisen called Mendoza in Miami and told him to cancel the search on Wienoshek. Then he went out and started the Powerwagon, thinking that he would go downtown to pick up the warrants on Wienoshek and Clippert.

The city snow crews were attacking the snow-filled streets with some success now, but there was still no traffic. Mulheisen was grateful for the high clearance of the Powerwagon.

He swung down Gratiot Avenue just before dawn. The snow was generally a foot deep on the street, with many drifts that were much deeper. There was a chewed-up lane that the plows had opened for emergency vehicles.

Just beyond Trinity Lutheran Church, where the funeral services for Jane Clippert had been held, Mulheisen glanced to his left and noticed the high-rise apartment buildings of the Lafayette Plaisance. Conspicuous among the buildings was the Seaforth Tower. A number of the apartment lights were on. Mulheisen thought that this probably indicated apartments where children had arisen to see what Santa had brought.

"Shirley Carpenter." He said the name aloud. Clippert might have gone there. He could even have walked there from Indian Village. It was just a hike down Lafayette Avenue. Not much farther than Mulheisen's walk to Oswald's Marina.

He pushed the big Powerwagon through bumper-deep drifts and pulled up in front of Seaforth Tower. A security guard looked at his badge and let him into the lobby. Mulheisen took the elevator to the twelfth floor. Outside Shirley Carpenter's apartment door, he opened his parka and put his right hand on his .38 Chief's Special. Then he knocked with his left hand and stepped to one side of the door, out of any possible line of fire from within.

The door was immediately opened and a small blond boy of ten or so stood there in pajamas. He looked at Mulheisen. Then he leaned out in the hallway and looked both ways.

"I thought maybe it was Uncle Arthur," the boy said.

"He's not here?" Mulheisen asked.

"No. He left."

"Are you Scott?" Mulheisen asked.

The boy nodded. He had a very round head, rather like his mother's. Mulheisen looked beyond the boy into the room. The floor was littered with torn wrappings from Christmas presents. There was a new bicycle, a very fancy racing model. A gift from rich "Uncle" Arthur? There were also a hockey stick, a Detroit Lions football helmet, phonograph albums, books, clothes and candy. The draperies had been drawn back on the big windows and dawn showed the white shroud that lay on a peaceful Detroit and Canada, with the black swath of the river running across it.

Shirley Carpenter came into the room. She wore a short robe that showed her nice legs. She had her hair in curlers with little pieces of tissue tucked into it and covered with a net.

"What do you want?" she asked, standing behind her son.

"Clippert," Mulheisen said.

"He's not here," she said.

"I'd like to see for myself," he said.

"Do you have a warrant?"

Mulheisen bared his teeth in a weary smile. "Do you really want me to get a warrant?"

She stood aside and let him enter. He drew the pistol, his eyes darting to all corners of the room. "I'd appreciate it if you and the boy would just stand quietly over there," he said. He didn't think Clippert was there, but he didn't want to take a chance. There might be gunfire.

Mulheisen moved cautiously from room to room, checking closets, draperies, even under the beds. He had found people under beds before. But not this time. Clippert was not in the apartment. As the boy had suggested, however, Clippert had been there. There was a rich tobacco smell in the air, from a pipe.

Mulheisen jammed his pistol back into the hip-grip holster and returned to the living room.

"How long ago did he leave?" he asked.

Shirley Carpenter stood with her hands resting on Scott's shoulders. The boy looked fascinated and excited by Mulheisen and his gun, but seemed quite unafraid.

"About an hour ago," she said. "Maybe a little less."

"Where did he go?"

"He didn't say."

"How did he get here?"

"He said he walked. I guess he did."

"What did he want?"

Shirley Carpenter shrugged. "I'm not sure. He said he was thinking of going away, for a few days. He wanted to say good-by."

"How long was he here?"

"He got here around midnight, I guess," she said.

That meant they had been together for six hours or so, Mulheisen figured. He wondered if they had been to bed together. He thought they probably had.

"Did he seem upset? Nervous?"

The woman looked thoughtful. "Perhaps. It's not easy to tell with a man like Arthur. He kept watching the time."

"Did he talk about his plans? Call anyone?"

"He didn't call anyone. Somebody called here, about two hours ago. He answered the phone. It must have been a brief conversation. He just said hello, then gave this phone number and hung up. It must have been a wrong number.

"He said he had to be out of town for a few days and that the cops might come around, but that I shouldn't worry."

"Aren't you curious what we want?" Mulheisen asked.

She shrugged.

"He didn't say where he was going? Or how he was going to get there?"

"No."

"You think he's coming back?"

The woman suddenly looked very bleak and lonely, but she answered, "He said he would."

Mulheisen nodded with a cynical grimace and went out of the room. Down in the lobby he questioned the guard. The guard said he knew Clippert and had seen him out the door at about five forty-five. He said he had seen Clippert set off toward Gratiot on foot.

The footprints were still visible. Mulheisen got into the Power-wagon and followed the trail up to Gratiot. There the prints ended at the plowed traffic lane. There were no further traces of a pedestrian. Obviously, somebody had picked him up.

Mulheisen stopped at a call box and called the precinct. "Dill," he said, "do you have an up-to-date road report?"

"Roads are terrible, Mul," Dill said.

"I know they are, I'm out on them. What about the highways?"

"The Interstates are still officially closed, say the state police, but they expect to resume their patrols shortly."

Mulheisen closed the box. That meant that there were open lanes, he thought. He went to a phone booth and called the airports, Amtrak and Greyhound. All runways were closed and not expected to open for normal traffic for many hours, probably late in the day at best. Amtrak said their 8:30 A.M. train to Chicago had been canceled. They were hoping to run the 5:45 P.M. train. Canadian National's morning train from Windsor to Toronto was delayed and probably would not run. They had high hopes for their 6:10 P.M. train. Greyhound was not running anything. Maybe later in the day.

So where could he go? Obviously, somewhere where he wouldn't need anything more than a car, probably a four-wheel-drive type of vehicle. And Wienoshek was in Traverse City. Mulheisen called the state police and asked about highways in the Traverse City area. They put him on hold and checked with their Traverse City barracks.

"Roads are not impassable in the northern part of the state," Lieutenant Ackerman said. "Traverse City barracks is checking for your fugitives but have nothing to report. They don't seem to be staying at the hotels or motels there, and they didn't rent a car. No reports of stolen vehicles, so far this morning. They didn't bother with roadblocks, 'cause they figure that if your guys do have a car they can only use it on a few roads and the chances are very good that they'll be spotted, unless they drove to a nearby city and holed up, or have friends in the Traverse City area who could have picked them up. Nobody at the airport saw them leave."

Mulheisen hung up. He sat in the truck and considered the possibilities. Kusane could have hidden Clippert away. He could hide out for a few days and meet Wienoshek later. But could Wienoshek afford to delay the meeting? He thought not. Probably they would want to meet as soon as possible, before the cops had a chance to get on their trails. But where would they meet? Anywhere, preferably up north. Perhaps in a northern city like Charlevoix, Petoskey, or even Sault Ste. Marie. The latter was comfortably close to the Canadian border, in case anyone wanted to get out of the country in a hurry.

Or they could meet at Clippert's Jasper Lake home.

For no conscious reason, Mulheisen took the Powerwagon down onto northbound Chrysler Freeway. The snow wasn't as bad as on the streets. Unimpeded winds had swept the road down to a more or less uniform foot of snow that had been broken by the passage of plows. There were only occasional drifts, and these offered little problem for a vehicle like the Powerwagon.

In a relatively short time Mulheisen found himself out beyond Eight Mile Road and headed for Interstate 75. What the hell? he thought, and stepped down on the accelerator. He knew he should have called in, but he figured that with any luck he might be able to make it to Jasper Lake in four or five hours. He thought it was worth the try.

The snow was worse around Flint, but there was still a passable lane. A plow had been through, not really clearing snow, but breaking a trail. It was heavier going around the Saginaw/Bay City area, but now it was after eleven and more plows were running. He even saw a state police patrol, fighting along in a blue Chevrolet. He tooted his horn and went by him at 45 m.p.h.

Gas was down to half a tank already, and there were few stations open today. But he had the two five-gallon cans sitting in the back. He went on.

The sky was a deep blue and the sun hurt his eyes as it reflected off the unbroken fields of snow. Even the cab of the truck was warm. He could take off his gloves.

By now, a hundred miles north of Detroit, Mulheisen had had time to reflect on what he was doing. He told himself he was either dumber than a run-over rabbit, or he was running in on target with both afterburners cooking.

He remembered a time when he'd sat in the control tower on a slow night and played hearts with the GCA crew. They played to a hundred points, at a quarter a point. An airman first class, a weatherman assigned to the tower, was "shooting the moon," but no hearts had fallen yet. The weatherman played into clubs and two tricks later saw his jack go down to Mulheisen's queen. A heart had fallen on the trick, blowing the weatherman's chances. "Hearts are broken, I guess," the weatherman said glumly. One trick later, Mulheisen slipped him the queen of spades, putting the man thirteen points down in one blow. "Hearts are really broken, now," Mulheisen told him.

Mulheisen grinned his wolfish grin and leaned forward to the wheel as the Powerwagon roared past Midland. "Hearts are broken," he cried out to the fields of snow.

The snow was lighter up here, he noticed. Not nearly as bad as in Detroit, and nothing like Saginaw. The Powerwagon was pushing sixty. He wheeled off the Interstate and into a small town called Clare. They had a sign on the highway that proclaimed the town "Gateway to the North." The hotel was open and Mulheisen got a quick lunch at the dining room. A pretty little waitress told him the name of a man who would pump gas on Christmas Day. A half-hour later, feeling a little better for the food and coffee, and with a full tank of gas, Mulheisen was back on the Interstate.

It was almost two in the afternoon, a beautiful day, and he was feeling high. Exactly like a man who has been up all night, smoked too much and drank too much whiskey, he told himself.

A sign said: JASPER LAKE, 31 MILES. According to the map he had gotten at Clare, Mulheisen could see that there was a small town called Jasper Lake, but it was near the Interstate. The lake itself was quite large, one of the earliest summer resorts to develop in the state, and it was ten miles east of the town that used its name.

It was twenty to three before he reached the Jasper Lake exit. Instead of stopping in the town he drove straight through it and out into the country toward the lake. It was only after he had driven some five miles along the snowy country road that circled the lake that he realized that he should have stopped to find out just where to go. There were too many little country lanes running off the county road. At last he spotted a white farmhouse, with smoke curling up from the chimney and a veritable battlement of stacked firewood encircling the house. The driveway was filled with four pickup trucks and two cars.

Mulheisen left the Powerwagon running on the road and went up to the back door, where a path had been broken through the snow.

There were at least fifteen people—men, women and children —sitting at a table laden with turkey, a ham, bowls of broccoli, yams, mashed potatoes and rich giblet gravy. There were two bowls of cranberry sauce, shimmering cylinders fresh from the can. Mulheisen felt like a visitor from another planet.

The kitchen was warm and the windows were steamed up. It

was a large room with enough space for the large table where the feasting farmers sat on every available chair in the house. The children were grouped together on a bench, except for a tiny child that a young woman carried on her lap and occasionally fed spoonfuls of mashed potatoes.

A color television in the adjacent living room had been positioned in the doorway so that the men could watch the Vikings play the Green Bay Packers, while they ate. Mulheisen was cheerfully urged to have dinner, drink a beer, watch the game. He thanked them, but declined. He asked for the whereabouts of Arthur Clippert's summer home.

No one had ever heard of him.

"It's a big place, I understand," Mulheisen said. "I think one of his neighbors is a Carl Joyner, the fellow who started the Black Beaver Lake development."

"Oh, that sonuvabitch, Joyner," said a lean farmer through a mouthful of mashed potatoes.

"That's right," Mulheisen said. "A fat man, with white hair."

"He's a albino," a ten-year-old boy said.

"He is not," said a heavy woman with an enormous bosom. "You be quiet, Jabe."

The lean farmer swallowed his potatoes and said, "You must mean the Bodnar place."

"That's it," Mulheisen said. "Clippert is his son-in-law."

"Is that right?" said another man. "I thought old Axel Bodnar'd sold it."

"No. Mr. Bodnar died a few years back," Mulheisen said.

"Is that right?" The man turned to a short, swarthy man who wore a thick black beard and whose pure-blue eyes actually twinkled. "Did you year that, Pat? Old Axel's died."

"Wal, I'll be damned," Pat said. He had a surprisingly Southern drawl. He forked a huge chunk of ham into the mouth that was nearly hidden behind the beard.

"You'll have a hell of a time getting there," said the lean farmer. "You go down here a quarter mile, take a left, go to the third road and take another left. It has a sign that says Blackman Lane. You go up that lane, which probably ain't plowed, till you come to a stone fence and it has a big iron gate. I doubt you'll get up that drive. You'll have to walk about a quarter mile to the house."

"Thank you very much," Mulheisen said.

"You'll know the place," the farmer said. "There's a name carved into the stone by the gate, says Valhalla."

"Valhalla?"

"That's what old Axel called it. I think it's a town in the old country, maybe, where his folks come from."

Twenty-seven

"This guy is something else," Joe Service said to Wienoshek. They stood in a cold upstairs bedroom. There was no furniture in the room, no curtains on the windows. The floor was hardwood and polished with a thin film of dust on it. Also on the floor was a cardboard box. They had found it in the closet, pulled it out and opened it.

The box was full of money. Negotiable bonds in tidy little stacks, denominations of five thousand and ten thousand dollars, some even larger. It wouldn't be too difficult to convert these bonds into cash.

"I didn't really expect to find it here," Joe Service said.

"So how come we got here early?" Wienoshek wanted to know. "I thought you wanted to make a search."

"Just a matter of form, really, Byron. I couldn't come into the house without making absolutely certain that the money wasn't here.

"But who would have thought he'd stash it here? It's not even hidden, really. The guy is a lawyer, smart enough to rip off a whole corporation, smart enough to be the only one of the bunch who isn't going inside . . . I mean, look at it! They're all ready to take a fall, and he's got the whole bundle. And the feds can't touch him. So why is twenty million sitting in the closet?"

Wienoshek did not answer. He took a sheaf of the bonds from the box. "Man," he said, softly. "Look. Fifty big ones, right here."

Service looked down at the big man, squatting over the bonds. He laughed. "That's more right there than he paid you, isn't it?"

Wienoshek flushed. He was embarrassed. "Twenty bills. That's all I got," he said. "And I would have got only ten, but . . ."

Service smiled. "I know, Byron. But it's payday again." He squatted down and put the bills back in the box.

"Hey, wait a minute," Wienoshek said.

"What's the matter?"

"What do you mean, what's the matter? The split!"

"Now?" Service said.

"Now."

Service looked as if he were considering it. Wienoshek stood up and unbuttoned his overcoat and his suit coat. The handle of the huge .44 Magnum jutted out from the holster. Wienoshek looked directly into Service's eyes. "Now," he said.

"You're making a mistake, Byron. You're forgetting things."

"Like what things?" the big man said quietly. Service didn't like the flat, unemotional tone of that voice. He knew he was going to have to do some fast talking. He didn't like standing in an empty room, in a closed-up summer house, miles from anywhere, while a man with a .44 talked like that. There was a whole cold lake just beyond the window where a body could get lost. It looked like a broad, flat field, covered with snow. It stretched several miles to a range of low, pine-covered hills.

"You're forgetting Clippert, for one thing," Service said. "And you're forgetting my clients."

"Screw Clippert," Wienoshek said.

"No. I'd do something about Clippert, if I were you," Service said. "You'll never really be safe as long as he's around. You ought to know that. You take this money and he'll turn you, for sure, just to save his neck with that gang of loonies who expect him to take care of their money."

"Maybe," Wienoshek said.

"Well, I'll tell you what isn't a maybe," Service said. "My clients. You better think about how you're going to get out of here. You need help. They can get you out of the country. They can help you. A million bucks is a lot of bucks, Byron."

"So is twenty million."

"Twenty million is nothing if you're in the can for life. Or if you've been knocked on the head. Think about it, Byron."

"I'm thinking about twenty million, Joe," he said softly.

Service shook his head with concern. "Don't think that way, Byron. Don't. My clients don't want to hit you. I think they'd like you. You'd like them. I mean it when I say they want to help you. But if you help yourself . . ." He spread his hands and smiled sadly.

"You see," he went on, "they aren't like the cops. They don't have areas of jurisdiction. They go anywhere. And they will, for a load like this, to say nothing of the bad precedent it would set if they let you get away with it. See, they don't have heavy case loads, like the cops. They aren't like the cops at all. They'll come for you wherever you go, no matter how long it takes . . . and they won't read your Miranda rights to you when they knock on your door that dark day."

Wienoshek smiled. "Who'll they send? You?"

Service shrugged. "Maybe. I'm their best. I'm better than you. That's a fact. A simple, unavoidable fact."

Wienoshek didn't seem impressed. "If you're still alive, you mean," he said. He stood very still, watching Service and waiting.

"Look at the way you messed up the job on Clippert's old lady. Was that good?"

"I didn't do that," Wienoshek said. "Elroy did that. I made a mistake there. I sent him in, instead of doing it myself. If I did it, it's just a nice clean accident in a bathtub."

"But why?" Service said. "Why did she have to have an accident?"

"I don't ask why," Wienoshek said. "It's not my business why. I just figured it was the insurance."

"The insurance? Ha hahahahaha. Are you kidding? There's twenty million at stake and you think he wants his wife's insurance? Hell, she was worth more alive. She would have inherited much more than a million in another year. Just a few months, really."

"I don't know anything about that," Wienoshek said. He looked puzzled. "So, you tell me why, then."

Service's mind raced. Why, indeed? he thought. The trouble was, despite some private research he did not know much about Clippert, he did not know the man's mind. The answer could be as simple as a girl friend, or as stupid as wanting the insurance money now, instead of waiting for an inheritance with a wife he may have hated. For all Joe Service knew, Clippert was insane, a raving maniac. Could be. Or maybe he wanted to split for Brazil and didn't want to take her, or leave her to talk.

It could be very complex, he realized. Perhaps a combination of all these things. Or maybe it was as obvious as twenty million dollars.

"So what's the answer, smart boy?" Wienoshek said.

Service smiled. "It's obvious," he said. "Twenty million."

"What? That don't make sense."

"Think about it, Byron. Clippert's no dummy. Now why is this money sitting in a closet in a summer house? Why did Clippert want you boys to fake a burglary?"

Wienoshek shook his head. "I don't know."

"And you, you're going to take the money and run." Service seemed amused. "You wouldn't get back to the goddamn highway. You couldn't even get the car out of that ditch you stuck it in."

"Knock it off, big mouth," Wienoshek said, "or I may have to let a little air into you." He gestured toward the .44.

"All right, I'll spell it out for you," Service said. "First of all, Clippert didn't have the money. I'll bet he doesn't know that it's here. And second of all, he wanted everybody, or at least a certain group of people—his Fidelity Funding buddies—to think that he didn't have the money anymore."

Wienoshek couldn't follow that. "What are you talking about?" he said. "Is this some kind of trick?" He actually rested his hand on the handle of the gun.

"No trick. Look, these people at Fidelity Funding, they knock off twenty of the best, but they do it a little at a time. What's it going to be, in cash? Maybe some of it, a little of it. But most of it is payments from other corporations, and it has to go into Fidelity Funding's accounts. A paper transaction. And then another paper transaction transfers it into other, hidden accounts. That's all right, for a while, but eventually somebody has to collect this dough.

"The people want to get paid off for their hard work. So they get themselves a bagman. A wise guy who can convert these accounts into cash, who will go and get the money—or what is approximately the same thing, bearer bonds. They want a trusty fellow like Clippert to carry that bag, somebody they can trust. They might even have already had some payoffs, for all I know. There might not even be twenty million here, though it looks like enough to be." He glanced down at the box.

Service went on, spreading out his explanation, his story, for his dangerous companion.

"Clippert could have put the bonds into numerous deposit boxes, all over the country. If a guy did that carefully enough, he could probably cover his tracks. But a deposit box can be red-tagged. There's always the chance. The feds might get some of it. But that's kind of a clumsy operation for Clippert, and anyway, if he does that the money is no more readily available than it was before. No, it's just as well to get it all and stash it.

"Then along comes Mrs. Clippert. One day, maybe she's looking in the basement for her golf clubs, she comes across a cardboard box full of bearer bonds. If she has any brains at all, and I imagine she did, she knows exactly what it means. And she's appalled to discover that her beloved hubby is a thief. So what does she do?"

"You tell me," Wienoshek said.

"She takes the money herself, and hides it."

"Why?"

"She's scared of what it means. She's worried for her husband, and she's angry with him for not telling her what he was doing."

"Maybe she's a thief herself," Wienoshek said.

"Maybe. The important thing is she did take the money. And she brought it up here. But she obviously didn't tell him where she hid it, or it wouldn't be sitting here, I can guarantee that.

"Then, she tells him that she knows and that she took the money. From the little that I've found out about her, she probably tried to get him to come clean. Turn state's evidence and cop a plea."

"Hell," Wienoshek said, "I wonder when she did it?"

"Why?" Service said.

"Me and Elroy cracked this joint ourselves, back in September, only Clippert nailed us. The money could have been here then."

"Clippert caught the two of you, at it?"

Wienoshek explained the whole thing to him. Clippert had been amused at catching them, and when he recognized Wienoshek he had let them go. But not before checking their identification to make sure that he knew where they would be, and who exactly they were, in case of any future trouble.

"He had some broad in the car," Wienoshek said, "and I don't think it was his wife. Some chick he brought up here to bang for a weekend."

"That must have been before his old lady ripped him off," Service mused, "or he'd have been looking for the stuff and would easily have found it. When did he contact you?"

"About six weeks ago."

"That's when it was then. I guess she found the stuff, threw it in the trunk of the car and buzzed up here in a couple hours, stashed it, and got back to town before he knew she was gone. He wouldn't have guessed that she'd taken it so far away."

Wienoshek nodded. "Makes sense, I guess. But why did he want to fake the burglary?"

"The burglary is a clever idea," Service said. "Just consider: it provides the cops with a reason for the killing, in case they don't buy the suicide bit. Not only that, Clippert is in a position to tell the Fidelity Funding boys that the money is gone. Probably he could blame it on the Mob. And he doesn't have to worry about the Mob trying to score the stuff, either, because they'll think it's gone, too. In fact, they sort of half believed it."

Service was beginning to believe the story himself. It was very likely, he thought. Best of all, Wienoshek clearly believed it. Service was glad to see him relax. He hated these kinds of hassles with partners.

"One thing, though," Wienoshek said, "he couldn't have a burglary and an accident, could he? What's the point of all that?"

"It gives him an extra option," Service reasoned. "For the last six weeks he's been looking all over hell for the money, and not finding it. I bet he was giving the old lady hell about it, too. Finally, he just decided to do her. He'd be rid of her pressure, and he'd be free to look for the dough. If I were him, I'd have figured that she put it in a safety-deposit box. After she's dead he can settle her affairs and then it's likely that he'd find her safety-deposit box.

"What was the deal," he asked Wienoshek, "was he supposed to call you before he came back to town and find out what the lay of the land was?"

"Yeah," Wienoshek said, "how did you know?"

"It seems reasonable. If you guys go in and get her, and everything goes right, he can come back to town and discover that she's had a terrible accident, but not before he carefully picks up all the stuff you guys were supposed to rob and puts it back in its place. But, if things go wrong, and you're caught, he is still in good shape. It's just a little option play, for him. Hell, even if things go well he could still use the burglary option, if it suited his purposes."

"I can see that," Wienoshek said. "Yeah, that's it."

"Sure it is," Service said. "I know if you had given it a little thought, Byron, you would have come up with it yourself. But I can see your point of view, too—do the job and get out. Don't get involved in complications."

Wienoshek was mollified. "I like things to be simple," he said.

"It's the best way," Service agreed.

"So now what?" Wienoshek asked.

"So now we deal with Clippert," Service said. "That's your job. He's your problem. Then we get you out of the state, get you safe. I take the stuff to Detroit and make my deal with my clients. I get the payoff, and I pay you off."

Wienoshek didn't like that, Service could tell.

"It has to be that way, Byron. Clippert will be here anytime now. We don't have time to sit down and make a count and then split the dough. Besides, my clients won't like that. You have to trust me. I'm getting ten percent. My clients won't burn me. And you get half of my cut."

"I got a better idea," Wienoshek said.

Service sighed. "All right, let's hear it."

"We just cool it. Clippert comes, we'll both take him off. Then we can sit down and talk."

Service was resigned. He was about to agree, when there was a noise at the door. It was Clippert.

Service knew it must be Clippert, even though his back was to the doorway and the open door itself screened him from Clippert's view, because Wienoshek's mouth fell open and he raised his hands with fingers spread wide, as if to ward off something terrible.

A .45 automatic came through the doorway and Service stepped back, out of view.

"My money!" said a voice, tight with controlled fury. "You've got my money! You son of a bitch." The hand with the gun came up and the finger tightened. Service kicked the door.

KABLAM!

The shot spun Wienoshek around and he fell down against the far wall. Even before he hit the floor, Service had his .38 out and put two fast rounds through the opening where Clippert should have been.

It was very fast, but Clippert was not there. He had fallen backward into the hallway, then scrambled to his feet and ran down the hallway to the end. A door slammed.

Service looked at Wienoshek. "You all right?"

Wienoshek was dazed, then got to his feet. He got out the .44. "I'm all right," he said. "He just burned me." He eased his overcoat off, still holding the .44. There was a hole in the sleeve of his suit coat and blood was seeping.

"You sure you're all right?"

"I'm all right," Wienoshek said coldly. "But he's not. He's dead."

"He's at the end of the hall," Service said. "You better be careful."

"I'll be careful."

"Wait a minute," Service said. "Let's think this out."

"Nothing to think about," Wienoshek said.

"Yes, there is. He's trapped himself, but he won't be easy to get at, and we can't leave him there."

Wienoshek stepped to the door. "I'll get him out."

"What are you going to do? Walk down there, kick the door down and then put on a lot of weight in a hurry when he unloads that clip on you?"

"So what's your idea?"

Service looked around. "I'm thinking maybe that room is like this one. Empty. He won't have much to hide behind. I'll cover you from here. You work down to that door, room by room. Then I'll put a couple shots through his door. I have a feeling he'll shoot back. When he does, you should get a good idea of where he is. Then you open up on him."

"And if we don't get him?"

Service smiled. "Why then, I think that cannon of yours could probably remove the hinges on that door and then the lid will be open on his casket."

"Right," Wienoshek said.

"Get going," Service said. He dropped to his right knee and sighted in on the end door as Wienoshek slipped by him and made for the next room.

Twenty-eight

The farmer was absolutely right, Mulheisen saw. There was the stone fence, then came the iron gate with its rock post that had "Valhalla" engraved on it. The gate was open and tire tracks led inside. Mulheisen turned into the gate and stopped. Within fifty feet there was a new Chevrolet Blazer, buried in the ditch. Just beyond it was an International Scout, also stuck. Mulheisen stopped right where he was and got out.

It was after four and starting to get dark already. The lane stretched up before him, curving away, lined by barren Lombardy poplars on either side. The snow was deep and in it were the tracks of three people. The shadows in the tracks were blue.

Mulheisen zipped up the parka and hurried on. He had the .38 in his pocket, in his hand. As the sun faded, the wind rose, and it made his eyes tear.

He was just around the first bend and had caught sight of a large stone-façade house when he heard the first shots. He jumped behind the nearest tree and thought, I'm a sitting duck.

The house was still three hundred yards away. It was very large, an old-fashioned-looking house. It would be called rambling. It had a faced fieldstone front, with a roofed porch. The porch ran right across the front and around one side. There was a second story with a big slope-roofed dormer. From his position, Mulheisen could see the newer section on the rear of the house, with a high wooden fence that probably enclosed the swimming pool.

On the other side of the lane was a stone fence. It ran on up toward the house, then angled off across the field. Mulheisen figured it could shield him until he was close enough to the cover of the fence around the pool. From there he ought to be able to get right up to the house. He ran across the lane and dove over the fence, burying himself in deep snow.

He moved along the fence, struggling through the deep snow in a stoop. He was sweating inside the parka by the time he reached the wooden fence around the pool.

He heard a couple more shots from inside the house. They must be shooting at each other, he thought. Mulheisen followed the fence around the pool area until he came to some outbuildings, a barn and stables, a large garage. From there he was able to slip comfortably around to the back of the house.

The back door was locked. It was locked and it wasn't going to be opened without a lot of noise. What he needed now, he thought, was the Big Four. Honcho Noell would go through that door like butter and the rest of them right behind him, Stoner rifles cooking. But . . . he was alone.

He got down in the snow and crawled, the .38 out in his bare hand and freezing. What a deal, he thought, crawling through snow, a houseful of guns waiting.

About halfway around the house he paused at a basement window. He looked inside. There was a storage room there, with cans of paint on shelves and boxes stacked in a corner.

Here's where I go in, he decided. He wrapped the gun in a glove and punched the window in. The glass fell on the concrete floor with a tinkle, but there wasn't much noise, and besides the door to the room was closed. He didn't think they would hear it upstairs. He cleaned the rest of the glass out and started to crawl through, when he realized that his parka was too bulky. He took off the parka and shivered.

He eased through the window and dropped down to the concrete floor, gun in hand. He went out the door and into the basement. The basement was not finished, though it had several rooms

202

similar to the one he had just left. Ducts radiated out from an old furnace. He shivered and wished that the furnace were on.

As he crossed the concrete floor he heard footsteps overhead and then, he couldn't be sure, but it sounded like someone went out the front door.

Mulheisen went up the stairs cautiously and opened the door that led into a large kitchen that had a red tile floor. The door to the dining room was open, and he crossed over to it. The room was empty. He went from there to a hallway that led past the living room, past something that might have been a parlor but now was a kind of music room with a piano in it and some bookshelves, a television. There was another room, apparently a den, with more bookshelves and another television. Beyond that was a bedroom. All the rooms were empty.

BOOM! It was the roar of a Magnum. It came from upstairs.

Well, that's it, Mulheisen told himself. They're playing upstairs. There was nothing for it but to go up.

The stairs were wide and solid. They did not squeak. There was a carpet runner, with iron rods holding it in place at the base of each step. At the top of the stairs there was a hallway about twenty feet long, with several oak doors opening off it. Mulheisen lay flat against the stairs and stuck his head around the corner of the hallway, just at floor level.

"No!" screamed a voice from the end of the hall.

BLAM! BLAM! BLAM!

The shots tore through the end door, flew down the hallway and smashed into the wall, knocking plaster down. Mulheisen ducked his head back down and around the corner.

After a moment, he peeked out again. He was just in time to see a large man ease out of the third room, a .44 in his right hand. He recognized him. It was Wienoshek!

Wienoshek moved quietly along the hallway, flattened against the wall but not making any sliding noises. He carried the gun forward, confidently. He slipped into the next room. It was the last room before the end of the hall, right next to the end door itself.

Wienoshek had not looked behind himself as he went. That seemed significant to Mulheisen. It suggested that Wienoshek knew there was no one behind him.

So, he thought, there's someone in that last room, and Wieno-shek's after him.

He waited to see if anyone else showed, but there was no sound. He made up his mind and stepped into the hallway, staying close to the wall on the same side as the room that Wienoshek had gone in. He moved quickly along the hallway, stepping into each doorway as he went and stopping to look around and listen. In one room there was a man's overcoat crumpled on the floor, but nothing else. All the rooms were empty but one, which had several mattresses stacked against a wall and the frames of beds similarly stacked.

He slipped out again and went to the room just next to the one Wienoshek had entered.

"Clippert!" he heard Wienoshek yell, "come on out of there! We'll make a deal!"

The answer was three shots through the door. They hit about where the other shots had hit and there was now a splintered hole in the door panel, three inches wide and running vertically along the grain of the panel for a foot or so.

Wienoshek's head showed out the doorway and Mulheisen could see him peering into the end room, his head moving sideways and up and down, as if trying to see where Clippert had positioned himself. Then they both heard a click and the clatter of an empty cartridge clip falling to the floor. Another series of clicks told them that the clip had been replaced, no doubt by a full one, and the slide was racked back to load and cock the pistol.

Wienoshek ducked back into his room and was silent. Mulheisen waited in his cold room, shivering. It must be ten below zero, he thought. He peeped out of his doorway, watching for Wienoshek to appear.

And then he heard Clippert. He was talking to someone, it seemed, but Mulheisen could not make out what he said very well. Clippert's voice sounded strange, excited and rasping. Then he laughed. Mulheisen decided he had flipped out. The voice swore violently.

"... then the tough get going," Clippert was ranting. "You're goddamn right! Ha ha! Can't go round 'em, go right through the bastards! Have to go it alone, by God! Always did! The ol' Flying Clipper!" He laughed again and swore.

Mulheisen shuddered.

KABLAM! Another shot tore out the center panel of the door. Mulheisen ducked back into his room and suddenly he was sweating. But not for long. The cold came back. He noticed then that it was getting quite dark. Soon it would be very dark and all the problems would be compounded. He peeped out his doorway again.

Wienoshek eased out of his doorway. Mulheisen could see that he'd been hit in the left arm by a bullet. There was a large bloodstain on the suit coat.

Wienoshek's right arm came up, bearing the .44. He aimed through the shattered center panel of the door.

Mulheisen took three quiet steps down the hallway, not disturbing Wienoshek's concentration. He laid his .38 next to Wienoshek's left ear.

Wienoshek froze. The .44 wavered and then was lowered. Nothing was said. Mulheisen reached out and took Wienoshek by the left arm. He drew the man completely out of the doorway and walked him backward, quietly along the hallway until they reached his room and stepped into it.

Wienoshek stood calmly in the room, still with his back to Mulheisen, the hand carrying the .44 hanging down at his side. Mulheisen gently took the big pistol from the man's hand and tucked it into the band of his trousers, keeping his own revolver on Wienoshek all along. Then he stepped back from Wienoshek and spoke quietly to him.

"This is the police, Wienoshek. My name's Mulheisen. Now go over there to that wall and lean against it, feet apart, both hands on the wall. That's it. Get those hands higher."

Wienoshek was having some trouble lifting his left hand. Mulheisen held his hand in the center of Wienoshek's back, holding the .38 in his right hand. He kicked Wienoshek's feet farther out from the wall and farther apart, so that the man would not be able to move without falling forward. Quickly he shook the man down. He reached for his handcuffs, and then realized that he didn't have any handcuffs.

"All right, Wienoshek, sit down, against the wall, feet straight out in front of you, legs flat on the floor."

Wienoshek did as he was told. Mulheisen looked at the pitted face with interest. He moved over to the doorway and pulled the door almost closed, so that he could still see the end door. He could hear Clippert still talking to himself.

Mulheisen gestured at Wienoshek's left arm. "He hit you?"

"Yeah," Wienoshek said.

"Bad?"

"No."

"Where's your buddy? Mulheisen asked.

"What buddy?"

"The guy who came on the plane with you."

"Service?"

"Service?"

"That's his name," Wienoshek said. He spelled it for Mulheisen. "I don't know where he is."

"Did he come here with you?"

"Aren't you going to read me my rights?" Wienoshek asked.

Mulheisen bared his fangs. "Yeah," he said, "as soon as I have time. Now tell me about Service."

Wienoshek looked disgusted. "I think maybe he split. With the money."

"What money?" Mulheisen said.

"The money Clippert ripped off."

Mulheisen looked at the man and shook his head. "You're not too smart, are you, Wienoshek? What happened here?"

"Ask my lawyer," Wienoshek said.

"Aw, c'mon now," Mulheisen cajoled, "don't be stupid. You've got nothing to gain by clamming up. In case you don't know, we've got us a problem here. You're bleeding pretty hard, it's cold in this house, damn cold, and getting dark. We've got us an armed madman down the hall and miles to go before we sleep. Now open up."

Wienoshek screwed his face up in a look of disgusted agreement. "Yeah, you're right, cop. What it is, old Goofy down there got the jump on us. We exchanged a few shots and he ran down the hall. Service was supposed to cover me, while I went after Goofy, but I guess Service decided he'd rather roll."

"Why didn't you go after him?"

"I didn't know he was gone, till you showed. Then I figured you wouldn't have got to me if Service was still around, unless you nailed him first, and I guess I would of heard something if you'd met up. So I figure he must of give you the slip."

Wienoshek slumped against the wall. Mulheisen watched him and thought, Now what? Down the hall, Clippert was still talking.

". . . what's a guy going to do?" he was saying.

"Clippert!" Mulheisen yelled.

Silence.

"Who's that?"

"Mulheisen. I came to help you, Clippert. Put the gun down!"

"What do you want?" Clippert yelled. "You won't help me. Nobody can help me," he snarled. "I can do it by myself!"

Mulheisen closed his eyes for a second and shook his head. He was beat, he was cold and he was having trouble thinking straight. He glanced up at Wienoshek and was suddenly filled with rage.

"I ought to just shoot the two of you," he said. "Save everybody a lot of trouble."

Wienoshek said, "You shouldn't have stopped me from killing the goofy bastard."

Mulheisen had to concede that Wienoshek had a point there.

"Clippert! I've got Wienoshek."

Clippert laughed. "Good. You can have him."

"But the other one got away," Mulheisen yelled.

"Got away? You let him get away?" Mulheisen could hear the anxiety and concern in Clippert's voice.

"That's right," Mulheisen yelled, "and he took the money, too."

"You let him take the money?"

"I couldn't help it, Clippert. He got by me, somehow. He's getting away, right now."

Clippert let off a volley of curses. "You idiot!" he screamed.

"We've got to get him, Clippert. I can't catch him by myself. I can't leave Wienoshek here. I need your help."

Silence.

"Clippert! How about it? I can't do it alone. The longer we wait, the farther away your money gets."

After another long silence, Clippert spoke, this time in a more subdued, cautious voice. "All right. What's the deal?"

"You help me with Wienoshek and I'll help you catch up with the other guy. He can't have gotten far."

"What happens when we catch him, Mulheisen?"

Mulheisen tried to think of a convincing answer, but the best he could come up with was, "We'll cross that bridge when we get to it."

There was no reply from the end room.

"Clippert! Did you hear me?"

"I heard you! It's a trap."

It was dark in the room now. Wienoshek was just a slightly darker lump. Mulheisen did not like the situation at all. At any moment he could have both these men at his throat.

"Clippert," he called wearily, "give it up. You've had it. Either you freeze to death in that room or I'm going to blast you. Now get your ass out of there!"

"You can't talk to me like that, Mulheisen," Clippert shrieked.

"He's nuts," Wienoshek said. "The bastard'll sit in there till we all freeze."

"You're probably right," Mulheisen said, "but I have to try.

"Okay, Clippert," he yelled, "it's time. Time to quit acting like a punk and start acting like a man."

"What would you know about it, Mulheisen?" Clippert answered.

"I'll tell you what I know," Mulheisen snapped back, "you killed your wife, you double-crossed all your buddies, and now you're hiding in a room waiting to get your ass blown off!"

"I didn't kill my wife!"

"You had her killed. It's the same thing. If you ask me, it's worse. You couldn't do your own dirty work. You're a goddamn coward, Clippert!"

"I'm a coward? I'm a coward?" Clippert shrieked. "I'll show you who's a coward!"

208

With that there was a terrific crash and the door to the end room splintered.

Mulheisen snapped on the light in his own room and leaped across the hallway into the security of darkness, using the light from the room he had just left to get a fix on Clippert. He saw immediately what had happened.

Clippert was tangled up in the wreckage of the shattered door. It had not simply flown open when he charged it because it was a door that opened into the room, not into the hall. Clippert struggled with the splintered frame, tearing his clothes and waving the .45 wildly.

Mulheisen stepped forward swiftly and slashed at the weaving face with his pistol butt. The butt caught Clippert across the bridge of the nose and he fell backwards into the end room, crashing onto his back.

A second later, Mulheisen heard crashing noise in the lighted room and tinkling of glass. He raced back to the room in time to catch Wienoshek in the act of crawling through the broken window onto the roof of the porch.

"Hold it!" he shouted.

Wienoshek stopped, one leg out the window. He stared at the pistol in Mulheisen's hand with frustration, then he gave it up. "Damn," he said. "Damn, damn, damn."

"Get in here."

They went into the end room and turned on the light. Clippert lay on the floor, groaning, his hands to his battered and bleeding face.

"Face the wall, hands outstretched," Mulheisen snapped at Wienoshek. The man obeyed calmly. Mulheisen kicked Clippert viciously in the ankle.

"On your feet," Mulheisen rasped. Clippert got up slowly, still clutching at his face. Mulheisen seized him by the shoulder of his overcoat and slammed him face forward into the wall across from Wienoshek. Clippert yelled with pain. Mulheisen hammered him across the back of the head with his left forearm.

"Shut up! Get your arms up. Higher! Get those feet spread!" He kicked Clippert's feet farther apart. The man was braced against the wall now, his head hanging. Drops of blood spattered on the polished hardwood floor. Mulheisen patted him down quickly.

He had the two men covered nicely now. He found Clippert's automatic where it had fallen and kicked it into the closet. He pulled out the .44 that he had taken from Wienoshek earlier and threw that into the closet with the automatic and closed the door.

Mulheisen stood back from the men and tried to calm his heavy breathing. When he was more relaxed he began to consider what came next.

"Is the phone connected, Clippert?"

"Service cut the line when we came in," Wienoshek said.

"Nice, real nice," Mulheisen said. "All right, that settles it then. We walk."

They collected Wienoshek's overcoat and Mulheisen's parka and set off. He marched the men in front of him, hands in their coat pockets. The lane was snowy and cold. It was well below zero, but at least there was no wind. Fortunately it was a clear night with a half-moon and a sky bristling with stars. They could see well enough.

The Powerwagon was gone, of course. Mulheisen cursed Service from the bottom of his heart. Not only had Service hotwired the Powerwagon, but he had disabled the other two vehicles, smashing the distributor caps and removing the rotors. They had a longer walk yet ahead of them.

The men gave Mulheisen no trouble. They stepped briskly along, their shoulders hunched against the cold and hands jammed deep in their pockets. It was three miles to the farmhouse where Mulheisen had stopped for directions. By the time they got there, their faces were numb and their feet were like blocks of ice.

Mulheisen had never felt so exhausted.

The Last Chapter

The prisoners sat at the kitchen table while Mulheisen talked to the county sheriff on the telephone. The farmer's guests, at Mulheisen's request, stayed in the living room but the entryway was crowded with faces and there was a lot of conversation.

The farmer's wife pressed food and coffee on her three unexpected visitors. Mulheisen accepted coffee and was grateful when the farmer got out a dusty, half-full bottle of bourbon from a top cupboard shelf and poured a generous portion into the coffee. Clippert would take nothing. He sat staring at the floor, occasionally fingering his broken nose with hesitant fingers.

Wienoshek was not so shy. He readily accepted a large plate of sliced turkey with warmed-up gravy and dressing. He talked cheerfully to the farmer as he ate, enjoying the audience that hung out of the living-room entryway.

"This guy's one hell of a cop," he told them, gesturing toward Mulheisen. "You should have seen him. A regular Wyatt Earp. Hey, anyone got a cigarette?"

"Shut up, Wienoshek," Mulheisen said.

When they had finished their coffee, Mulheisen herded his prisoners into a bedroom. He sat by the open door, covering them. They sat on opposite sides of the bed. Wienoshek smoked a cigarette. The farmer's wife had bandaged his arm wound, which turned out not to be serious, although he had lost a good deal of blood. It didn't seem to bother him.

While they waited for the sheriff, Wienoshek chatted. "Where did you get that parka, Mulheisen?"

"Air Force."

"No kidding? I was in the Air Force."

"I know," Mulheisen said.

"What outfit were you in?"

"AACS," Mulheisen said. "Control tower."

"No kidding? I was in AACS."

"I know."

"I didn't really care for it, though," Wienoshek said. "Before that I was a gunner. I was one of the last gunners in the old B-36's. It was good duty."

Mulheisen didn't say anything. Clippert stared at the floor.

"I knew a guy one time," Wienoshek said, "he was a gunner on a B-24. In World War II. Flew all over France and Germany. You know what he told me?"

"No," Mulheisen said.

"He said they were on a bombing run over Germany one time and a bomb got hung up in the bay. The bombardier came back and tried to free the bomb. Finally, the guy got to kicking at the bomb, to get it to fall out. You know what happened?"

"What happened?"

"The bomb finally let go and the bombardier lost his balance and fell out right behind it! He fell right out the damn bomb bay, right onto Germany, with no parachute. And you know what his last words were?"

"What?" Mulheisen said.

" 'Oh fuck!' Those were his last words."

Mulheisen stared at Wienoshek. "Is that the truth?"

"My buddy was right there, he was the waist gunner. His name was Johnny Wood. We were in B-36's together."

Mulheisen studied Wienoshek. "I see," he said.

After a while, Wienoshek said, "Where do you think I'll go?"

"What do you mean?"

Wienoshek nodded at Clippert, "Well, I know where he's

going." He made a stirring motion with his forefinger near his temple. "But me," he said, "there's only two places in Michigan for me: Jackson or Marquette."

"Marquette is for the bad men," Mulheisen said.

Wienoshek smiled. "That's me."

Mulheisen smiled at that.

"I think I'd rather go to Marquette, anyway," Wienoshek said.

"Why is that?"

"It's north. The Upper Peninsula. That's my kind of country."

"You like the north country?" Mulheisen asked.

"Always have," Wienoshek said.

"How about your pal, Service? Where's he going?"

"Service? Who knows?"

"We'll get him," Mulheisen said.

"No, you won't," Wienoshek said. "Not him. Besides, don't be so greedy. You got me, and you got him." He pointed to Clippert with a thumb. "You ought to be satisfied with that much."

Mulheisen laughed, despite his fatigue. "Well, I've got you, anyway," he agreed. "I'm not so sure about this one, though."

Clippert ignored them. He seemed far away. Wienoshek was puzzled, however. "What do you mean?" he asked. "Of course you got him."

"Not necessarily," Mulheisen said. "He's got good lawyers. The best. Hell, wouldn't surprise me if I get called for police brutality."

Wienoshek turned a look of utter contempt upon Clippert. He looked back to Mulheisen and leaned forward. He was very serious. "Don't worry, Mul," he said, "you'll have him."

"I will?"

"You're damn right. No matter what happens to me, I can give you Clippert."

Mulheisen could see that he meant it. Clippert appeared not to have heard. "All right," Mulheisen said. "We better not discuss it any further, for now. Wait until you get a lawyer."

Wienoshek nodded. "Right. But you can count on me, Mul. I won't talk to anyone but you."

Mulheisen felt a little nauseous. He smiled at Wienoshek in a friendly way, however. He thought, Oh, let that sheriff come soon. He was thinking that he had to talk to Lou.

"It was no summer Progresse. A cold coming they had of it . . . The waies deep, the weather sharp, the daies short, the sunn farthest of *in solstitio brumali,* the very dead of Winter. . . ."

—Lancelot Andrewes
From "A Sermon Preached Before the Kings Majestie, at White-Hall, on Wednesday, the XXV of December, A.D. MCDXXII. Being Christmasse Day."